FEEL THE FIRE

ANNABETH ALBERT

carina
press

carina
press®

Recycling programs
for this product may
not exist in your area.

ISBN-13: 978-1-335-45952-7

Feel the Fire

This edition published by arrangement with Harlequin Books S.A.

For questions and comments about the quality of this book,
please contact us at CustomerService@Harlequin.com.

Carina Press
22 Adelaide St. West, 40th Floor
Toronto, Ontario M5H 4E3, Canada
www.CarinaPress.com

Printed in U.S.A.

To the ones who got away,
the ones who got second chances and the
ones who earned their shot at forever

FEEL THE FIRE

Chapter One

"You want me to go *where*?" Luis paced the narrow length of his boss's office, ignoring the visitor's chair in front of where Rosalind sat. His pulse alternately revved and sputtered, struggling to keep up with the freaking live grenade Rosalind and the Forest Service had just lobbed into his life.

"Central Oregon. The Painter's Ridge air base is there along with an interagency hotshot crew and, of course, a large forest service office. It's a big operation."

"I know what's there." Even now, he could picture exactly what was there—endless sky, big ranches, surprising number of cowboys, and Tucker. But not the Tucker of his memories. Chestnut hair. Gap between his teeth. Floppy hair over his ears. Penny in his sneakers. That boy was gone forever, replaced by a fully adult Tucker, who undoubtedly had a happy wife, happy life, maybe a half-dozen kids by now, all with Tucker's damn smile. That boy—*man*—had roots as deep as a two-hundred-year-old fir in that area, and no way was Luis getting lucky by him having moved away or something.

"I had a feeling you might. You grew up near there, right?" She gave him an encouraging smile, sun glinting off her short gray hair. She was one of the few in the building with a window in her office. Usually he enjoyed visiting her and her collection of houseplants and stacks of forestry manuals, but not today.

"Something like that." His voice was probably terser than Rosalind deserved, as they'd been good work friends before she'd taken this promotion, but damn, he was still reeling. "I grew up in Riverside mainly, but we spent some years up in Oregon when my dad was transferred there to manage a new bank branch. All my family's back here in California now though," he added in case she was under the mistaken impression that he was pining for the area. No, he'd gotten all the pining out of his system years ago and all that was left was a bitter, ashy taste and a major distrust of toothy grins and careful promises.

I promise to write.

I'll wait for you. I'll wait forever.

You're the one. My one.

"Hmm." Rosalind's mouth twisted. "I'm not saying this assignment will be easy. Extended travel is never fun. And I'm sure your family will miss you. You're not seeing anyone right now, are you?"

Ah. There it was. The real reason Luis was being shipped north. In a large office with several fire behavior specialists, he might well be the best, but he was also the only single guy, only one without kids. And that made him expendable. This wasn't the first time the forest service had loaned him out to a region with great need—he'd spent a few weeks in northern California last year, and in Montana with the big national park fires the year before that. But fucking Oregon? That he wasn't prepared for.

"If I say yes, will that get me out of this?" He gave her his best smile, but she simply sighed.

"Sorry. I know this is short notice. But you'll get the

travel per diem. If you're frugal with food, that can be a nice little bonus for you, maybe?" Her dark eyes pleaded with him to understand and not make her day that much harder. And anywhere else in the country and he'd already be back at his desk, making arrangements. But this was *Oregon* and he was going to dig his heels in.

"I'm not worried about the money. But you're saying this could be more than a couple of weeks. I've got…" He cast around for some good reason. His coworkers had softball games and kid day camps and family reunions this time of year, but he was rather low on excuses for himself. A hollow feeling bloomed in his chest as he tried to remind himself that he liked his life, liked his freedom from entanglements and encumbrances. After Mike, he hadn't wanted anything to do with domestic bliss, not ever again. And sure, he had a social life, but nothing he could point to as a commitment. Those he stayed away from. "The cat and—"

"You took her with you to Mendocino. I remember." Smiling, she shook a finger at him. He'd let her assume he was an indulgent pet parent instead of a guy who was reluctant to pay sky-high pet-sitter fees while he was stuck with someone else's cat. "We'll make sure we find you a pet-friendly extended-stay place with a kitchenette. I know you like to make your own food. And assuming you want to drive it, I can arrange mileage too."

"It's thirteen hours, give or take." He'd had that number memorized for decades now, dating back to when it had seemed to matter with life-and-death urgency, each mile an endless chasm between him and what he really wanted. But now it was simply a scar, a wound he'd rather not acknowledge, let alone reopen.

"Do it over two days," she urged, apparently assuming

that was him agreeing. "And come on, Luis, don't look at me that way. I wouldn't ask you if you weren't seriously needed. They've been shorthanded all season thanks to this hiring freeze we're all under, but now it's reached crisis level there with a maternity leave, a stroke, and an abrupt move. They're dealing with a much greater number than usual of spot fires."

"Arson?" He didn't want to be curious, but his neck prickled all the same.

"That's the working theory. They don't have anyone with your level of expertise right now. Their crews are overworked, and management is stretched thin. They need help getting through this peak of the fire season, and they need a specialist with your qualifications. So when an old friend called in a favor, I immediately thought of you."

The single guy. But he only nodded. He could tell when something was a losing effort, and trying to get her to send someone else surely was. Just like he'd been well and truly screwed at sixteen when his parents had moved back to California partway through his junior year.

They're making me go.

I don't have a choice.

I'm gonna miss you forever.

At least at thirty-five he was a touch less dramatic. He'd get through this. Somehow.

"You're exactly what they need."

Somehow, he doubted that. "Wasn't that you last week complaining that I'm too headstrong and that I don't take critique well?"

"Oh that." Rosalind made a dismissive gesture. "I mean, you're the best fire behavior specialist I know of. It's why Mendocino asked for you last year. And it's why

I know you're going to do excellent here. And I'm going to owe you. Seriously."

"Yeah, you are." He managed to keep his tone almost playful, not petulant, but it was a close thing. Her flattery wasn't unnoticed either—she'd known the mention of arson would pique his professional interest, and he did have an excellent reputation in his specialty of identifying and predicting how a particular fire would react to given variables like wind, weather, and type of response available. He was used to working with various incident commands and interagency teams of wildfire fighters, and he tried his best to be adaptable and good with crisis situations. In short, he'd be perfect for this job. But, *Oregon*.

Rosalind leaned forward, expression kinder now that he'd agreed. "Isn't there anyone up there you'd like to see again? Old friends?"

"Nope." He had a vibrant social media life but not a single Oregonian on his contacts list, hadn't for years now. Then, as Rosalind frowned because that was kind of harsh, he added, "I fell out of touch with my high school friends. I'll be okay though. No warrants for my arrest up there or anything."

"Better not be." She laughed and offered him the bowl of candy she kept on her desk. "This will work out. You'll see."

"Hope so." He crunched into a cinnamon hard candy, letting the heat fill his mouth and tamp down some of his reservations. Maybe this wouldn't be so bad. It was a big area. Fair number of people spread out through several small farming communities. And he hadn't checked— thank you, iron self-control—but chances were high that Tucker was off running his dad's ranch by now. Him and that smiling wife and half a dozen kids. He'd be way too busy to be concerned about what the forest service was up to. Luis would simply get a room for himself and Blaze and plant his ass there when he wasn't working. If he didn't have to see Tucker, this didn't have to be anything other than a pain in the neck temporary assignment.

"I'm sorry, we're getting *who*?" Tucker was usually all about getting through the morning meeting as quickly as possible, and he'd learned through years of working with Fred that too many questions would slow the boss down, lead to tangents and rambles and a lost morning he could have been working. And a lost morning meant being late getting out of here in the afternoon, meant another hasty dinner for him and the twins and grumbles all around. So he made a point of paying attention to the announcements and getting information right the first time, but this time he had to have heard Fred wrong.

"New fire behavior specialist out of California— Angeles National Forest is sending him since we're still under a hiring freeze and now down to a bare-bones operation. You know all that. You were complaining about overtime last week."

"I get that we need some more boots on the ground. But I've been working as burn boss the last several fires, and Garrick's coming along too. Would be nice if they'd send us some more admin support and not someone who's going to expect a leadership role."

"Don't get your feathers ruffled. You're both an asset to incident command, sure, but we need this guy's fire behavior experience, especially as it pertains to arson. He's got the analytical skills we can use and the experience to back it up."

"Glad they're finally taking the arson suspicions seriously. And what did you say the name was?" That last part was what he really wanted to know. He could deal with the problem of too many chefs in the kitchen, but he could have sworn Fred had said—

"Luis Rivera. Comes to us with great experience."

"Sounds good." He managed a nod, even as his head swam. *Fuck.* Maybe there were a lot of guys with that name in the LA area. Maybe it was some stodgy near-retiree and not the darkest, deepest pair of eyes Tucker had ever known. The voice husky and earnest. The smile he'd never forget.

"Apparently he knows the area at least a little is what his boss told me on the phone."

And with that, Tucker's cornflakes and coffee turned to bricks in his stomach, a heavy weight he hadn't felt in eons. There might be plenty of guys with that name in California but there had only been one Luis Rivera in central Oregon, the one who'd left with Tucker's heart all those years ago.

"They're making me go." Luis's voice had wavered, first time Tucker had seen him cry since he'd broken his arm back on a fourth grade dare, and even then, he'd been more mad than sad, all sputtering bravado. This was a level of devastation Tucker had never seen from his friend.

His chest hurt, like he was some hapless cartoon character and his heart really had been cleaved in half by this news. Scooting closer, he wrapped an arm around Luis's slim shoulders, trying to be brave for both of them.

"You could stay with us to finish school. Share my room and—"

"I'm hardly your parents' favorite person." Luis's weighty sigh hit Tucker like that time a swing had

slammed into his gut, because he was right. Tucker's par-
ents weren't going to come charging in to save the day.

"I'll wait for you," he promised.

Only Tucker hadn't. And if it was that same Luis, well, there wasn't going to be any avoiding him. As short-handed as they were, it wasn't like Tucker could claim some of his mountain of unused vacation days. Fred would want him working closely with this person. But maybe he could figure a way around—

"Should be here any minute."

Or not. Damn it. He needed time to sort himself out, time he apparently wasn't going to get because here came Fred's assistant, Christine, knocking at the conference room door, ushering in…

A stranger.

Not the boy Tucker had known. A *man*. One with a couple of flecks of gray in his dark hair, which was neatly styled, not all choppy and goth, and he had a lean, muscular build, taller than him by a couple of inches, not some scrawny kid. His shoulders were solid, a man who had known his share of heavy labor, and the biceps peeking out of his forest service polo said he kept that work up. The edge of a tattoo played peekaboo with his sleeve. Tucker's memory had miles of smooth tawny skin, no tattoos or scars like the one this guy had on his other arm.

But right when Tucker's shoulders were about to relax, the pit in his stomach starting to ease, the guy frowned, and Tucker would recognize that hard, defiant look any-where. Luis's head tilted, revealing the familiar curve of his neck to his shoulder that Tucker remembered all too well.

"Tucker?" The Californian accent drew out the vow-els in his name, an effect that could make him feel spe-

cial and singled out when whispered on a starless night. But add a little disdain and a deeper timbre than Tucker recalled, and it made him feel like an unwanted extra in a surfing movie.

"Yeah." He nodded, head feeling untethered, like a helium balloon about to escape.

"What the—" Luis blinked, then drew his shoulders back, professional distance taking over, smoothing his facial features and softening his next few words. "Sorry. Wasn't expecting…"

"Y'all know each other?" Fred stood to greet the new-comer with a hearty handshake. "Now, that's just great. Small world, right?"

"Right," Tucker echoed weakly, unable to take his eyes off Luis. "Small world."

Too small. Especially considering that he'd once seen the miles between them as an uncrossable sea, a distance so great it made his brain hurt almost as much as his heart. Once upon a time, he would have given anything to end up in the same room again, weeks of working together looming, and now he'd trade an awful lot to avoid it.

"We went to school together a few years," Luis said dismissively, body-slamming eight years of best friend-ship to the ground, reducing everything they'd been to a chance acquaintanceship.

Tucker almost couldn't breathe and sure as hell couldn't get the words out to correct Luis. And even if he could find the power of speech, what the fuck was he supposed to say?

Nothing. That was all he could do, so he managed a nod without meeting Luis's eyes.

"Good, good." Fred continued talking, explaining the

office management structure to Luis and asking about his
drive up from the LA area, but Tucker's ears were ringing too loud to register Luis's answers. Luis was here,
invading the office Tucker had worked out of a good decade plus now, never a problem. Now here Luis was after
all these years, looking all grown up and pissed off and
way, way too good to ignore. He might not be the same
boy anymore, but he was a *man*, and that was possibly
more devastating to Tucker's sanity.

Tucker had spent almost two decades working around
wildfires, first on a line crew, then engine and hotshot
outfits, paying his dues before moving into fire management. He'd worked hard on his reputation for being
unflappable under pressure. No one wanted a burn boss
who startled easily or who couldn't keep his temper. And
after all that time on the front lines of fires, not much
scared him anymore. Except maybe Luis and the prospect
of needing to work alongside him and pretend that they
hadn't once been everything to each other. And more to
the point, Luis had every reason in the world to still be
pissed at him, even after all this time. Tucker couldn't
expect him to simply forgive and forget any more than
he himself could.

As Fred talked, Luis kept glancing over at Tucker,
mouth still twisting like he couldn't believe his rotten
luck. Or maybe like he was expecting to wake up any
minute from this bad dream. Lord knew Tucker felt the
same way. *Wake up, damn it.* He had plenty of other
stuff to worry about this summer more than Luis's sudden reappearance.

"So Tucker can show you around the office, introduce
you to our support staff, show you where we keep the coffee." Not even looking at Tucker, Fred nodded like this

was a done deal. "He'll bring you up to speed on our various projects. This is undoubtedly a smaller operation than you're used to, but we're family here. Everyone pitches in, and we get the job done, one way or another. You'll see. I've got a good feeling you're going to fit right in."

Tucker had the exact opposite feeling. And family or no, he wasn't exactly eager for their past to become office gossip. These were his work colleagues, people he'd do anything for on a professional level, although personally, he'd always kept to himself and he'd like to keep it that way.

But it wasn't like he could argue with Fred or volunteer someone else—that would only raise suspicion, start that gossip mill chattering. No, he'd have to face this head-on.

"Yup. I can do that." There. He sounded normal. Distant yet helpful even.

"I appreciate it." Luis spoke more to Fred than him, not bothering to glance Tucker's way until they were in the hall. Together. Alone.

Forget all his usual cool resolve. This was fucking terrifying. Every cell in his body took notice of Luis's nearness in the narrow space, the way he smelled like an unfamiliar spicy and citrusy aftershave, the way he was too big, nothing at all like Tucker's memories, tall enough now to glower down at Tucker.

"What the hell, Tucker?" Luis's voice was low, but the fury there was unmistakable. Yup. Two decades might have passed since they'd last locked eyes, but he was still angry.

Before he could reply, Christine came bustling down the hallway with a cheery "It's Selma's birthday today! There's cake in the break room. Make sure the new guy gets a piece."

"Sure thing." Tucker managed a nod her direction before she disappeared into the copy room right next to where they were standing. Goodbye chances of a long conversation he undoubtedly needed to have with Luis. What he wanted to say wasn't going to happen with an audience. Instead he took a deep breath and forced a hearty tone. "Let's start your tour there, then. Get you some coffee and cake. Follow me."

Luis's eyes narrowed like that was the very last thing he'd like to do. He opened and closed his mouth a few times while he darted his eyes to the copy room, posture tense until finally he exhaled.

"Fine. Lead the way." His tone was every bit as fake as Tucker's.

Damn. This was going to be a long-ass day of pretending things were fine. Wait. Long-ass *weeks*. Luis was here for weeks. And that meant at some point they *would* have to talk. It was inevitable really, and Tucker was already dreading it with his entire being. Hell, he'd live through the twins' colicky phase again if it meant avoiding having it out with Luis. But one glance at Luis's stiff shoulders and tight mouth told him no amount of bargaining with the universe would save him from Luis's barely controlled anger. Weeks. It was going to be *weeks*, and he might not survive.

Chapter Two

"Where's this coffee you promised?" There was plenty else Luis wanted to say to Tucker, but they'd passed several other coworkers on the walk to the break room alone, and now here they were standing, staring at each other again while some women chatted at a table and two older men helped themselves to the large white sheet cake on the table at the rear of the room.

"Over here." Tucker led the way to a large industrial pot, same brand and size as Luis's office back in California. Probably same low-quality coffee, but his French press and bag of small-batch dark roast coffee was still in the car, waiting for him to be assigned a desk. Preferably far, far away from wherever Tucker's working space was.

"Thanks." He accepted the ceramic mug Tucker handed him, a dark green number with a smiling elk in a hunter's cap and plaid shirt on it. Powdered creamer had zero appeal, so he resigned himself to drinking the weak brew black.

"No sugar?" Tucker raised an eyebrow, like he knew anything about Luis and his dietary preferences these days. Oh, he still had a sweet tooth, but he was way more sane about it than he'd been at fifteen making weird soda combos at the convenience store. A lot of that had to do with losing his dad, but he wasn't about to get that personal with Tucker.

"Nope." He might be coming off as rather curt, but he couldn't seem to chase the anger from his tone. It wasn't really anger at Tucker though. He'd made his peace with the past years ago, but this tension was more of the same frustration he'd had ever since Rosalind handed him this assignment. He didn't want to deal with old hurts and old memories and old guilt, didn't want to have to interact with Tucker, and was mainly mad at himself for how much he was letting all this affect him.

"Ah." After pouring himself a cup, Tucker doctored it up with plenty of creamer and sweetener. Maybe some things didn't change, even if it seemed like damn near everything else had. Tucker at sixteen had had a habit of helping himself to the dregs in his parents' coffeepot, but more milk than coffee in his cup. He'd been a flagpole—tall and skinny with a long neck and lots of brown hair. He'd played running back on the football team that year, and it was entirely possible his gear had weighed more than him. And he'd been more cute than hot—pale skin, freckles across his nose, earnest eyes.

This Tucker, the one in front of him, was ruggedly handsome with a chiseled face that had clearly spent time in the sun as squint lines had started to form around his eyes. Broad shoulders and biceps more suited for tackling than darting between defenders like he'd made a name for himself doing. And most startling, he was actually shorter than Luis. Only an inch or two, but still this was the kid who'd come into his height early while Luis had waited patiently for his growth spurt to finally arrive.

"So…about that tour?" There was only so long Luis could stand in one place, trying to dodge bullets of old memories along with the disconcerting present knowledge of how damn attractive Tucker had turned out to be.

"Right." Tucker blinked like he too had been deep in memory land. "I take it you're going to skip the cake for now?"

"Yeah." Luis didn't want to be rude, but cake this early in the morning was far from appetizing to him, especially since he'd skipped having an actual breakfast. He'd been too worried about making sure Blaze was settled and then finding the forest service office.

As he gave Luis a tour of the one-story building, Tucker pointed out water coolers and supply closets and introduced the reception and administrative support staff as they made their way through the office, which was a mix of open workspaces, cubes, and narrow hallways leading to small offices and conference rooms.

"This the new guy?" A guy with a broad build and biceps even bigger than Tucker's, who was in a wheelchair, stopped them as they passed his cube. His hearty smile and easy demeanor said he was happy for the interruption.

"Garrick, this is Luis Rivera. He's from the Angeles Forest region. He's a fire behavior specialist." Tucker made the introductions as handshakes were exchanged. "Luis, Garrick is one of our more experienced dispatchers. Former smoke jumper. He's gonna be a hell of a burn boss soon. Been working his way into more management and oversight this year."

Tucker's tone had a defiant edge, an underlying message that they didn't truly need Luis and his expertise. Whatever. Luis wasn't going to stand in the way of Tucker's friend advancing in the ranks, but he also wasn't here for petty power struggles either. He was damn good at what he did, and they'd summoned him for a reason.

"That's great." Luis kept his own voice professional. Garrick looked vaguely familiar, like perhaps he'd seen him around here when younger. He had a fun collection of little fidgets on his desk—springs and finger puzzles and a hand-knit bear with lopsided ears. And interestingly, Garrick had a pic of himself with a long-haired hippie sort of guy near his computer monitor.

Hardly definitive proof that Garrick wasn't straight, but it sure as hell would be nice if Luis wasn't the only openly rainbow-flag-waving person in the office. Unexpected around here, that was for sure. He was used to being quieter in these rural offices, not going back in a closet but still toning it down, so finding allies and other LGBTQ folks was always very welcome. And he probably wasn't going to be able to count on Tucker for either of those things. He had no idea how Tucker identified these days, but he'd put money on that closet door being padlocked shut, no matter what he'd said all those years ago.

"I...I think I'm gay." It was the first time Luis had said the words aloud. Heck, he hadn't even let himself write the words in his private notebooks. But the words had been pounding in his head, louder and louder, until now when alone with his best friend in the loft of the barn, he couldn't keep them back anymore.

"No kidding?" Tucker didn't sound particularly shocked, which said that maybe Luis hadn't done such a good job hiding it after all. He kicked at some straw, not looking at Luis, but not moving from his spot right next to him, hips and shoulders mere centimeters apart. The barn smelled musty, their whispers the only sound in the old structure.

"Yeah. I mean... I've thought it for a long time now, but at Sam's party last weekend, when Chelsea kissed me, I couldn't wait for it to be over. I'm not sure what other guys feel when they look at girls, but for me...it's not happening."

"Wow. I thought..." Tucker gulped in a breath and Luis's heart galloped. He wasn't sure he could stand it if his friend condemned him. "Thought I was the only one who felt like that."

Best. Feeling. Ever. Luis's whole being soared. "Seriously? Katie told everyone you were a good kisser."

"She's...nice. But kissing..." Tucker made a sour face. "Not sure what the big deal is."

"Maybe we're not kissing the right people." Luis leaned in, pulse pounding like he'd slammed half a case of Mountain Dew. Any second now, Tucker would pull away and the bubble would burst, but far from recoiling, Tucker scooted closer, denim-covered thigh rubbing against Luis's, the most electric sensation he'd ever felt. Then their lips met, clumsy and unsure, noses bumping as they shifted around, trying to sort out how to do this. The glancing contact at first wasn't that different from other kisses, but then Tucker gave a happy sigh, mouth parting, and a ball of energy gathered in Luis's middle. He felt like a superhero coming into his powers, a strange new force taking over. Yeah. He was gay. That was for sure. No more maybe about it. And far from scary, it was nothing short of amazing because his best friend was right here with him, kissing him back.

But apparently while the memory was etched on Luis's soul, Tucker hadn't had any such revelation, and he had either figured out the "big deal" about kissing women at some point or slammed the door shut on that part of himself, consigning himself to something less than the perfection they'd found in the barn loft that day. And whichever it was, Luis had no business caring.

Indifference was tough to maintain, however, especially when Tucker finally moved on from Garrick and some small talk about who had been in which grade in school. He led Luis to a nearby office. It had a door with Tucker's name on it, which spoke to his management role in the organizational hierarchy.

"We can talk about your duties in here." Tucker held the door open. He apparently rated a window—a high one, with a shelf of hardy plants in little pots. Scrubby cacti with two of the pots looking painted by a child's hand. Figured that he was the kind of dad to display gifts like that. A large bookcase dominated the room, and a few more kid-centric mementos like a Lego structure and a lumpy clay something lurked along with the textbooks and manuals Luis would have expected. The wall held a diploma for a degree Luis hadn't known he had, and next to it was one of those collage frames. And there they were. Little clones of Tucker. Babies and small boys and awkward tweens. He couldn't tell whether it was the same two kids over time or if maybe it was a whole soccer team of miniature Tuckers.

Not caring. Right. Without intending to, he coughed, still unable to look away, and that was enough to draw Tucker's attention as he shut the door.

"That's Walker and Wade. I need to get some more recent pics in here. Walker's always on me to stop showing off baby pictures whenever he stops by."

"Uh-huh." He managed a noncommittal sound, but something of his unease must have shown on his face because Tucker frowned.

"Damn it, Luis. Am I supposed to pretend that they don't exist? How precisely would you like me to play this?"

"Not sure," Luis admitted. Then the question that had been searing his brain all morning finally escaped. "How's the wife?"

A strangled sound echoed in his small office, and it took Tucker a moment to realize that it came from himself.

"Wife?" He blinked. This was one of those inevitable conversations, but he still was far from ready for it.

"You know, Heidi, that sweet thing you ran off with when you weren't even old enough to buy booze yet? Are Walker and Wade the only two mini-Tuckers?" Luis's gaze was still on the collage of the twins through the years, God knew what running through his mind. Couldn't be jealousy, not after all these years. Condemnation maybe, censure that he'd waited almost two decades to dole out.

Hell, he hadn't even ever replied to Tucker's message attempting to explain what had happened. Not that he'd entirely understood it himself, but he'd *tried*. And all he got back was silence. So, Tucker had been forced to imagine his judgment, picture his reactions. Had he yelled? Punched something? Not cared enough for anger?

Tucker might never know his initial response, but this sarcasm was pretty good proof that it hadn't been positive. And Luis not knowing anything about who Tucker was now was also evidence that he hadn't been social-media stalking him, wasn't interested enough to go snooping. Not that Tucker had done that either—he hadn't wanted to know, hadn't wanted to see grown-up

Luis with a life of his own. Seeing him frequently in his dreams was bad enough.

"We divorced. About seven years ago now." He kept his response brief because no way was Luis entitled to the whole story.

"My...condolences?" Luis's mouth quirked, like he was unsure of the polite response. And that was okay. That made two of them.

"Thanks." Tucker gave the same response he'd handed out over and over back then when well-meaning people had crawled out of the baseboards to express sorrow. "And yes, we only had the twins. We split custody, and while I'm not one to overshare at work, I'm not about to deny the presence of the two most important people in my life simply to make you more comfortable."

"I'm not asking you to." Feet shuffling restlessly, Luis looked more ready to stage a fast getaway than to continue this conversation.

"Sit." Tucker pointed at the visitor's chair near his desk. "Let's admit neither of us really knows who the other is right now. And that's fine. No one's demanding we forgive and forget."

Luis muttered under his breath, something about hard to forget, but then settled into the chair, leaving Tucker to seek out his own office chair behind his L-shaped desk.

"If it helps, you're not the only one with some... baggage." Damn it. He was *not* going to unpack everything that stood between them, all the years and hurts and wrong assumptions, not now. His heart pinched, memories of those last few tense conversations, ultimatums and arguments making his chest muscles go tight.

"Fair enough." Clenching and unclenching his hands,

Luis stretched before nodding. Clearly, he was as uncomfortable as Tucker, but they had to find a way forward.

"But here we are. We're not stupid teens any longer, thank God. And I've been in this office too many damn years to let any personal issues interfere with my work. We simply need to focus on the job at hand."

"Agreed. I'm still shocked your family let you off the ranch, though. Seeing you here…working together…that I didn't see coming."

"That makes two of us. Figured you'd end up going Hollywood, not wildfire chasing."

"Just because I was a theater nerd at sixteen doesn't mean I stayed one." Luis gave him a defiant stare. "And you know I did the fire explorers, same as you. Wasn't only in it to be your sidekick."

"Point taken." And honestly, Tucker *was* guilty of that assumption—he'd been the one to sign up for shadowing the local volunteer fire department, part of their high school outreach program. Back then, Luis had been more interested in the allure of fireworks and bonfires, not putting out fires. "And as to your question, my brother runs the ranch with Dad now. They don't need me underfoot."

That was the understatement of the fucking century, a chasm he had no interest in exploring with Luis.

Luis's eyes narrowed like he was about to ask a follow-up question, but then he shook his head. "So, leaving the past where it belongs, tell me how you envision my role here. I take it Adams is my supervisor, not you?"

"You're right. But I'm in charge of a lot these days." He tried to make sure his tone wasn't too defensive, not liking at all the look of relief on Luis's face. "The fire behavior specialist role is under Adams in terms of management. He wants me to bring you up to speed, but you'll report to him, not me. I'll tell you right now, though, that he's getting close to retirement and I've been taking more and more of the burn boss duties, especially when it comes to the controlled burns. We've got one coming up that I've been working point on, and Garrick's been helping me."

"Not interested in upsetting your fiefdom." Luis leaned back in his chair. His tone might be this side of bored, but he radiated the sort of take-charge persona that didn't always function well in a team environment.

Their last group project had been decades prior. Tucker seriously didn't have any clue about who this stranger was in front of him, what he liked, who he was with, what his work personality was, and wasn't likely to find out as Luis hardly seemed eager to make friends.

Showing impatience with Tucker's ruminating, Luis made a little gesture with his hand. "Go on."

"I'm also the main liaison with the interagency crews when there's an emergency or an ongoing situation like what we've got going this summer with all the spot fires."

"Tell me more about those. My boss said you're investigating the possibility of arson. That's one of my specialties. I wrote my graduate thesis on the different fire spread patterns with deliberate burns, particularly looking at behavior that's indicative of arson."

"You've got a graduate degree?" Tucker shouldn't be surprised—this was a specialist role after all, but he was still having trouble reconciling this clearly professional, competent man with the academic-hating boy he'd once known.

"You need my full résumé? I worked on a city crew first, then took an opportunity for wildfire work. An injury to my back forced me back to school, and I was thinking of becoming a fire investigator, but the forest service found me and I've been at this a few years now. Paid my dues with big fires and small operations alike. Apparently, our bosses think I can be of assistance here." More of that hard, defiant stare.

And honestly, Tucker probably deserved it as he wasn't exactly acting professional here himself. "I'm sure you can. I'll share what we're working with in terms of the spot fires and the damage they've caused. Avoiding significant spread has kept the smoke-jumping base busy along with ground crews too."

"You were always hard-charging to be a smoke jumper yourself." A small smile played with the edges of Luis's mouth, like maybe he too was remembering their time as fire explorers, the sunny dreams of an adrenaline-packed job and life together Tucker had confessed to him alone. "What changed?"

"Kids." Much as Luis might not like the mention of them, they were central to everything Tucker had done with his life since their arrival. "I needed a stable year-round job with benefits. I did some years on engine and hotshot crews early on, but I pretty quickly realized that the boys needed me around more than I needed that tryout."

"Ah." Luis's eyes went predictably distant at mention of the twins. "Too bad. I've worked with them some over the years. You would have made a good jumper."

Tucker wasn't sure whether that was praise or a subtle dig, but he nodded all the same. "Just wasn't how life worked out."

"Yeah." Nodding thoughtfully, Luis exhaled hard. And wasn't that a good motto for this whole divide between them, the decades of no contact, the past that once was and the future that might have been. *Just wasn't how life worked out.*

He wouldn't trade his boys for anything, not even that murky future he'd once wanted with all his heart, the one where he'd be a smoke jumper and Luis would be in school, and they'd make a little life for themselves under warm, blue California skies. He might not regret how life had worked out, but he was sorry for the hurt he'd caused them both, and still wasn't exactly sure how or when to apologize. More dwelling in the past seemed like a terrible idea, and he really didn't need coworkers overhearing an argument, but the urge to try to make things right was there nonetheless.

"I'm—"

"Knock, knock," Christine called before opening Tucker's door. "Fred said Luis can use Marjorie's office while she's on leave. I'm going to go in and clear the desk for you now."

And the good news just kept on coming. Marjorie, a pleasant woman out with the arrival of her first kid, occupied the office right next to Tucker's. Nice that Fred had found something other than a cube for Luis, but man, he didn't need more reasons to run into Luis.

"Thank you." Luis gave her a nod and tight smile, and Tucker did the same, because there wasn't really an alternative.

"You were saying?" Luis asked as she left again.

"Nothing. Just that I'll get all the documentation on the fires together so you can look that over, maybe you'll see something with fresh eyes that the rest of us missed."

Whatever else he'd been about to say could wait for better timing. Or maybe never, because it wasn't like anything he could say now would make a lick of difference in how Luis saw him. Them being friends again, that was probably never going to happen, so he might as well put his head down, focus on work and work alone, and simply try to survive the next few weeks best as he could.

Chapter Three

Even by lunchtime, Luis still didn't know what he wanted. Or expected. He hadn't expected Tucker working for the forest service, that was for damn sure. And now that working together was apparently a requirement, Luis didn't know what came next. They were both defensive and prickly, and even fetching his French press and coffee from the car hadn't been enough to settle him down. *Let's admit neither of us really knows who the other is right now.* Tucker wasn't wrong. Luis had no freaking clue who the other man was—a devoted dad judging by his office decor, a competent worker given how his coworkers all sang his praises and how organized his process seemed to be. He'd turned Luis loose to get settled in his borrowed office, which smelled like lavender. However, like Tucker's, it had a sliver of a high window, which Luis cracked to get a little air circulating.

He gave the absent Marjorie's spider plant some water and carefully set her nesting doll figurines aside to make room for the few things he'd brought with him—laptop, some field equipment and gear like his boots and hard hat, and his favorite coffee mug, a stainless steel tumbler that kept his titanium-strength brew at the perfect temperature. All in all, it was a single trip out to the car for his things, followed by a meeting with Adams about some specific responsibilities.

Then Adams had headed to a lunch meeting, leaving Luis with a strange wobble in his stomach as he made his way back here to his office. Outside his window, people headed to the parking lot while others mingled in the hallway on their way to the break room, chatty clumps of twos and threes. It was fine. He'd been the new guy before. He'd figure something out, and this weird feeling could go fuck itself.

"Hey, new kid!" The boy with the floppy hair and big ears poked Luis's shoulder as their class lined up for lunch, making Luis brace for trouble.

"It's Luis. Not kid. And what do you want?" He gave the boy his best don't-mess-with-me stare, the one he'd learned from his big brothers.

"Miss Martin said to ask if you brought a lunch or if you need a hot lunch. Hot lunch kids get in the other line."

"Brought one." Luis held up his box, which had dueling space fighters on the front. His mom had insisted on packing him food for his first day in this strange school. He still didn't know why they'd had to buy a house here, in this tiny school district. His dad's new job was bad enough, but Luis didn't care how big the yard was or how nice the basement playroom was. Nothing made up for this stupid school with the kids—including this one— all looking at him like he had green hair or a third eye. You'd think they never got anyone new around here. And even the teachers were nothing like his old school. He'd loved his old teacher so much, but Miss Martin was old and smelled funny.

"Cool." The boy—Travis? Trevor? Something with a

T, whatever. Too many new names that morning. But the boy continued his appraisal of Luis, his eyes lingering on his new sneakers. "Follow me. You can sit with me."

"You don't have to sit with me just because the teacher said," Luis protested even as he let the kid lead him to the lunchroom.

"She didn't say to sit with you." Frowning, the boy's tone shifted to one more defensive, making Luis regret his sharpness. "I'm tired of sitting alone with the girls, that's all. The other boys in our class this year are stupid. And my mom sent salami. Again. No one ever wants to trade with me anymore. But I figured...maybe you like salami?" His smile, both hopeful and more than a little bashful, did something to Luis's insides, made him need to smile back.

"I don't mind salami."

"Good. And I'm Tucker." He led Luis to a table filled with chatting girls, pulling out a battered blue lunch bag with a seam that had been repaired, possibly more than once. That smile came out again, soft and shy as he pointed at Luis's lunch box. "You like that movie?"

"Yup."

"Me too."

And there he'd sat the rest of that year and the one after that too, eating Tucker's sandwiches for him, introducing him to Mami's preferred brands of snack cakes and chips, and listening to Tucker's opinions on popular movie franchises and video games and the wisdom of listening to older brothers. Now here he was, years later, the new guy all over again. But nowhere near as desperate to fit in and not nearly as susceptible to puppy-dog looks from freckle-faced boys.

And no more time for wallowing in memories, either.

He ate his lunch at his desk, a prepackaged protein box. It wasn't that he was antisocial, but he was still figuring out the lay of the land here, the particular office politics that every place had. That and he hadn't particularly wanted to run into Tucker in the break room. Which might make him a coward, but so be it.

"Hey. Adams wanted me to bring you this." Tucker stuck his head into Luis's office. Apparently thinking about him was enough to conjure him up. "Oops. Sorry to interrupt your lunch."

"It's no bother," Luis lied.

"Is that all you have?" Tucker set a thick folder on the corner of Luis's desk. "That reminds me of the little snack boxes the boys loved when they were small. If you're still hungry—"

"I'm not." Luis hated how curt he sounded, so he forced himself to try for a lighter tone. Tucker was trying. So could he. "And it's aged cheese, an egg, some nuts, and chorizo. Not exactly kid food."

"You always did like spicy meat…" Tucker trailed off and rubbed his jaw, apparently realizing a little too late how that sounded. "Sorry. Never mind. But I've got extra snacks in my office if you get hungry. Accidentally grabbed some of Wade's chili chips a couple of days ago."

"I'm too old to be eating food you don't like." Despite himself, Luis smiled as decades sped past. Somehow he knew without asking that Tucker was thinking about that first meeting too and all the many lunches that followed. "But congrats on having a kid with bolder taste buds than you."

"I think it's payback from the universe. He even likes those cinnamon candies you were always addicted to, the ones that burn my tongue. And he adds hot sauce to everything. Walker and I had to ban him from cooking, which was possibly his objective." Tucker gave a crooked grin, one that invited Luis to smile back, and damn if some rogue muscle in his chest didn't flutter. He had no business being flattered that Tucker remembered his candy preferences. And Tucker's smile had always been appealing, but now, coupled with rugged adult looks, it was nothing short of devastating, and Luis had to look away. The worst thing wasn't having to work with Tucker. No, the absolute worst thing would be getting any sort of attraction to the person he was now.

He had to be smart here. And that meant letting Tucker explain the file he'd brought with a minimum of sneaking more glances at him. The papers included photographs and evidence from some older area fires that weren't yet digitally archived, along with instructions for how to reach the records on the office server of the more recent fires that were still under investigation.

"Tomorrow I'm supposed to take you out to the field— show you the site for the next controlled burn as well as one of the suspected arson spot fires."

"Sounds good." And it did—not the spending hours together, but getting out of the office was always his favorite part of the job, and he always felt like he did his best work hands-on rather than merely crunching data in front of a screen. Which was what loomed after Tucker retreated to his own office, slow-moving hours of reviewing records and getting up to speed on various projects, becoming more familiar with their procedures and ways of doing things.

At least he had his favorite music playing in his headphones, an indie band he'd been lucky enough to see live a few months back, and he didn't need to see Tucker again until they were packing up at the end of the day, encountering him in the hallway with a leather messenger bag on one shoulder, another reminder of how far he'd come from the kid who'd been inseparable from his hand-me-down backpack with graphics from their favorite movie franchise.

"Heading out?" Tucker's gaze swept over Luis, a cursory examination, but still one that made Luis both want to stand taller and to glance away.

"Yup."

"You…uh…find a place to stay okay?" Tucker shifted his weight from foot to foot.

"Yeah. Newer extended-stay hotel out by the highway. It's got a little kitchenette at least so I can handle some of my meals." He added that last bit in case Tucker was about to issue some sort of guilt-induced invitation. But he also purposefully didn't mention the cat—didn't need to invite opinions on the merits of traveling with a pet.

"Good. Good." A muscle worked in Tucker's jaw and an awkward silence stretched out between them. "Uh…see you tomorrow?"

"Bright and early." Luis dug deep for a cheerful tone. It was a day in the field. Might be with Tucker, but he'd survived worse. Surely he could make it a single day in close quarters with the last guy he'd wanted to see.

However, back at the hotel, heating up a packet of rice while Blaze ignored the new treats he'd bought her, his resolve wavered. Why did adult Tucker have to be so darn attractive? And by all counts, a decent person? *A decent single person*, his traitorous brain added. That little detail did *not* matter. Divorced did not equal out, even in his most optimistic of imaginings, and for all he knew, Tucker had some pretty rebound cowgirl on the string.

That. He had to keep reminding himself that he didn't know this Tucker at all, didn't know how he spent his time, what he valued, what he hoped and feared. And that wasn't likely to change. Their friendship was buried two decades deep. No sense in unearthing it, even if such a thing was possible. And he had no business being sad about that either because chances were high that Tucker was having no such similar pangs. No, the best he could hope for was making it through these weeks with his emotions firmly in check and his psyche unscathed.

"Is this all there is?"

It took Tucker a minute to take in Wade's expectant expression and to realize he meant dinner, not whatever existential crisis Tucker's brain was mired in. His head was cluttered with so many stray thoughts that he'd had a hard time keeping track of little details like it was Wednesday, and he'd arrived at Heidi's with only a few minutes to spare before their family dinner tradition.

"It's two pounds of pasta. Surely you can make do." Isaac carried the last of the food to the table. As usual, Heidi's husband had cooked enough for an army, no matter what Wade thought, and his steaming bowls of rotini coated with some sort of creamy from-scratch sauce and seasoned roast vegetables were far more gourmet than what Tucker usually offered up when they repeated this ritual most Sunday nights. The meals had started as a way of easing the custody split transitions on the boys, a tangible way to show them that they were all still family even if they had separate houses, but over the years they'd evolved into something more, part command appearance and part beloved ritual.

"The start of football means I'm hungry all the time."

Wade took his seat at the large oval table adjacent to the open kitchen. The house had been built in the same year as Tucker's own smaller house down the street, and the great room was similar but more expansive here. However, Heidi and Isaac favored chunky, dark wood furniture and colorful dishes whereas his own setup was more utilitarian.

"No, that's you every day." Walker slid into the seat next to Wade, matching grin and equally damp short hair. They'd arrived minutes after Tucker, full of stories of football practice and with twin gigantic appetites.

"Hey! Like that wasn't you ordering double at lunch." Wade bumped Walker's shoulder.

"Ordering?" Heidi placed water glasses in front of both of them before taking her own seat across from Isaac. "Isn't the fridge stocked with bread and lunch meat for you guys? I thought you were going to pack lunches?"

"Oops. Sorry, Mom."

"The other guys wanted to go out." Walker matched Wade's contrite tone. "And we ate some of that stuff anyway."

"Thank goodness you're your dad's grocery problem for the rest of the week." Heidi took a sip of the wine Isaac had already set by her place.

"Gee. Thanks." Tucker took the bowl of pasta Isaac passed and helped himself to a reasonable, non-Wade-sized portion. He'd accepted the wine, a rarity for him, but between Luis's unexpected reappearance and other work stuff and the twins' exuberance over all things football, he figured he was entitled. "I did a run to the warehouse store in Bend yesterday. I don't think you guys are going to starve."

"Good. Did you get protein powder?" Wade made the same pleading eyes his mother had a wicked talent for.

"Yes, Hercules, I got you some of that brand Coach recommended." Tucker was fairly sure that Coach's sheet of tips for nutrition and strength training hadn't changed in twenty years, but he wasn't going to cut into Wade's enthusiasm for following the advice. "How was practice?"

"Great. Tons of running." Walker answered for Wade, who had taken a mammoth bite of broccoli.

"I worry about you guys out there in the heat." Heidi delicately plucked a piece of pasta with her fork. She was still in her suit from work, makeup impeccable as always, but the executive persona never stopped her from taking her mom role seriously too. "You drank lots of water, right?"

"Yes, *Mom*. What are you gonna do without us to nag next year?" Wade's eyes sparkled. The last thing Tucker wanted was another reminder of how little time they likely had left before the boys flew the nest. Wade might be counting down the days, but he sure wasn't.

"What do you mean? I'm going to have you guys forever." Heidi was even more in denial than Tucker, but the sharpness in her tone said that she too was feeling the slide of time slipping away. "Doesn't matter how far away you end up, we're still going to nag. It's what parents do."

"Yep." Tucker nodded, keeping his tone pragmatic. He knew from long experience that the more he clung to the boys, the faster they ran. Any nostalgia he had for their younger selves was best kept to himself, but that didn't mean he didn't feel it. "And you better get as serious about test prep as you are about football if you want to go anywhere."

"Don't worry. We've got test prep classes after football

all next week. I'm as good as gone. Just gotta see which recruiters come calling."

Yup. There it was. Wade already limbering up those wings, ready to fly even if that meant a nosedive toward the ground, fearless as ever. Another year and they'd be weeks away from college move-in dates, and all these hypothetical future plans would be all too real. Wade's eagerness was, however, an excellent reminder that he couldn't get hung up on Luis's unexpected return. The boys had to be his number one priority, this year especially. They needed him fully on his dad game, not muddled and distant like he'd been guilty of prior to the food being served.

"For me, it's all about where Mary Anne ends up." Walker sighed dramatically, glancing down at the phone next to his plate like that might make his girlfriend appear at the table.

"Smooch. Smooch. Can't believe you dropped shop to take AP English with her this year." Wade might be all in on a football scholarship, but academics weren't his strong suit. Tucker bit back another "partying is not a major" lecture.

"She'll help me study," Walker countered.

"Uh-huh. Better be *safe* with studying and—"

"Little ears," Isaac said mildly, gesturing at Angelica, who sat between him and Tucker. Isaac was possibly the least flappable person on the planet, and the rare occasions when he spoke up, he tended to get results, as evidenced by both boys nodding.

"Hey, I'm not that little!" At five, Angelica still had a talent for getting more pasta on her face than in her stomach, but the promise of kindergarten in the fall had her asserting her desire to be one of the big kids at every turn. Her dark eyes mirrored Isaac's but her pout was pure Heidi.

"Sure you're not, squirt." Walker, like Wade, tended to spoil her, the whole family doting on the little girl. Tucker supposed he was something of an honorary uncle to her royal cuteness. But even so, her presence often made Tucker become more aware of his outsider status—Isaac might be the bonus dad for the boys, but with Angelica at the center, this was a tight five-person family unit. Oh, they were all happy to have Tucker in their orbit, but he never felt truly needed here. Especially now, as the boys got older and all this talk of college dominated dinner conversations, he wondered how much longer this twice-a-week tradition would last.

Appreciate it while you have it. Soon enough it was going to be him and a stack of frozen meals with the boys off on some new adventure, him not wanting to impose on Heidi and Isaac's cozy hospitality any more than he had to.

He wasn't jealous of their relationship in the typical sense—God knew he'd made peace with his slew of complicated emotions where that was concerned years ago, but he did envy them each other. On the nights he had the boys, they still had plenty of companionship, no painfully quiet rooms or forgetting to eat.

You could date. Heidi had said it so often that the words echoed in his brain in her persistent tone. But for many, many reasons that wasn't happening, and that was one more reason to make the most of the limited time they had left with the boys at home. So he tuned out melancholy thoughts about the passage of time as well as the replay of every conversation he'd had with Luis earlier in the day, and focused on the swirl of dinner activity—

Angelica talking about day camp, more football stories from the boys, and Heidi weighing in with a funny anecdote from her work as an exec for a solar energy company.

However, maybe he didn't do the best job at staying in the moment, because as they were cleaning up, Heidi turned to him. "What's up with you? You were quiet enough at dinner that I wondered if you'd caught a buzz off the wine, and now you've washed that pot three times."

"Nothing," he said quickly. Probably too quickly. He glanced away even as Heidi made a clucking noise. Over in the living area, Isaac was reading Angelica a story while the boys had disappeared to grab backpacks for going to Tucker's. No one was that strict about which nights they slept where anymore, but they did usually split the week between the two houses.

"Uh-huh. Tell me another one." She dried the extra-clean pot for him. Theirs was a comfortable partnership. Isaac cooked. The boys cleared. They cleaned. Even if he did sometimes feel like an outsider, he liked it here, always had. And he and Heidi had far too much history for him to lie to her too long.

"Work stuff. We got a fire behavior specialist transferred up from California."

"And? Are they horning in on your territory already?" She laughed because she knew all too well what a control freak he could be, how he didn't like sharing jobs he could do fine on his own.

"It's Luis Rivera." He moved on to the next pot, watching the suds swish around instead of waiting for her reaction.

"No sh—crap?" A piece of silverware clattered to the

floor. They both bent to retrieve it at the same time, narrowly missing bumping heads.

"Yeah."

"Oh boy." Heidi gave him a sympathetic pat on the shoulder. "But it's been what…twenty years. Surely you've both moved on. Changed. Grown. No sense in holding a grudge or hurt feelings."

"You'd be surprised." He wished the whole world could have Heidi's optimism and faith in the power of positive change. Her impressive résumé was proof of that belief, the way she never stopped striving for self-improvement. And she always had believed in the best of other people, including him, even when he didn't entirely deserve it.

"Seriously? He's still upset?" She shook her head, a few strands of red hair escaping the knot of hair on the top of her head. "You were kids. Younger than the twins are now."

"Don't remind me." Man, he didn't want to think about that. The memories didn't feel that far away, still vivid and real. And they might have been kids, but it had been important. Vital. He'd had plenty of other friendships but nothing that seared his chest quite like Luis had. And his reappearance only intensified those memories, made that time feel that much more poignant and significant.

"Maybe there's still something there?" She turned her attention to wiping down the counters as he loaded the dishwasher with the plates and silverware.

"There is not." Not likely, at least, the way Luis had been shooting him dark looks all day, like he simply couldn't believe his rotten luck. "We're both grown up now. Feelings change, especially when there's no contact. He's lived a whole lifetime I have no clue about."

And damn it, he was irrationally curious about that life, in a way he had no business being. What did it matter to him if Luis had a partner or spouse, pets, a house, all of that, or how his family was doing? Heck, he might even have kids of his own. Tucker didn't know, didn't have any right to know, and that both bugged and intrigued him far more than it should have.

"But you want to know."

"Nope." His lie was firmer this time, no telltale warmth or wobble to his answer, and Heidi exhaled hard before resuming scrubbing around the stove with extra force.

"That's probably the right attitude." Less teasing now, Heidi sounded more pragmatic, which was good. Last thing he needed was anyone pushing a reconciliation of any type. "No sense in rehashing the past, really. He's only here a few days?"

"Weeks, but yes. Not sticking around." He needed to remember that, tattoo it on his soul. Luis hated it around here, and no matter if they could find their way back to anything resembling a friendship, it was destined to be short-lived.

"Yeah, no sense in reopening old wounds then. Not like anything could come from it."

"True." Tucker nodded and wrung out the sponge. His back tensed—the tight, uncomfortable feeling that had lingered all day. "But… I still feel guilty. Even after all these years."

"Just treat him like any other coworker."

"Exactly." That was the right advice and what he needed to hear. Treat Luis professionally but distantly. No more awkward rehashing of the past. But somehow, he already knew he'd fail because Luis was *not* simply another coworker. He might be an adult Tucker knew little about, but he was also *Luis*, the embodiment of all those memories and feelings from so long ago. All the longing and yearning. Tucker wasn't sure he could figure out how to move forward as if their past didn't exist, but he needed to try.

Chapter Four

"Ready?" Tucker's easy smile hit Luis square in the chest, made him blink, like that might dim the power it held over him.

"Sure." *No.* Luis was anything but ready for spending the day away from the office alone with Tucker. They'd both attended the morning meeting, then Tucker, who had been strangely courteous since he'd shown up for the day, had been raring to get on the road.

"Good. I already checked out keys for one of the Jeeps." Tucker led the way to the parking lot where a line of Forest Service vehicles waited. "Figured I'd drive since I know where we're headed, but if you'd rather, I can set GPS for you."

"You can drive," Luis said grudgingly because it was only practical. Tucker had a lot more years driving these back roads into the federal lands than he did. Even if ordinarily he preferred to drive himself and hated being a passenger, he didn't want to start the day by being difficult. This was bound to be awkward enough.

"Thanks. You want a coffee on our way out of town? There's a new drive-through place that H—*people* seem to like. I noticed you didn't have a chance to use that French press of yours yet this morning."

Luis was both strangely appreciative that Tucker had observed his coffee habits already and irritated at his continued attempts to act like he was no different from other coworkers. Which, honestly, should be what he wanted, a chance to play it casual and pretend they had no history. But they did. And the near-namedrop of the ex-wife didn't escape his notice either, a sign that things weren't as free and simple as Tucker wanted.

"Coffee sounds good." He buckled up while Tucker started the Jeep. "And you can say Heidi's name around me. Promise I'm not going to pout or throw a tantrum."

He was fully aware he hadn't been at his best the previous day, hadn't reacted well to Tucker's pictures of his kids. He could do better, and if Tucker was going to make an effort, then the least he could do was try to act like an adult.

"Appreciated." Tucker backed out of the space, the sort of effortless driving that ordinarily would put Luis at ease about being the passenger, not make his pulse hum with fresh awareness. God, the last thing he needed was to get turned on whenever Tucker revealed himself the least bit competent at daily tasks. The flex of his muscled forearm and concentration lines around his eyes should be of exactly zero consequence.

"Man, it sure is strange to think of Heidi Keating as a *mom* though," he admitted, in part to get his brain off the subject of Tucker's forearms. "Wait. Is it Heidi Ryland these days?"

"Heidi Arnold now. She remarried after we divorced."

"That…" Damn it. He couldn't get a read on what Tucker thought of that turn of events. "Sorry?"

"No condolences needed." Tucker gave a tight nod as he turned onto the main road. "Her husband is a great guy originally from Detroit who works IT for the same solar energy firm she's an exec for in Bend. They've got a little girl. Saw them last night for our twice weekly dinner with the boys."

"Wow. You guys need your own blended family sit-com," Luis teased, trying to keep his voice light, not biting. Heidi happy wasn't a bad thing. It had been too many years to wish her ill or keep some sort of grudge going. Besides, she too had been a friend way back then, volunteering with him backstage on the school plays, walking him through choir choreography when he'd picked up music as an elective to get out of gym. Because their parents went to the same church, she'd always been more Tucker's friend than his, but she'd been kind and funny. It wasn't her fault that she'd won the Tucker sweepstakes.

"All we need is a nosy neighbor peeking over the hedge and relatives walking in unannounced. We've got know-it-all kids and clueless parents covered."

Luis had to laugh at that. It made sense that Tucker would still be funny, still have that dry way of delivering a punchline, but the familiar warmth in his gut, that was the unexpected and unwelcome part, the reminder of how that subtle humor always undid him.

"Unexpected guests happen more with my family. Swear my mom is still happiest when someone turns up for dinner. She keeps the fridge stocked like it's Easter week all year."

"I can believe it. God knows she fed me often enough."

"Guess I can always take credit for being your first…" He deliberately drew the pause out until Tucker's cheeks turned pink. "Tamale."

Tucker gave a sputtery cough that said his brain had gone right to kissing. And maybe all the other firsts along the way—Tucker's first homemade Mexican meal when he'd come for a playdate, then first sleepover, first time camping out in Luis's backyard, first time at the movies with no adults, first day of high school.

"I still think about them. The sweet ones especially."

It took Luis a minute to figure out that Tucker meant Mami's cooking, not the memories, which indeed could be sweet enough to make his teeth ache. "Be jealous. She made several types for my birthday a couple of months back. I was full for days."

Tucker pulled into a small hut with a drive-up window. Not a chain place and the signage had a distinctly homemade feel, but the toasty smell of fresh ground coffee beans was promising.

"Triple shot, extra foam, no sugar, and whatever you're getting." He passed Tucker a twenty.

"You don't have to pay."

"It's no problem." Luis tried to tell him with a pointed look that this wasn't worth arguing over. "Get whatever your regular is."

Frowning, Tucker relayed the order to the young barista, adding an iced hazelnut latte in a mumble that made Luis smile.

"Your health kick is making me feel guilty for my sugar addiction," Tucker grumbled as the barista turned to make their drinks.

"You always did love dessert most," Luis teased before sobering. Maybe it wouldn't hurt to tell Tucker a little of his truth. "My dad died a few years back. Complications from diabetes."

"I didn't know. I'm sorry. He was a good guy."

"He was." They hadn't always seen eye-to-eye, but that didn't stop Luis from missing him every day. "Too many years behind a desk for the bank took their toll. Died a little over six months after taking his retirement. I'm not saying I never indulge in sweet stuff anymore, but I'm a lot more careful."

That applied to so much in his life beyond sugar—he wasn't as brash and reckless these days in all areas. And he wasn't sure what to make of the part of himself that wanted Tucker to see that, to see him as an adult and not some flicker of the kid he'd once been.

"I can see that. My dad's heart attack was a similar wakeup call for the whole family. Mom changed how she cooked for his recovery, and I picked up some of that. A lot fewer fries, that's for sure."

Luis's mouth went chalky and dry. As always, he tried to push away the memory of the hasty phone call when Tucker had revealed his dad's health crisis as the reason he couldn't make the move they'd planned for years. He'd always admired Tucker's family-first stance, but hell, it had hurt back then.

"So anyway, with Dad sick, no way can I leave. Not now." Tucker's voice had crackled, a bad connection for even worse news.

Luis slumped down on his bed, glad he was alone. "But—"

"They need me." Tucker's voice was firm. It was deeper now, subtle changes after a year apart, and Luis missed him with a fierceness that had him hugging a pillow tight against his chest, trying to keep his emotions in check.

"So do I. I need you too." It was true. He needed Tucker, needed his smile, the way he grounded Luis, needed him to keep Luis steady.

"I know you do, but we'll have the whole rest of our

lives together." Tucker was whispering now, cautious even though Luis had heard the door to his room close.

"Which is going to start when?" Luis hated the edge to his tone, but he liked even less feeling as though Tucker was patting him on the head, dismissing his concerns so easily.

"I...don't know." Tucker's exhale echoed across the crackly connection, static that scraped down Luis's tense spine. *"Might be a while."*

"I can't keep waiting, Tucker. It's not fair."

And that was where Luis had to end the memory, had to stop before he remembered all too well his role in how things had ended—his ultimatum, his own failure to be there when Tucker needed him. It was no wonder he had been in such a bad mood the past few days—all those old frustrations resurfacing along with a healthy dose of self-condemnation that he'd thought he'd put behind him.

"Your dad's still around though?" Luis forced himself back to the present, to making small talk.

"Yeah. Moves a lot slower these days, and Aaron does most of the ranch business, but he's still with us. Guess that's a blessing." Tucker didn't sound entirely sure, and there was probably a story there but before he could pry, their drinks arrived in the window.

"I've got no idea how you can drink hot coffee in this heat." Tucker shook his head as he slipped a tip in the jar on the windowsill.

"Tastes better." Luis laughed. "Mike and I had this argument all the time. He always said..." Fuck it. He trailed off awkwardly because he had not meant to mention Mike at all to Tucker, ever.

"Mike?" Tucker's question as he pulled away from the coffee hut was soft, curious without being demanding.

"Boyfriend."

"Ah." A Grand Canyon's worth of meaning existed in that single syllable, and hell if Luis could unpack it all.

"He died the same year as my dad." Honestly, it might have been easier if he'd used present tense for Mike, pretended to have something waiting back home, another layer of distance between them, but while he was many things, a liar wasn't one them.

"Wow. That's…something. Must have sucked." Tucker's eyes were on the road, but the sympathy was clear, both in his eyes and his voice. "You were together a long time?"

Luis had to swallow hard, both the unwanted empathy from Tucker and his own churning emotions making his throat tight. "Yeah. Almost six years. We were on the same crew. He died in the same fire where I injured my back. Shitty year doesn't begin to cover it."

"I'm sorry. That's terrible." There was something in Tucker's tone, something personal and compassionate, and it wiggled under Luis's skin, burrowing deep in ways he wasn't prepared for.

"It's okay." It wasn't, not really, not any of it, but accepting the sympathy, giving in to voicing more of his pain, that he couldn't do.

"Still. I hope you had a good support system. I don't like thinking of you—anyone really—going through that much alone."

"I had people." Luis focused on staring out the window at the narrow road and waves of trees broken up by a few signs of modern life. Usually he found a certain peace in vast spaces like this. He might enjoy urban amenities like live music and a wealth of dining options in his off time, but he also loved the outdoors, particularly the sorts of vistas many weren't privileged to see. It opened up his chest, loosened his shoulders, made his worries small and insignificant, balancing him. But today, the gorgeous surroundings might as well have been rows of concrete pylons for all the effect they were having.

"Good." Tucker's nearness was a problem, as was his unexpected caring. The last thing he needed or wanted was Tucker having an opinion about what he'd done with the past twenty years. He didn't need evidence that Tucker's sensitive side had survived adulthood, that somewhere under those muscles and rugged features lived the sweet boy who had rescued kittens and stood up for his friends.

For his own self-protection as much any other reason, Luis let them drift off into silence as they passed into increasingly hilly terrain before Tucker came to a stop.

"This is the first stop. Edge of where we'll be doing the controlled burn. Fred wants your perspective on the plans."

"Hills always make it more challenging," Luis said as they exited the truck, slipping back into work mode, a little less comfortably now. It was harder to stay distant when Tucker was being nice on top of being professional. Distance was in even shorter supply when his body responded to how good Tucker looked in the summer sunshine, light glinting off his short hair, sunglasses giving him a certain badass vibe, muscles flexing as they walked around. *Fuck.* It was one thing to appreciate Tucker's manners and another altogether to go noticing him physically—that would only lead to more awkwardness.

You're not sixteen, he reminded himself. He didn't do crushes anymore, and it didn't matter how good Tucker's ass looked in those work pants, admiring it was only going to get him in trouble. No, it was better to take a cue from Tucker. Be polite. Nice. But absolutely, positively no infatuations.

Luis was good at his job. Like infuriatingly good, to the point Tucker had to appreciate his skills. The sun beat down on them, getting on to midday, making Tucker grateful for his hat and sunglasses as he kept up with Luis's long, fluid strides. He needed to quit making assumptions about who Luis was as an adult. The kid who had staged paint wars backstage at play rehearsal and been more obsessed with pop lyrics than algebra had grown into a professional who knew his way around a burn zone. He walked the entire perimeter of the planned area, asking smart questions about the procedures in place as he examined everything from soil to wind.

Never once did the conversation stray back to the personal, but that didn't mean his presence wasn't unnerving. If anything, the focus on matters at hand allowed Tucker's brain to wander back to what he'd learned earlier as they picked their way through the trees. Six years. Luis had been with someone that long. Another firefighter. He'd loved someone and lost them. It made Tucker's jaw clench thinking about that kind of loss. And that sympathy was accompanied by something else, a weird twinge in his chest.

Couldn't be jealousy. Not possible. He hadn't really expected Luis to spend decades pining for a teen romance that had only a handful of kisses to its name. He should be happy that Luis had built a life for himself, one where he was loved, where he could freely share that love...

Maybe that was it. A little *what if* game pinging around

in Tucker's head about how different his own life might have been if he'd had Luis's kind of bravery sooner.

"I'm gonna tell my parents. Feels weird them not knowing." Luis's legs swung back and forth as he sat on the edge of the old fort in his expansive backyard.

"Don't do that!" Tucker leaped up, risking crashing through the brittle wood floor. His heart hammered, lips going numb at the same time, breath coming in gasps.

"Why?" Luis turned to look at him, holding out a hand to get Tucker to sit back down. He didn't take it. Couldn't.

"Mine would kill me." He knew it in his bones. Maybe not literal murder, but nothing would ever be the same if they knew about the kissing and hand holding with Luis.

"Well...okay. But I'm not hiding forever." Luis nodded with the sort of certainty Tucker wasn't sure he'd ever have. Not here, at least. He liked playing the what-if game with Luis, imagining a future together, but it was always away from here, one of the funky little Californian neighborhoods Luis was always going on about where two men could be together and where Tucker's family's judgment couldn't reach him.

And now here he was, decades later, older and wiser, and Luis was too, and he'd apparently stuck to that resolve. Good for him.

"You said you also wanted to show me a recent suspect spot fire?" Luis asked as they rounded back in sight of the Jeep.

"Yup. Did you get all the data you needed here?"

"Yes, it should be a fairly straightforward burn unless we get wind. I'll discuss contingency plans at the next meeting and work with Garrick to make sure Dispatch is ready for any changes that might come up."

Huh. That was usually Tucker's role, readying the

team, working on alternative plans in case of weather, and coordinating the various crews that would be needed on site. However, he couldn't deny Luis's expertise. In keeping with his goal of treating him like any other coworker, he nodded curtly. "Sounds good. Keep me in the loop."

"Will do. Now lead on."

Tucker didn't call him on his bossiness there either. And if he was honest, it wasn't merely in the interest of keeping the peace either. He maybe liked Luis take-charge, and that was something he needed to sit with a bit. Attraction like this didn't come along very often for him, and he needed to remind himself how foolish it would be to let it get out of hand.

The drive took them farther into the federal lands, winding roads that gave way to an unpaved logging trail that required tight concentration to navigate and not as much opportunity for conversation.

"When was the last rain?" Luis asked as they got out, his head apparently already deep into the job. Unlike Tucker.

"Two weeks ago or so. I can get you exact precipitation data tomorrow back at the office."

"Good. I'll need that." Luis continued to pepper him with questions as he examined the scorched trees and blackened earth, looking at the burn pattern, tracking even minute details.

The aftermath of a spot fire was always almost spooky—burnt trees dancing next to ones that had been spared, a weird stillness settling in the area like the terrain itself was wounded, retreating to attempt to heal.

"I'm pretty sure this is intentional versus natural causes, but I want to do more examining." Luis straightened from examining a particular stump.

"You always did love a puzzle," Tucker observed, still trying to reconcile who Luis had been with who he was now.

"Oh yeah." Luis gave him an unexpected grin. "My niece and nephews all love me. I'm the *tio* with all the Legos and contraptions. And now that the nephews are getting older, they call for me to come help out at science fair time too."

"Raul and Carlos had kids? How many?" Tucker remembered Luis's older brothers as gangly college-bound sports-obsessed teens, not dads. *Wait. You're a dad too, Ryland.*

"Three boys in four years for Carlos, God love him and my poor sister-in-law. Then Raul's two came along a little later, a boy and a girl. Five grandkids for Mami to dote on. Makes for loud holidays, but it keeps her from bugging me about adding to the numbers."

"She…ah…" Tucker wasn't entirely sure how to ask what he wanted to know, but he bumbled ahead anyway. "She liked your guy? Mike?"

"Yeah." Luis's smile took on a softer edge, fond and distant. "She really did. Papi took longer to warm up to him, but then they'd sit and watch Dodger games together. Mike let him talk historic stats all he wanted. That probably got him in his good graces faster than a grandkid even."

Tucker laughed at that. "Sounds about like your dad. Win him over with math."

"Yup." Eyes clouding, Luis nodded. "Mike wasn't out for a long time, and his family never quite knew what to make of me even after he came out. We fell out of touch pretty quickly, but my mom still brings flowers to his grave. He was a good guy."

"Anyone lucky enough to land you better be." Tucker meant the words to come out as a tease, but his firm belief in the sentiment took on a more emphatic tone.

"Ha. More like anyone crazy enough to put up with me."

"I'm glad you had him." Still resolute, his voice shifted to something quieter. "You...deserve to be happy. And for what it's worth, I truly am sorry that you lost him."

"Thanks." Luis swallowed audibly, looking away at the valley below them. The air itself seemed to shift in that moment, warm breeze coming through. "Guess we should head back?"

"Yeah." Strangely reluctant to leave this spot, Tucker turned back to the Jeep. This time their silence felt more comfortable as they made their way back to the main road. Predictably his personal cell beeped with Walker's ring tone as soon as they were back with a decent signal. "Can you do me a favor and glance down at my phone? I just want to make sure it's not an emergency with the boys and don't want to pull over if I don't have to."

"Sure." Luis grabbed Tucker's phone from the console. "Nice case."

"Wade gave it to me last birthday." It was a metallic case with subtle imagery from the reboot of the space franchise he and Luis had been obsessed with back in the day.

"Message says, 'FYI that we're having dinner at Mary Anne's tonight. Her cousin is in town and wants to meet Wade.'" Luis laughed as he set the phone back down. "Setup much? I'd say poor kid, but maybe he likes that sort of thing. So maybe lucky kid?"

"It's Wade. As long as the cousin likes football and hearing about workout plans, he's good. And darn, you and I skipped lunch. I'm absolutely starving. Was counting on cooking with the boys." A rogue thought wiggled into his brain and refused to leave. "How about you? Hungry? Want to get something after we return the Jeep?"

If Luis truly were another coworker from out of town, he wouldn't hesitate to make the invitation. He didn't like eating alone, and he'd eaten countless meals with contacts in the firefighting community. It didn't have to mean anything. But still his pulse sped up as he stopped at a four-way intersection and waited for Luis's answer.

Releasing a whistling breath, Luis shook his head. "That's probably a bad idea."

"Come on. You need to eat. I need to eat." Strangely, the more Luis shook his head, the more invested Tucker was in his suggestion. "This doesn't have to be complicated. Surely we can share a simple meal together?"

"Simple?" Luis raised an eyebrow. "When have things ever been simple between us?"

"They could be." Shrugging, Tucker looked away to make his turn. "They were. Once upon a time. We were friends. Nothing says we can't be friendly again. The way I see it, we're stuck working together. Figuring out how do that is a smart idea."

"There's a lot left unsaid." Luis's voice was quieter now, more considering.

"Yeah." Tucker couldn't dispute that. And yet he still wanted this, bad idea or not. Maybe Heidi was wrong— maybe they did need to clear the air, at least a little, if they were to find a more amicable way forward. "And maybe that's more reason to spend a little time away from work. Eat. Talk."

"Talking is possibly an even worse idea than dinner."

"Possibly."

"Well, at least you're honest." Luis's laugh was part snort, but not as dismissive as before. "And I am hungry. Blaze can wait, I guess, for us to grab a quick dinner."

"Blaze?"

"My cat."

"Ah." Another part of Luis's life he had no clue about. Tucker had always been the animal lover, not Luis. *People change*, he reminded himself yet again. "Well, we won't keep Blaze waiting too long. I know a brew pub with good wait times even at the height of the summer season."

"I still say this is a bad idea."

"You're probably right." Tucker laughed, but he wasn't entirely kidding and doubted Luis was either despite his lighter tone. But perhaps more troubling than dread over the coming talk was the satisfaction at having won Luis's agreement and the anticipation for more of his company. Yeah, Luis was right—this was a terrible, risky idea, and he was still counting down the minutes.

Chapter Five

This wasn't a date, not by any stretch of the imagination. Luis had been on plenty of dates. He would know. But somehow knowing something logically did nothing for the churning in his stomach as he pulled into the restaurant Tucker had chosen. The place wasn't far from his Bend hotel and the department headquarters, and Luis was unreasonably glad that Tucker wasn't making him drive to Painter's Ridge. Less chance this way of running into people one or both of them might know.

While he waited for Tucker to pull in, he stretched his back, which was tight after hours in the Jeep. He'd need more than some basic stretching that night if he wanted to sleep. Exercise followed by the hotel's hot tub sounded like a good prescription for getting rid of not only his sore muscles but also the tension that had plagued him ever since Rosalind had given him this assignment. The day spent with only Tucker hadn't helped any, especially with him showing compassion and concern. Damn it. He didn't want conflicting feelings where Tucker was concerned. Frustration was much easier to deal with.

"Hey. You found it okay?" Tucker exited a dark blue SUV with bumper stickers promoting the Painter's Ridge Football Boosters and the high school's honor society.

The large vehicle looked particularly suited to hauling half a soccer team and dwarfed Luis's little compact.

"Yeah. Which twin got Heidi's brains?" Gesturing at the academic brag bumper sticker, he managed the joke easily, which boded well for him surviving this outing.

"Walker. They both play football, but Walker's the one with the grades. He's wanted to be a marine biologist since he was seven and we took him to the aquarium on the coast. Wade…" Tucker laughed, that sort of fond paternal chuckle Luis's brothers did well, and shook his head. "It's a shame Wade's not taller. Pro football's probably not happening. Maybe college ball. But I'm not sure that my asserting that he'll need a major is getting through."

"Maybe he'll get a decent college coach." Luis followed Tucker up the sidewalk toward the restaurant's doors. It was a low building with the sort of faux log cabin styling popular around these parts. They were a little early for the dinner rush, but the air still carried hints of sizzling meat. "Raul went to USC on a baseball scholarship, but an assistant coach talked him into getting serious about his business major. Now he's got an MBA, three cell phones, and enough underlings to make my head spin. Doubt anyone would have predicted that back in high school. Bet your kid will be the same way."

"Hope so. God knows he's not listening to me." Tucker paused as they reached the host, a fresh-faced young guy with two earrings, something Luis wasn't used to around this area. Maybe times truly were changing here too. The host led them to a back booth by a window. The woodsy, vaguely Western theme continued for the restaurant's interior—lots of pale wood and sepia-toned ranching pictures with oversize leather booths dominating the space.

"You still eat meat, right?" Tucker asked as they opened their glossy menus.

"Yes, Tucker. I still eat meat." Taking advantage of the chance for a joke, Luis added a wink, which made Tucker's cheeks darken. "Everything in moderation. Including beer."

He didn't imbibe all that often, but if he was going to survive any sort of real conversation with Tucker, he might need it.

"Good idea." Tucker nodded sharply, like he too wouldn't mind some fortifying. They each ordered a local IPA when the server, a near-clone of the host, arrived at their table with water. Tucker got short ribs with mashed potatoes, while Luis ordered an intriguing portobello mushroom and steak salad with a side of sriracha cauliflower just to watch Tucker's face at his selections. His wide eyes lingered even after the server disappeared again.

"Man. Wade would love you…" Tucker trailed off, seeming to realize how unlikely it was that Luis would ever meet the kid.

"I'm going to make you try a piece just to have a story to tell him," he threatened, enjoying this a little too much. Probably inching too close to flirting, but banter like this felt so much better than constantly being on the defensive.

"Fine. They do dessert hand pies here with in-season berries that are totally worth the sugar splurge. You taste that and I'll have a bite of the cauliflower."

"Deal." Their eyes met across the table, mid-laugh, Tucker's eyes still twinkling, and Luis's next breath caught. Damn. It really was too easy to fall right back into old habits. Basking in Tucker's presence was so simple—and dangerous. And something in his expression must have given him away, because the light gradually faded from Tucker's eyes, replaced by a frown.

"What's wrong?" Tucker asked as their beers arrived.

"Nothing." Luis sighed then because that wasn't the truth, and they both knew it. "I guess…it's just weird. Being here with you. Talking."

"Yeah, it is strange, that's for sure." Tucker fiddled with the coaster. "Honestly, never expected to see you again."

"Totally. After all these years, it's just…"

"Weird," they said in unison, and somehow, that connection between their brains relaxed Luis more, made it easier to speak the truth.

"I spent a lot of years mad at you, even though I knew rationally that the anger wasn't justified. And yeah, I know it probably went both ways as far as pissed off goes."

"You're not wrong."

"And then, I did get over it." That part wasn't a lie either. He hadn't spent two decades this jumbled up—he'd laughed and loved and traveled and while maybe lately fun and connection were a little more…infrequent, he wasn't some hermit locked away muttering about the one who got away either. "I laid the past to rest so to speak. But now I'm here, and seeing you…it all comes crashing back, you know?"

"Yeah. I get it." Rotating his beer glass a few times, Tucker finally stopped fidgeting with it enough to take a sip. "Same. I just keep thinking…what the hell happened to us?"

"Exactly. I'll be honest, much as I still had this…raw

spot, it had been years since I really thought about...
everything."

"Understandable, really. You've lived a whole life
since you were here. Mike. Your nieces and nephews.
Your dad's passing. All of it. And same here. I was busy
with raising the boys. But I'm surprised at myself, at
how much I want to hear about what you've been up to."

Luis took a long sip of beer at that revelation. Tucker
angry would be far easier to dismiss than Tucker curious, pushing this "let's be friendly" agenda. However,
all the memories that accompanied Tucker were the real
problem. The pining and emotions kept bubbling to the
surface as if the years apart hadn't happened, intense as
ever. "I wish I could stop thinking about it. What went
right. What went wrong. How it all fell apart."

"It feels too simple to say we were kids, but that was a
huge part of it. We were kids, and a year and a half was a
long time to be apart, to have to rely on letters and emails
and the odd chat."

"Yeah, it was. We were...pen pals, I guess. But we
had a plan. And then that fell apart."

"We'll make it work. You'll see." Luis made himself
sound way more certain than he felt. "Rest of this year
and then senior year is nothing. All we need is to make
it to graduation."

"Yup." Tucker wasn't looking at Luis, instead studying
the empty football field from their perch in the bleachers.

"You'll come to LA. We'll both go to school and get
jobs and a little place." Luis loved this particular day-
dream, and he stretched as he warmed up to the topic.
"And in the meantime, there's email. And regular mail.
And that chat thing my cousin was telling me about. We
can try that."

"I'm not the most on writing. Like what do I say?"
Tucker studied his sneakers.

*"Tell me about school. And about the horses. And what
your mom cooked for dinner. I want to hear all of it."*
Glancing around to make sure they were still alone, he
patted Tucker's knee before grabbing his hand, squeezing.

"Okay. I can do that." Tucker nodded, but his eyes
were still brimming with uncertainty.

And now, with adult pragmatism, Luis could see how
doomed they'd been, despite all those big plans. They'd
been so *young.* Him especially, believing all the way to
his sneakers that sheer force of want would be enough to
produce the future they both wanted. But that same stubborn optimism had made him less than flexible. Their
falling-out wasn't all on Tucker by any means.

*"My dad's heart attack changed so much. I couldn't
leave."* Tucker's dad's massive heart attack had sent his
whole family into a tailspin.

Luis could still remember the way his chest had
pounded and his eyes had burned at the news. "I know.
And I was stupid and hurt and made that ultimatum."

*"Damn it, Tucker. He's always so mean to you. You
don't owe him anything. And you promised."* Luis knew
he sounded petty, but his whole body was vibrating, sense
of doom coursing through him.

"I know," Tucker said softly. *"But I also promised
my mom."*

"You don't want to tell them." Luis's voice was flat
because he knew the answer.

"I can't." Tucker sounded like he was in mortal agony
and maybe he was.

"You mean you won't. If you can't come, can't even

*give me a date, then I'm not sure what kind of friends we
are anymore. I'm tired of saying no to fun."*

*"I don't want you passing up fun either. But I can't
promise some deadline either. Might be here awhile."*

*Awhile might as well have been a decade for the level
of devastation that descended on Luis. He wanted to wait
for Tucker, but damn it, he needed some sort of light at
the end of the endless tunnel of waiting. He'd wanted this
for so long, he almost couldn't remember a time when he
hadn't been waiting and wanting. It colored everything,
his time at school, his friends here, the way he framed his
future. His ribs ached, almost like they couldn't hold back
the heartache any longer, dam of feelings moments from
bursting. "I keep turning down chances, and I'm tired
of it. It's one thing if you're coming, but if you're not..."*

"I get it. You're done waiting."

"I'm only human."

Only human. It had made so much sense at the time,
his own hurt foremost in his mind, but he'd forgotten
somehow that Tucker was too. But now, looking across
the table, seeing the pain in Tucker's eyes, he could own
his role in what had happened—he'd been selfish. Maybe
shortsighted too. And young. It always came back to that.

"You were disappointed. I don't think you meant to
be...dunno...cruel with what you said. It was just the
truth. We weren't going to make it."

"Yeah. I never expected you to immediately start dating Heidi though. And maybe that was naive of me."
Talking this out, he could feel the resentment leaving
his body, one tense muscle at a time. He'd been deeply
wounded by how fast everything happened after their
last conversation, but taking responsibility for his own
behavior made it hard to keep on blaming Tucker.

"I didn't." Tucker's eyes went wide as his voice dropped even further. "It wasn't dating. Wasn't even... the other."

Luis raised an eyebrow because the mere existence of the twins disputed *that*.

"It was one time. You and I had argued, and I was crushed—not blaming you, just explaining my state of mind. And she'd just broken up with this total jerk of an older guy. Her parents were out of town, mine were at the hospital still dealing with dad's condition, graduation had been a total bust for both of us, and we were drinking. Zero tolerance back then. Bad idea, but there we were. And somehow..."

"I see." Luis had to smile because he could see how that could happen, and honestly, while he had no business caring either way, knowing there hadn't been some grand romance between Tucker and Heidi helped with the whole letting-go thing.

"Anyway, it would have simply been an ill-advised one-time thing, but..."

"Twins."

"Yup. We knew there were options, but we were also such good friends, and I wasn't going to make her do it all on her own or pressure her into another choice she didn't want to make. Plus, we knew the families were likely to do enough pressuring of their own. So, we did what we thought made sense and eloped. And as bad of an idea as that probably was, I can't bring myself to regret it. My boys...they're everything to me."

"I can tell. And I'm not asking you to regret it." Luis was surprised how true that was, the weight of certainty pushing out more of the tension he'd been carrying in his back the past few days. "I'm not blaming you either.

I need to take responsibility too, but in the end, it was what it was."

"Yeah." Tucker exhaled hard, face going slack.

"And maybe it worked out how it was supposed to. God knows I had a lot of growing up to do myself."

"We both did."

Luis nodded right as their food arrived, a big steaming platter for Tucker and one of the largest salads Luis had seen. The food was a welcome distraction from the heaviness of the conversation. This was a lot to unpack, truths replacing decades of assumptions, and new, adult understanding replacing adolescent hurt and anger. But he wasn't sure that letting go of his regrets and resentment was entirely a good thing where Tucker was concerned because with understanding came caring, and *that* he simply couldn't have. Healing old wounds presented risks he wasn't prepared to deal with.

It was what it was. I don't blame you. Even as he tried to eat, Luis's words pranced around in Tucker's brain, inducing a giddy sort of lightness that kept threatening to overwhelm him. He'd had private guilt and shame pushing down his shoulders for so long whenever he allowed himself to think of Luis that he hadn't been prepared for the rush of finally clearing the air between them. The acknowledgment that they'd both made mistakes felt like a benediction he hadn't known he'd been waiting for.

His food tasted sharper, flavors popping in fresh ways, and the background music resonated, like his senses were waking up from a long slumber.

"How are the short ribs?" Luis asked, motioning with his fork at Tucker's plate. He too seemed lighter, more relaxed now.

"Really good. It's one of my favorite things to get here because they slow cook them until they practically melt. Here. Try." He slid a small bite of meat on the edge of Luis's plate. He was being nice, same as he'd be with one of the boys or Heidi, but he'd vastly underestimated the effect of watching Luis try his food. Luis's eyes went darker as he chewed with deliberate and rather sexy slowness, making unexpected heat unfurl in Tucker's belly.

"Yeah, that's nice. I think the stout really enhances the beefiness. And the fresh herbs add a brightness. I'm going to try getting a deeper sear like this next time I make short ribs," Luis mused so thoughtfully that Tucker had to laugh.

"Look at you. You turned into a foodie."

"I can cook." Luis's casual shrug said that he was probably damn impressive at it. "And you said you'd try this."

He passed over a piece of the spicy fried cauliflower. This was…well, not exactly flirty, but something. Tucker might be out of practice for any sort of dating, which this decidedly was not. But it was comfortable. Cozy. Way friendlier than they'd been the past few days. Gamely, he chewed the vegetable. And nearly seared his tongue off, scrambling for his water.

"Yup, same old Tucker." Luis's laugh was as welcome as rain this time of year, soft and easy. "I might have gone and learned how to cook, but apparently expanding your palate wasn't on the agenda."

"I was too busy plating nuggets and fries for toddlers. And then Wade went and ate a jalapeno slice on a dare and didn't cry."

"You were screwed."

"Yup. I don't even try to keep up with him these days.

I can cook, but with teens, it's more about the quantity of calories I can produce than any sort of gourmet dish. Heidi's husband, though, is a fabulous cook. You'd like him. His homemade mac and cheese almost made *me* be the one to propose."

"Now that would be fun. Your own little poly triad. Too bad he doesn't swing that way?" Luis raised an eyebrow.

He had to chuckle at that. "This is central Oregon. A poly anything is gonna catch a lot of flak, especially from folks like Heidi and I were raised with. Not that that was ever on the table. I've never come out and asked, but I assume Isaac's straight and he's a fairly traditional guy to boot. Can't see him having any wild threesomes."

"And you?"

"Me? You asking how I identify these days or if I would have been into the idea of a triad?"

"Both maybe."

"I'm sure threesomes and moresomes have their appeal, but I…uh…no. Not for me. Not with them, particularly. And as for the rest…it's complicated."

"Want to tell me about it?" Luis's head tilted, but he didn't lean forward and kept his focus mainly on his salad.

That was nice, the way Luis was offering, without pushing. And honestly, apart from their past, there weren't many people he could talk about this sort of thing with, and it was…refreshing to not have to carefully word each statement. Heck, even joking about threesomes was fun because this was someone he could be honest with, and he didn't have that many people like that.

"Heidi knew…back then. About us. She was the only

one I told." The back of Tucker's neck heated and he kept his voice down.

Nodding, Luis made a small affirmative noise, but his eyes were pleased. Tucker hadn't wanted to keep him and their special friendship a deep secret, but back then he simply hadn't felt like he had many choices.

"And we talked about…some stuff. We were always the sort of friends who could talk about anything. Made us good parenting partners, even if *that* part of our relationship was…kind of a dud."

"You never?" Luis's eyes went wider.

"We did. Not often, but…we tried, more the first couple of years than later on. Then she was in a psych class that talked about sexuality as a spectrum. Showed me the book, and I spent some time reading it myself."

"I'm enjoying the image of you so studious." Luis's smile was kind.

"Yeah. Anyway, I realized that for me attraction is more of an emotional connection thing than a physical thing. I was never one to see the appeal in random stranger hookups, and while I can appreciate good looks in various genders, it doesn't make me want to go there with them unless that emotional closeness is there first. Which is all a convoluted way of saying the book showed me that demisexual makes a lot of sense for me."

"I see. It makes sense then that you and Heidi…" Luis made a vague gesture. "You were close. Friends. Comfort sort of thing."

"Yeah. Exactly, and as time wore on and we drifted further and further apart, that emotional connection was…less, and it was harder for me to…connect on that more physical level too. It wasn't the marriage either of us needed, to be frank."

"I'm glad she found something that makes her happy. But you? What about what would make you happy?"

That was a loaded question, one Tucker still wasn't quite sure how to answer for himself. He took a minute to study a picture of a salmon on the wall. "Attraction is pretty rare for me, but I'm not opposed to the idea of someone in my life romantically. Most often that attraction seems to be other guys I feel a significant bond with." His face heated and his lips went dry. He wasn't sure whether he wanted Luis to know how much he actually did yearn for connection, how lonely he got sometimes. He liked the idea of someone in his life, in his bed very much, but finding that person hadn't seemed very likely. Until, of course, Luis strode back into his life, and that old connection kept sparking present attraction. "And in any event, I'm not exactly…"

"Out." Shoulders slumping, Luis shook his head like he hadn't expected any different but was disappointed nonetheless.

Tucker had been about to say *looking*, but he figured he might as well address Luis's implicit assumption. "Well, that's where it gets complicated. I'm not out at work, no, but after Heidi and I split, my family was… damn, it was bad, the things they said about her, the way they treated her. Like she was a cheater and abandoning her duty to her family."

"That had to be hard." Luis shifted, moving his hand restlessly, almost like he wanted to reach for Tucker but thought the better of it. Tucker liked that impulse, though, maybe more than he should. He felt the warmth of Luis's concern almost as surely as if they had touched.

"It was, yeah. I just couldn't stand their assumptions and attitude anymore, and finally, one day when I was helping Dad and Aaron in the barn, I just had enough and told them it wasn't Heidi's fault that we split. Wasn't her fault that I was mainly attracted to men and that she deserved a marriage that made her happy in every area."

"Wow." Luis fumbled his fork, narrowly avoiding it hitting the table. And wow was right. Tucker wasn't one to get fanciful about single decisions, but that right there had been a defining moment in his adulthood, the point where he finally felt like his own man.

"Well...that went over about as well as you're probably thinking. Nothing's been the same with them since. Frosty with no sign of thaw, guess you could say." That was putting it nicely, but he wasn't going to let his feelings over their reaction join his already raw emotional state. "But at least they laid off Heidi, and honestly, it was...freeing. Them knowing. Haven't felt the need to share it with the whole town or work, but it's also no longer this...dark secret either."

"That...that's something." Luis nodded sharply. "I know it probably doesn't make any difference, but I'm proud of you. Standing up for her like that. Standing up for both of you. It couldn't have been easy."

Luis was wrong. It did make a difference, him saying that. Tucker hadn't told many people this story, and having Luis proud of him made his shoulders lift, filled him with new certainty that he'd done the right thing.

"Dessert?" The young server, who had been blessedly absent during their talk, arrived to clear their dinner plates.

"I believe there was a promise of pie?" Luis grinned, seeming to sense that Tucker needed lightness right then, not more heavy conversation.

"Yep. Marionberry. Bet you can't get those down in LA."

"Not easily at least. Get a piece for you and I'll taste it."

"Sure." Tucker placed the order with the server, who seemed to find their little exchange amusing judging by his small smile, and he arrived back with the pie and two forks in short order. The menu called it a hand pie, but eating it by hand would be asking to spend the rest of the evening wearing berries.

"Try it." Tucker moved the plate to in the middle to encourage Luis to take more than a single taste. And again, he was unprepared for the eroticism of Luis eating. He took a small bite, but savored it, tongue sweeping out to catch the last drop of berry juice. Eyes briefly fluttering shut, he gave a small smile, one that hit Tucker low in some warm and sensitive spot.

Tucker wasn't someone who got crushes easily and didn't generally get turned on by random acts like eating. Honestly, Heidi's textbook had gone a long way to repairing his self-esteem. He didn't have a broken sex drive, nor was he a failure as a husband, two worries that had plagued him before he came to a place of self-acceptance. It wasn't that he never got turned on, but generally it happened after he knew someone for a long time, a slow smolder versus lightning-quick ignition.

You know Luis, his body seemed determined to remind him. Yes, he did. But acting on the rogue heat in his belly would be ill-advised. They were only now starting to inch their way back to something approaching friendliness, understanding replacing the bitterness and old hurts. It would be foolish in the extreme to try to pursue…well, anything really. Luis wasn't sticking around, and Tucker didn't have a clue how to do casual. *Bad, bad idea.*

But that reminder faded as they split the check, body thrumming with awareness of Luis's nearness as they walked out. Strangely reluctant to end the evening, he followed Luis over to his car—a sporty little red compact. No bumper stickers, but two figurines in the rear window—some baseball player and a superhero, same franchise as Tucker's phone case.

"Guess I'm not the only one who liked the reboot." He gestured at the window.

"Eh. It was okay." A little smile teased the edges of Luis's mouth as he fiddled with his keys. "Thanks. This dinner suggestion…it was a good idea."

"Yeah, it was. One of my best." Tucker meant the conversation, how good it had felt to lay everything out there, but then their eyes met, and the meaning shifted to something personal and intimate, an expression of how much he'd enjoyed the company and how much he rather desperately wanted to do it again.

Luis held his gaze, not wavering, and when his tongue darted out to lick his lower lip, the harsh kick of arousal almost stole Tucker's next breath. God, it would be so easy to lean in and—

Honk. Damn it. A car wanted into the empty space where he was standing. And with that, whatever spell had had him on the verge of kissing Luis was broken. They nodded and waved, a hurried goodbye. He wanted to imagine that Luis was as flustered as he was, but Luis probably had hundreds of near-kisses to his name and might not have even noticed Tucker's deliberation.

Yeah, that was it. He hadn't noticed. And that was what Tucker told himself the whole drive home. The car the boys shared was parked haphazardly in the drive, and he prepared another lecture about how to share the driveway as he let himself into the house. Not surprisingly, he found the boys with their heads in the fridge.

"Didn't you eat at Mary Anne's?"

"Yeah, but asking for seconds might have been rude." Wade gave him a grin. "And there wasn't any dessert."

"Found it!" Walker came up with a carton of the local brand of moose tracks ice cream Tucker had hidden in the back of the freezer. "You want some, Dad? And you're later than usual."

"Nah. I stopped for dinner with...a friend from work." He'd paused way too long trying to decide what to label Luis and stumbled over the rest of his explanation. And damn him for forgetting to text both of them. "That brewery with the short ribs I like so much. And we lingered a bit over dessert, so I think I'm good on sweets."

"Dessert?" Walker's mouth quirked. "Lingering?"

"Was this a *date*?" Ever more direct, Wade's eyes narrowed as he considered Tucker.

"Date? No, no, I don't do that," he blustered as Wade grabbed a pair of bowls for Walker who already had the ice cream scoop. Tucker had to turn away from Wade's continued speculative gaze. "It was just a friend. Someone I knew a long time ago. That's all."

"You forgot to text us where you were," Walker mused as he scooped the ice cream. "You never do that."

"And you had dessert." Wade wasn't dropping this any more than Walker, apparently, and Tucker groaned and grabbed himself a bowl. Maybe he did need some sugar to survive this conversation.

"Yeah. Are you *sure* it wasn't a date?" Walker gave him a small scoop while giving himself and Wade monster portions. He might know Tucker's ice cream preferences without being asked, but he was wrong here.

"I'm sure." Tucker was not trying to start something with Luis. That moment when they could have kissed notwithstanding, he knew better. But damn if his stomach didn't still quiver with the memory of it. He might *want*, but he wasn't going to *have*, and that was what mattered.

"Good." Walker was surprisingly emphatic, to the point that Tucker had to tilt his head, try to decide if something else was going on with the kid.

"Don't listen to him." Wade rolled his eyes and jostled Walker's shoulder. "He's thinking that one lovesick dude is enough around here. I'm thinking that it's past time that you got la—"

"Hey now." Tucker shook his spoon at Wade. Him meddling in Tucker's sex life in any way was the last thing any of them needed.

Wade, however, wasn't deterred, sly smile and impish eyes. "Even Mom thinks that you need—"

"And she's entitled to that opinion." Tucker had determined years and years ago to never badmouth or contradict Heidi in front of the boys, but she too was wrong about this. He didn't need to date. And even Heidi and the endless "don't be lonely, Tucker" refrain would agree that anything with Luis would be foolish. "But I don't need or want to date. I'm good. Promise."

And he was. Two great kids. Roof over their heads. Job he enjoyed. Friends. He didn't *need* anything else, but even hours later as he climbed under the covers, a part of him still *wanted*. Damn it.

Chapter Six

Tucker had been about to kiss him last night. Of that, Luis was sure, and even now as he reviewed fire data, the restless night and a dragging morning behind him, he was still obsessing over what hadn't happened. And what had—them finally talking everything out, him seeing some more of the man Tucker had become. Strong, standing up to that family of his. While Luis's teen self had wanted Tucker to be willing to make that choice at seventeen, as an adult Luis understood better what a hard position Tucker had been in as a kid. His super-strict family wouldn't have taken well to news of Tucker being anything other than straight and destined for ranching life. Asking a kid with few employable skills to break from the life he'd been raised to accept was a big ask, and Luis got that now.

Respect. That was what Luis kept coming back to as he shuffled through papers, letting admiration for who Tucker was now chase out bitterness over who they'd both once been. But with that respect came a dangerous attraction and endless replaying of that almost-kiss. He would have let Tucker kiss him, would have happily met him halfway, would have greeted him with a hunger that he knew better than to feed. Any kissing would have been a mistake, and he should have been relieved, not driving himself up a wall all morning over the way the energy between them had all but crackled.

Crackled. Wait. He thumbed back several photos. Yes. There. More evidence of a burn pattern indicative of an intentional fire, but the pictures were blurrier than he liked. He really needed to see this particular site in person, preferably before another summer rain surprised them. He'd just finished a hasty lunch at his desk, and as he hoped, he found Adams in his office, returning from his own break.

"There's a spot fire location we didn't hit yesterday that I really want to see in person," he explained after exchanging a few pleasantries. "I think it might be key to tying the sites together, establishing a pattern. Permission to head out to visit it? I might also visit the air base, see if I can talk to any of the smoke-jumping crew that was initially on site there. I already reviewed the procedures for Tuesday's burn, so I'm ahead on work."

"Sure, sure." Adams nodded, not looking up as he logged into the computer behind his big desk. "That makes sense. Check out a Jeep and take Tucker with you."

"Excell— Hang on, I don't need to bother Tucker. I've got GPS."

"And so does he. It's a ways out there, backcountry, two different logging roads to reach it, then a hike in. You shouldn't go alone, and he knows the management at the air base if you end up needing to go there as well. He'll get you in to see who you need to talk with easier than you on your own."

This wasn't bad logic, but he still didn't need to bother Tucker, who undoubtedly had work of his own to get done, and he tried telling Adams that, but he held firm.

"It's a Friday afternoon. He'll be happy to get out of the office."

Effectively dismissed, Luis wandered over to Tucker's office, steps slower because as much as the tension had been lowered the night before, he still wasn't sure about more time alone. Tucker's door was open, as seemed to be his habit, and he hung up the phone as Luis stuck his head in the doorway.

"Adams says I'm taking you out in the field." Gesturing at the phone, Tucker smiled broadly. Damn him for still having dimples.

"If you're busy with other work…" Luis managed weakly, knowing it was a losing proposition.

"Nothing that won't keep." Tucker stood, chest muscles rippling as he stretched. "It's a gorgeous day out. No way do I want to be cooped up here. And we don't want you hiking alone to this site. I could send someone else with you, but I'm not passing up that sunshine."

"Fair enough." Luis still resented the idea that he needed a tour guide of sorts, but nothing was going to be gained by continuing to protest other than ruining Tucker's good mood. After he changed into his hiking boots, he grabbed his travel coffee mug and some extra water and met Tucker by the same Jeep as the day before.

"Still good with me driving?" Tucker was already heading to the driver's side, so Luis stifled his inner groan and nodded.

"Sure. More time for me to review this data as we go."

"Yeah? How's that going?" Tucker easily swung himself up into the Jeep and behind the wheel as Luis settled himself.

"Going well. This is actually one of my favorite parts of the job, not that we ever welcome arson. But like you said yesterday, it's a puzzle. I'm trying to build a model of what's happened with the suspect spot fires so we can more effectively interpret the data and possibly aid investigative and law enforcement efforts."

"And maybe predict where the next one could be?"

"Yup."

They talked fire behavior most of the way out of town, taking a winding road past several campgrounds and hiking trailheads. Eventually even Tucker had to rely on the GPS to lead them to the logging access roads. They'd intersected a popular hiking trail, but this was far quicker than doing the entire distance by foot. The midday sun was still beating down as they arrived at the best place to park, having driven as close as they were going to get.

"Smoke jumpers must have had their work cut out for them," Luis observed as he exited the Jeep. The rugged terrain would not have been easy for the people hauling hundreds of pounds of gear with them. Taking the water with them, they set out at a brisk pace.

"This is nothing. We had a fire last year, week-long operation plus cleanup time, with a remote fire camp and the jumpers were battling wind and elevation the whole time. Finding landing zones was a challenge and a half."

Something about the way Tucker spoke about the smoke jumpers, a certain reverence maybe, gave him away, and Luis had to chuckle. "You still play the what-if game, don't you? Part of you really wanted to be out there with them."

"Maybe." Tucker shrugged as they continued walking, but a little smile played with his lips. "Okay, yeah, just between us, giving up that dream…wasn't easy. The adrenaline. The planes. The camaraderie. The variety."

"I remember. Heck, you even had the action figures."

"Yeah, I had it all planned out. And I did start on summer ground fire crews because I could be the primary caregiver over the winter while Heidi was in school. But then the boys got bigger and things like health insurance and tuition assistance for me to go to school myself mattered more than being on the front lines. Anyway, I've built a good life for myself in this job. Too old to see myself switching, that's for sure."

"You're not that old," Luis protested both because if Tucker was old then so was he, and because part of him resisted the reminder that Tucker was one hundred percent married to this area and this job, no matter how his family had treated him. Not that Luis got an opinion there and not that it made a lick of difference to how bad of an idea it would be to get involved with him. "And with your experience in both supervision and fire management, you could probably either be the most qualified rookie they've ever had or get some sort of support role."

"Rookie." Tucker snorted. "Think I'll leave that to the young guns."

"I'm just saying, all routine makes you old before your time." Said the guy who had spent more weekends than was healthy with his cat that year, but maybe Luis was better at giving advice on how to avoid ruts than getting out of them himself.

"Yeah? What's your endgame then? Aiming for your boss's job?" Eyebrows raised, Tucker seemed to sense that Luis was more talk than action.

"I'm happy in my role right now. Getting all the required certifications wasn't easy. Maybe less travel would be good." He gave Tucker a pointed look. Travel might have brought him here, and he might not regret the chance to smooth things over between them, but he also couldn't deny that the emotional upheaval of getting to that place took a toll. "Long-term, I'll simply have to see. A position with an interagency crew isn't outside the realm of possibility. Likewise, moving into a role where I could do even more investigation would be good. I'm open to whatever comes my way. Complacency isn't good."

"Yeah." Tucker's tone was thoughtful as they approached the site, and then it was back to business, Luis combing the area for an up-close examination of the burn pattern. The initial smoke-jumping crew had done a fabulous job of containing the blaze, keeping it from spreading, but the scorched trees and downed limbs spoke to how close of a call it had been from spreading into something more unmanageable.

The first thing he did, as with any fire site, was to walk the perimeter as much as possible, getting a feel for where the fire likely originated, moving from the general area of the fire to a more specific origin area, looking for possible ignition spots. He was looking for possible modifications to the fuel bed—places where branches or other fuel had been deliberately arranged to aid in the ignition and spread of the fire. And sure enough, he found subtle but still telltale signs that certain charred branches and other debris had been specifically placed.

"Again, this looks intentional, not lightning or other natural ignition, but I doubt it's kids—whoever is responsible is clean, not leaving behind much if any evidence and is trying to cover their tracks, make it look like a spontaneous fire."

"Yeah, I had a feeling we might be dealing with a pro. Damn it." Tucker's frown stayed in place as Luis finished up his inspection.

He didn't find any obvious ignition sources—no

mechanical devices or burnt remains of matches—but he collected a number of other clues to compare with the other fires.

"You're good at this," Tucker observed as Luis came back to stand next to him and take a drink of his water.

"What part? Telling you what you don't want to hear?" Luis laughed, the praise feeling damn good. "Or you mean the data collection? That's the fun part. Like you said, it's a gorgeous late summer day. Who wouldn't want to be outdoors? I always get way more insight hands-on like this."

"I bet. I just meant... I like watching you work." Tucker's cheeks went pinker than exertion alone would warrant. Damn. He was so appealing when he went shy and honest like that.

"Thanks." Luis stepped away before he could be tempted to do something foolish like kiss Tucker's cheek. It might be that professional respect was his newest turn-on, but he couldn't go there, even if they were alone in the middle of nowhere. He might be able to convince himself that only the trees would know, but *he* would know. And he would want a hell of a lot more than a peck on the cheek.

So, he kept it professional and responsible as they made their way back to the Jeep. They talked Luis's arson suspicions until they were back at the main road, when Tucker's phone rang from its spot in the console, flashing a picture of a smiling kid.

"It's one of the boys. Could you put it on speaker for me?" Tucker asked. "Wish this old vehicle had easier hands-free tech."

"Sure."

"Hey, Dad!" A youthful voice filled the car, and Tucker's

answering smile was another checkmark in the "too cute" column as the guy really did seem to love his kids.

"Wade? You're on speaker. I've got a coworker with me." He glanced over at Luis, pained expression on his face.

Luis had had to handle family stuff in front of coworkers before too, though, and tried to give him a reassuring smile.

"Yeah, it's Wade," the kid answered.

"Is this an emergency?" Tucker demanded in a hurry-up sort of tone, but not mean either. He did concerned dad well.

"Not exactly emergency, but I've been trying to catch you. I need the car. Walker's got a date with Mary Anne—"

"You know you're supposed to work out sharing your car with him, not me." Tucker groaned, the sort of long-suffering sound of someone who'd had this conversation a few hundred times.

"Yeah, I know. And I'm sorry. I really am." Wade sounded contrite, but also barreled ahead on his apparent mission to sell Tucker on his plan. "But the guys want to go watch this rodeo tonight, and your car holds more people. Is there any way you could catch a ride home with Garrick or something? Walker can take me to pick up your car then he can have that one and I can have yours. Easy, right? We've done it before."

"Easy huh? I'm not back at the office yet, and I've got another stop before I'll be free. I'm not sure what time Garrick's working to either." Eyes still on the road, Tucker scrubbed at his hair one handed before returning it to the wheel.

"Please. I'll owe you big time." The kid was good at the hard sell.

"You already do." Tucker's voice was stern, but the slackness in his features said he was close to caving. "Let me call Garrick and get back to you, okay?"

"I can give you a ride." The words came out without permission from Luis's brain. *Bad idea, bad idea, abort!* No way did this end well, but he also couldn't recall the offer, especially once Tucker gave a crooked smile.

"Seriously?" Relief was clear in his eyes.

"We'll be at the air base." Luis was trying to talk himself into this as much as Tucker. "It's not that much trouble to head into Painter's Ridge, drop you off wherever. I can return the car as easily as you. No big deal."

Except for the part where he'd told himself he might not have to go back into Painter's Ridge at all. And the whole more-time-alone-with-Tucker thing straining his already shaky resolve. No big deal. Right?

"Well, in that case…" Tucker was already nodding, no time for second thoughts. "Yeah, okay. But Wade? You owe me and my…coworker now, you hear?"

Tucker's hesitation over what to call Luis wasn't lost on him. Could they get back firmly into friend territory? It was ill-advised and not one of his smarter impulses, but he still couldn't stop the tug of longing in his gut.

"Thank you. You're the best, Dad!" Wade crowed, cutting in to Luis's churning thoughts.

"Tell me that when you come home safe. By curfew, okay? I want text updates from the rodeo too." Tucker was back into concerned-dad mode now, full of several other reminders that Wade took in stride before ending the call.

"Thanks. You didn't have to offer. I appreciate it."

"No problem." Luis lied with a smile because he had gotten himself into this mess. But surely he could survive a trip to Painter's Ridge with Tucker. All he had to do was drop Tucker off, after all.

"You're a lifesaver." Tucker smiled then, wide and easy, and somehow Luis knew, deep in his bones, that he was already screwed, but hell if he could see any way out of the coming calamity.

Chapter Seven

There was nothing weird about getting a ride home. In a two car/three driver household, it happened, way more than Tucker would like. Garrick probably would have been happy to provide a lift had it come to that. Luis playing taxi shouldn't have felt any different, and yet, the whole time they were at the air base, his neck tightened every time he thought about it. Which was often because there was plenty of downtime as Luis peppered the smoke-jumping team with questions and handled the inquiry expertly, clearly in his element. He'd been right that he didn't need Tucker along, but Tucker was happy for the chance to see him work.

Should he ask Luis in when he dropped him off? Would that look like an obvious pretext? Some sort of move that he wasn't even sure he knew how to make? *Get over yourself.* He sounded worse than one of the boys, all hung up on some crush who had no clue about his inner dithering. Not that this was a crush. Even if he enjoyed Luis's company beyond their past connection, it still wasn't any sort of infatuation. He had plenty of coworkers whom he enjoyed spending time with. Luis didn't have to be any different.

"Thanks again for the ride," he said as they walked

back from the main offices to the parking lot at the air base. "Are you sure Blaze won't miss you?"

"You remembered my cat's name?" A small, pleased smile danced across Luis's face, early evening sun still plenty bright and glinting off his dark hair. "She's remarkably independent. I'm honestly not sure she even likes me."

"Of course she likes you. You're her human and you feed her." Tucker had had more than enough animals to know that food generally equaled love and devotion.

"Well… Mike's the one who rescued her. It's been years, but I don't think she's ever forgiven me for him not coming home."

From Luis's regretful tone Tucker gathered that maybe the cat wasn't the one who needed to do the forgiving. Tucker knew a little about guilt, and he wanted to touch Luis's arm or shoulder, tell him that whatever had happened wasn't his fault, but it wasn't Tucker's place to touch him.

"That's rough." He shoved his hands in his pockets. He'd never lost someone, not like that at least. He struggled for the right words. "But Blaze travels with you. There's got to be some bond there."

"She deigns to accompany me rather than terrorize a pet sitter," Luis joked, but his smile was tight and narrow.

"How about you?" Tucker tried to keep his voice gentle, not pushy. "Have you coped better than her? Something like that…it had to take some time to get over."

"It's not really the sort of thing you get over." Even his tight smile was gone now, replaced by a more somber expression. "You move on, sort of grudgingly because there's no choice but to put one foot in front of the other. But over? If there's a secret recipe for that, I haven't found it."

"I'm sorry. I didn't mean to make light." Tucker paused on the edge of the parking lot.

"It's okay. One thing I learned is that people who haven't been there seldom know what to say. Even Mami, who should know better, harps on the idea of me finding someone new. Not happening."

There was a warning there, a note of caution, and it landed square in Tucker's chest. *Don't get attached. He doesn't have anything left to give.* Tucker wasn't sure that was entirely true, but he got the message, loud and clear. He wanted to say something else, maybe probe why Luis wasn't looking for anything romantic, but then he heard his name called.

"Ryland! What brings you around here?" A smoke jumper, Lincoln Reid, strode across the gravel lot toward them. Tucker had gone to school with him as well as Garrick, and they were at least friendly if not close friends. "Are we about to get a big callout?"

"No callout. Hate to disappoint you. You look like you're spoiling for a jump."

"Maybe so. I'm working as a spotter this season though, so less jumping for me. Old knees."

"Ha. Now you're going to make me feel old too. We're here on an arson investigation. This is Luis Rivera. He's taking point on that and some other fire behavior work."

"I know you." Linc stuck out a hand for Luis. "You were in school with us, weren't you? Through…sophomore year maybe?"

"Right as junior year started, yeah. Surprised you remember." Eyes narrowing, Luis returned the handshake. Back then, Linc had had his own rougher crowd, which had crossed with Tucker via football, but neither Tucker nor Luis had been high on the invite list for any of that crowd's parties and hell-raising.

"Of course I remember you. You're the one famous for starting a fight of some kind with paint. I forget what play it was though…"

"*The Grinch*. I was green for weeks." Luis grinned.

"Yeah, that was it. How's it been? Are you back for good?"

"No. Just helping out a shorthanded office here. On loan from Angeles National Forest." Luis's emphatic tone was a good reminder that his time here was short and finite. He rather clearly didn't have any desire to rekindle a fondness for the area—or anything else for that matter.

"Ah. Good. We can use all the help we can get around here. Busy fire season this year, that's for sure. I hope we can get to the bottom of the arson."

"We will." Luis stood taller. His pride in his work sure was appealing.

"Great. And speaking of busy, I better head home. It's Jacob's night to cook. Pray for my stomach."

"I'm sure you'll be fine." Even as he laughed, Tucker's chest gave an odd twinge. He'd known Linc was living with someone, of course. It was a small town with a smaller firefighting community, and word got around, but seeing Linc, the former badass, all domesticated… well, that was something. And somehow they were managing a life for themselves here. Garrick and his guy too. Maybe…

No. Tucker tried to picture a universe where he wasn't coming home to an empty house half the week, but all his brain supplied were flashes of Luis's face, which weren't helpful. Even if Tucker ever did find the inclination to date, Luis wasn't going to be here to see it, let alone participate. And on that fun thought, he let Linc continue on his way home while they reached the Jeep.

"I'll drive to my place, then I'll help you set your GPS—"

"I'll be fine. Save the parenting for the boys." Luis laughed as he climbed in the passenger seat.

"Hey, I can't help it. Worry. It's in my DNA now."

"I know. You're cute." Luis didn't give Tucker a chance to digest that little comment before he was asking, "Who's this Jacob?"

"Linc's boyfriend, although it might be fiancé now. Another smoke jumper. They've got a pack of dogs and a place out in the country. You'd remember Jacob's brother Wyatt."

"I remember." Luis's mouth pursed, probably because Wyatt had been something of a bully. "Lincoln Reid, though. With a boyfriend. Sure didn't see that one coming."

"Me either, but my radar for that sort of thing has always been off." That got a laugh from Luis, and he waited until he completed the turn out of the air base before continuing. "They're good together though."

"Nice. It can be tough, being on the same crew." Luis's attention was on the rural landscape, not Tucker.

"Was it for you?" It was surprising how much Tucker wanted to hear about Luis's LA life, Mike in particular.

"Oh yeah. Especially at first. We were trying to keep it secret and probably failing at it. I suck at secrets. Stress."

"I imagine so," Tucker said mildly. Again, there seemed to be a message there, a note of defiance that Luis wasn't about to be secret again. They passed the

edge of town, ranch land giving way to a few neighborhoods and small downtown.

"He...it wasn't perfect. He could be stubborn. We used
to butt heads over the stupidest shit." Tone fond, Luis
shook his head. He straightened as they passed the high
school, older brick building with only a car or two in the
lot since it was summer. "Same old building?"

"Yep. They've added on here and there, but I doubt the
town has money for new. We make do. Boys are pretty
happy there. Some of the same teachers even, old-timers
hanging on."

"Wow. It was so weird, going from such a small school
where all the teachers knew my name to one with over
two thousand kids. So many choices."

"I bet." Tucker tried to match Luis's reflective tone.

"I went a little overboard signing up for clubs. Maybe
part of that was trying to outrun how much I missed that
place, ceiling cracks and few electives and all."

"Understandable. And glad you missed...something."

"I did."

At a stop sign their eyes met, and there it was again,
that energy between them. Not so much a crackle this
time, but an ebb, a mutual wave of understanding, same
as at the restaurant last night. The harsh edges of the
past were softening, and he wasn't entirely sure what to
make of it.

Painter's Ridge wasn't nearly big enough because here
they were, turning into his neighborhood, and he still
felt rather dazed.

"New housing?" Luis's mouth tilted, quizzical expression on his face.

"Yep. Even Painter's Ridge expands. And Heidi and
I wanted houses close together at decent prices, so it

worked out for us," he explained as he pulled into his short drive. "The tradeoff for me is a tiny yard. No room for a garden."

"I imagine that's a hardship for you. You always did like helping your mom with hers."

"Yup. I've gotten creative with some containers, but it's not the same. And the boys wanted me to get a puppy after our old dog passed on, but it wouldn't be fair to the puppy, no room to roam."

"You need a cat…" Luis got a sly look on his face.

"Oh no, you don't. You're not pushing yours off on us, and no way am I getting talked into a kitten." He laughed as he shut off the engine. "Say…you want to come in?"

"Come in?" Luis raised an eyebrow, that way he had of saying volumes with a single look.

"Uh…yeah…maybe you want a tour? And…" He cast about for another reason to not send Luis on his way. "It's Friday. You've had a week what with the drive up from California and starting with our office. Perhaps you want a beer?"

Head tilting, Luis considered him for a long moment, probably trying to figure out what he was up to, and honestly, Tucker would like to know that too. Finally, he shrugged. "What the hell. Sure. Give me the tour, and we'll see about the beer. I'm picky about brands."

"Yup. You went and became a foodie," Tucker teased as he led the way up the sidewalk. "I can remember when we couldn't wait to get our hands on any beer, no matter the kind. But as it happens, I've got bottles from the brewery we ate at last night. You liked that IPA, right?"

"Yeah. It was decent." Luis waited for Tucker to unlock the door, then surveyed the open main area of the house. Tucker had let the boys pick a lot of the furnish-

ings, and unlike Heidi's carefully matching scheme, the
room was a bit haphazard. Luis didn't seem to mind,
though, nodding as he took in the oversize leather couch,
multitude of kid artwork on the walls, and the farmhouse-
style table with benches that the boys had made into
everything from a pirate ship to a covered wagon when
they were younger. "This is nice. My condo's in an older
building. I kind of moved in a fog after Mike and Dad
passed. Tiny kitchen is the big drawback there. I do like
the great room like this."

"Thanks. And sorry about your place—moving sucks
enough as it is. Can't imagine doing it after a loss and
injured as well."

"Yeah. Next time maybe I'll pick better." Luis
frowned, making Tucker want to chase his hurts away,
tease out another of his smiles instead.

"Here, let me grab the beer and I'll show you the
patio and what I've done with the container garden." He
plucked two beers from the back of the fridge and opened
them before leading the way to his favorite spot in the
house. He had a padded porch swing flanked by group-
ings of containers, facing the postage-stamp yard, which
sloped precariously upward, and he'd taken advantage of
the incline to terrace more plantings up to the tall privacy fence. Leaving the door open so that the breeze
would cool down the living area, he motioned for Luis
to have a seat.

However, he hadn't thought this through enough.
Neither twin had the patience for sitting outside with
him anymore, so it was mainly his own private thinking space. He didn't need a lot of seating in an already
cramped space. Which meant the two of them sitting side
by side on the swing, way too cozy, but claiming a seat

on the concrete patio felt like too obvious a retreat. Damn it, why did this have to be so complicated?

Even keeping to his side of the swing, their shoulders still brushed, electricity zooming down his arms. He'd gone years without feeling this kind of desire, and now he was drowning in it. The wind brought a whiff of Luis's aftershave, the scent quickly becoming Tucker's new favorite. Luis took a sip of the beer, and the simple act of him swallowing had Tucker close to groaning.

"Damn it, Tucker. Quit looking at me like that."

"Like what?" Maybe playing dumb would help him.

"Like you're dying for me to kiss you."

Or not. Luis always had been the more direct of the two of them. "Sorry," he mumbled into his beer.

"Sorry? That's not a denial." Luis's laugh was warm and intimate.

"Can't lie to you." That was the truth. He never had been able to keep things from Luis—every secret wish and private transgression had been shared once upon a time, and that kind of trust apparently didn't evaporate even with years apart. "And you can't tell me you're not curious."

If Luis was going to be bold enough to bring up the tension that had been simmering between them, then Tucker was damn well going to call him on his share of it. This wasn't all Tucker's overheated imagination.

"I'm curious about lots of bad ideas." Luis shrugged but his eyes sparkled.

"I'm not denying it would a big mistake," Tucker was quick to add even as his pulse sped up.

"The worst." Luis held his gaze, those sparkles giving way to scorching heat. Somehow they'd drawn closer, faces mere centimeters apart now.

"Can't do it," he whispered, voice little more than air now, especially once Luis's hand landed on his shoulder.

"Nope." Luis was so close now that his breath was warm on Tucker's cheek.

And then they were kissing, simple as that. One second bantering, the next desperately kissing. No preamble, soft exploration, or tentative feeling out. No, this was flat-out hunger, and Tucker couldn't get enough. Luis used his grip on Tucker's shoulder to haul him closer. Groaning, Tucker met him partway, clutching at Luis's biceps as he welcomed in his questing tongue. Damn. Felt like Luis wanted to devour him, his aggression sexy as fuck, and Tucker moaned against his lips, letting him deepen the kiss. He tasted vaguely like cinnamon and beer, but there was also a familiarity there, a flavor that was Luis's alone that dominated Tucker's senses.

"More," he demanded, pulling Luis until they were well and truly tangled together, chests meeting, hands roving, swing swaying.

"Yeah, I got you." Claiming another kiss, Luis went from raw hunger to something more refined, but no less effective at silencing every reason Tucker had for why this was a terrible idea. Indeed, the longer they kissed, the more it seemed like the smartest thing he'd ever done. Initially he'd been content to let Luis drive the kiss, taking in all that sexy assertiveness, but the longer they kissed, the more he met Luis's frantic energy with his own. He used his tongue to explore the contours of Luis's full lips and was rewarded with Luis sucking hard when he ventured inside.

"Damn." He shivered despite the warmth of the day, desperate to get himself under control, yet loath to stop.

"So good." Mouthing along Tucker's jaw, Luis moved

his hands more purposefully, sweeping over Tucker's back and arms before dancing his fingers along Tucker's belt. He couldn't remember his cock ever being this hard, this needy, abs already trembling. Sexual attraction for Tucker usually stemmed from feelings of intense closeness and was rare, making this desire that much more overwhelming. Like he was a teenager again with Luis, his lust was already at a full, raging boil and all they'd done was kiss. And when Luis's fingers skated closer to his fly, he had to pull back, bat his hand away.

"Don't...too close."

"Already?" Eyes widening, Luis took on a sly, pleased expression.

"Been a long time." Years since he'd felt another's touch, an omission his body was reminding him about in vivid detail.

"Too long." Luis went in for another kiss, this one soft and seductive before he nibbled along Tucker's neck, doing devious things to his ear.

"God, keep that up and I might..."

"Damn, you weren't kidding about having a hair trigger." Luis laughed, darkly.

"Sorry." Tucker's face heated even as his body strained toward Luis.

"Don't be sorry." Giving him a fast, hard kiss, Luis returned his hand to Tucker's waistline. "You want to come, baby? Want me to suck you off, right here? Because that's all I can think about right now, finally finding out how you taste, what you sound like when you come."

"Yeah." Like he was going to turn that down with his whole body in this feverish state. "Do—"

"Dad? You home?"

Walker's voice carried from inside the house, and Luis

instantly slid back to his side of the swing, easy as if they hadn't just been seconds away from a massive error in judgment. They'd been outside, for Pete's sake. And still Tucker cursed the interruption. But there was no time for curses, literal or figurative.

"Out here," he called right before Walker appeared in the patio doorway.

"Figured the Forest Service truck out front was you. Oh—you're not alone. Sorry." Walker nodded at Luis, who was casually sipping his beer like he hadn't just been making Tucker sinful promises in between getting intimately reacquainted with his lips and tongue.

"Walker." Unlike Mr. Cool and Casual, Tucker had to work for his normal tone. "This is… Luis. My co-worker, who—"

"Was just about to head out. Thanks for the beer, man." Standing, Luis stretched. "Nice to meet you, Walker. I'll leave you to your dad."

And with that he was gone. Somehow Tucker knew that they could try all they wanted to pretend that kiss hadn't happened, but it had, and any pretensions they had of pretending to be amicable coworkers was gone. And hell if he could bring himself to regret anything other than Walker's ill-timed appearance. He wanted more. Wanted to do that again. Soon.

Chapter Eight

Luis's phone buzzed early Sunday morning, and somehow he knew it was Tucker.

"Sorry to wake you—"

"It's okay. I was up," he lied, but only partially because he'd been half awake, lying there in bed, debating whether to get up and face another boring day off or indulge himself by jerking off and sleeping in. Saturday had been long without the routine of going into the office. He'd reviewed several files from his room, gone for a long walk, and used the weight room at the hotel, but he'd still been restless all day. "Distract me. Please. There's a fire?"

He knew even before he asked that this wasn't a social call. He hadn't heard from Tucker after he'd sped away from his place Friday, when he'd been saved from his stupidity by Tucker's kid. God. Apart from all the other reasons why getting involved would be a bad idea, Tucker was a *dad*. A rather devoted one, who put the kids first before anything else. Luis was still trying to wrap his mind around that, but regardless, a guy like Tucker deserved commitment. Romantic seduction at the very least. Not a semi-public blowjob from a guy destined to leave town.

So yeah, he knew this was a business call, and he told himself he wasn't the least bit disappointed over that. Almost believed himself too.

"Yep. There's a fire. And early word is that it's fitting our arson profile. Crack of dawn ignition, small fire size, anonymous tip, no reported lightning or nearby campers. The smoke jumpers were called out, and they seem to have it contained, but I figured you'd want to be on scene ASAP."

"You guessed right." Luis was already out of bed and pulling on pants. "Got directions?"

"Hang on there. It's a pretty remote location. You shouldn't go alone. Also, I'm worried about that little car of yours on the back roads. I'll pick you up. My SUV will be fine, so no need to switch to an official vehicle."

"Okay, okay. Bring on the dadmobile." He didn't put up too much of a fight because Tucker sounded like a man with a plan who wasn't about to be deterred. And Luis did want to be out there quickly. That was all. Couldn't possibly be that he wanted to see Tucker.

"Good. I'm already on the way to you."

"I'll feed Blaze, then head down to the front of the hotel." Sensing food was coming, the cat stretched from the chair where she'd been snoozing but like always she ignored his outstretched hand. No head scratches for her royal highness.

"Sounds good. I grabbed you a coffee, but you might want some food and water if you've got it."

"I'm on it." He stuck two bottles of water and some energy bars in his bag. "And thanks."

"No problem. See you soon."

Tucker memorizing his preferred coffee order was

oddly…touching. Sweet. Different, being taken care of like that when he was usually the one fussing over his—

Wait. This was *not* a relationship. Wasn't even a permanent work relationship. Tucker was simply being considerate. That was all.

And when Tucker arrived a few minutes later, he was sure to say thanks but kept his tone distant. Professional. Definitely not mentioning that kiss. But then one glance at Tucker sipping his iced drink through a straw, and he was right back to the unwanted lust that had woken him up. Damn but he wanted this man, wanted him eager and begging and—

Not happening. Be professional. He forced himself to focus on his coffee, which was the perfect temperature and right balance of bitter and smoky flavors. At least Painter's Ridge had found its way to decent coffee if nothing else.

For his part, Tucker didn't seem any more inclined to discuss the kiss than Luis was. They kept the conversation to the fire, checking in with the air base on the status of the operation as they made their way through winding roads. It was a gorgeous Sunday morning in the mountains, blue skies, and soft winds sweeping through the trees and scrubby terrain. Not too hot yet, but the sun overhead said they'd be sweating before too long.

"Like the other fires, it's not too far from a hiking trail, but the nearest ranger station doesn't report any backcountry camping permits," Tucker explained as they drove. "It's a long, challenging trail for experienced hikers, but we'll only have a couple of miles to hike in from the closest access road. You wore your boots?"

"Yup. Gear in my bag too."

"Good. We'll need it." Tucker navigated the access

road to a clearing where several other vehicles were already parked.

They got situated with hard hats and other gear while one of the smoke jumper supervisors brought them up to speed on what had been happening. Nearby, exhausted-looking jumpers who'd carted their heavy equipment out from the site were hydrating and tending to their packs.

"The fire was contained by our initial team, but we're still on the lookout for hot spots," the supervisor explained as the wind ruffled her short hair. "We've got a small mop-up crew in now."

After the update, they started the hike to the site. The air was heavy with the scent of charred wood, smoke lingering despite the fact that the blaze was out. But he was well used to the smell of smoke. Harder to take was the growing tension between him and Tucker. They were alone on the walk, no fire updates or navigation to distract them, and the memory of that kiss seared his brain. Forget hot spots in the woods. His body was a mess of flare-ups every time their eyes met.

Finally, he couldn't stand it any longer. "So…about Friday night?"

Tucker predictably groaned and slowed down his brisk pace. "Do we really need to talk about it?"

"Are you wanting to pretend it didn't happen?" That had been his personal approach all weekend, but now he wasn't so sure, didn't know if he wanted Tucker to so easily dismiss everything simmering between them.

"No. Couldn't even if I wanted to, which I don't."

"Good." Damn it. He wasn't supposed to feel relief over that. "It…was okay?"

Tucker laughed, deep and hearty, sound echoing. "You

wanting compliments on your technique? Something tells me you already know you're a damn good kisser."

"Thanks. I meant more… I didn't take advantage?" That was the other question that had plagued him the past two days. He wasn't exactly sure what Tucker's boundaries were. Kissing him had been like pounding shots, a heady burn that pushed out good sense. "I'd hate to push you into something."

"You didn't push." Tucker frowned as he navigated a rocky outcropping. The terrain was getting steeper, not unlike this conversation. "I was right there with you."

"I noticed." And how. Tucker's active participation and needy sounds had been on constant replay in Luis's overheated thoughts all weekend. "I more meant…"

"The demisexual thing?"

"Yeah." Luis had had his share of boyfriends and casual partners, but no one who'd identified as demi or ace. He wanted to be careful to not misstep or misread Tucker's signals.

"It's…hard to explain." Adjusting his backpack, Tucker surveyed the terrain, lowering his voice despite their isolation. "It's not that I dislike sex at all, but I can go long stretches without it. Then along comes someone I connect with, and it's like a furnace turning on. It's all about deep, emotional connection for me, I guess. And there's your compliment for you. Not saying that you've got like some sort of magic touch, but there's…something there."

"Yeah, there is." Luis couldn't deny it, same as he couldn't deny the thrill coursing through him at Tucker's words. He liked being different for him. Special. And there *was* a connection, one that seemed to go beyond their shared past even. He'd be attracted to Tucker even if they didn't have that—he was competent and funny and sexy as fuck. He was Luis's type and the past simply underscored that fact. "But I'd be lying if I didn't admit it would be easier if there weren't."

"Amen to that." Tucker nimbly climbed past more rocks.

The rugged terrain reminded Luis of some of the more challenging wildfires he'd been a part of, the delicate balance between wanting to reach a spot quickly and not wanting to lose his footing. And it was similar to how he felt about Tucker right then too.

"We probably should avoid more...entanglements. I don't want to lead you on."

"Entanglements? It was a kiss. Not a marriage proposal." Tucker laughed, but Luis couldn't join him, couldn't ignore the way his pulse pounded at the very suggestion. "I don't have any illusions here—you're leaving first chance you get, and I know it."

"Yeah." Luis's voice was weak in a way that had nothing to do with the altitude.

"But I'm also not ruling out more. Bad idea or not. I want—"

Voices up ahead made Tucker abruptly stop and they turned their attention back to work and examining the fire site. *I'm also not ruling out more.* Damn Tucker for that little proclamation, which burrowed under Luis's skin, made his senses hum even as he forced himself to focus on work and uncovering signs of arson.

As with the other sites, there were no obvious signs of human intervention—no gas cans or other debris—so he had to look for more subtle calling cards, like a similar seemingly deliberate arrangement of branches near the suspected ignition location. No matches or other ignition device, but he still looked for other physical evidence that they could use to establish a pattern later. This was the sort of puzzle he'd always excelled at, looking for clues, examining how things worked together.

While he worked, he was cautious, knowing full well that arsonists often hid nearby a fire to see the fire suppression efforts, an added layer of danger even after the immediate fire situation had been handled. His eyes kept scanning the tree line, looking for unusual movements or possible hiding spots. However, the culprit was good, with no obvious missteps that might make apprehension easier. But Luis was determined. He'd get them, one way or another.

Between his own investigation and questions from the personnel on site, he kept busy but not so busy that he forgot about his unfinished conversation with Tucker. However, they weren't alone on the trek back to the parking area. Surrounded by sweaty, sooty workers climbing over rocks and scampering down the trail was hardly the place for even thinking about kissing let alone a serious talk.

"Damn. That was a trek." Back at the SUV, Tucker removed his hard hat and wiped off his forehead with a bandanna from his pocket. "I'm going to need a shower as soon as I'm home."

"Yeah. Same." It was the perfect opportunity for Luis to suggest that they share said shower, and the flirty response rose in his throat only to die as one of the workers came over to ask Tucker a question. Just as well. Sex would be foolish.

Even knowing that, he still wanted it, his body buzzing the whole ride back. His brain might be debating the wisdom of starting something with Tucker, but his cock knew exactly what he wanted. And as for his heart…well, it knew his brain was in denial. There was already something going on, whether they got naked or not.

As they pulled into Luis's hotel, he was still deliberating asking Tucker to come up. Unlike Tucker and his "tour" of his house, Luis didn't even have good pretext. If Tucker accompanied him up to his suite, it would be for sex, and there wouldn't be any more pretending that they could ignore this...whatever it was.

Tucker parked in the back of the lot near a clump of trees, and when he turned toward Luis, all calculations ceased, desire winning out the instant their gazes met. The same heat he'd battled all day was right there in Tucker's eyes. His face was smudged with dust, and tired lines bracketed his mouth, and Luis had never wanted anyone more. His body leaned in, no longer waiting for his brain's permission, and Tucker more than met him halfway as they slid into a kiss as easily as if they'd been doing this for decades.

When they kissed, the years fell away, and Luis was right back to being a hyper sixteen-year-old, every touch thrilling, each brush of their tongues going straight to his cock.

"Come up with me," he panted as he pulled away to get a breath, forehead still resting against Tucker's.

"Can't." Tucker managed to sound genuinely pained. "I called Heidi after I found out about the fire. We usually do Sunday dinner together with the kids. It was my night to cook, but Isaac volunteered to grill instead. I shouldn't skip out."

"Family first." Untangling himself from the console, Luis retreated to his side of the car. "See you tomorrow?"

"Wait." Tucker touched his arm. "I'm not trying to blow you off."

"I know." And he did. It was the dad thing again. And the kids did have to come first. Luis got it. He didn't like it, but he did get that Tucker had priorities that didn't include getting laid right then. Tucker kept his grip on Luis's arm when he would have escaped, holding his gaze with steely eyes.

"Just so you know, I don't have the boys every night."

"Is that a proposition?" Luis tilted his head, considering. Tucker was way more tempting than their common sense should allow.

"Maybe more like a promise." Tucker's grin made him look far younger and more mischievous.

"It's a bad idea." He groaned, but his pulse was already speeding back up, anticipation curling low in his gut.

"The worst," Tucker agreed, still smiling.

"Until your next terrible idea, then." He leaned in for a final swift kiss, and this time Tucker let him leave.

As he walked back to the hotel, damn if Luis wasn't already looking forward to their next non-work-related encounter. Oh hell. *Work.* He had to see Tucker again tomorrow. At work, where he would need to pretend that he wasn't dying to kiss him breathless again. Fuck. He was so damn screwed.

Chapter Nine

"You're late." Walker greeted Tucker at Heidi's front door with a scowl so fierce that Tucker was afraid that even his hasty shower hadn't been enough to erase any signs of his kissing session with Luis.

"Sorry. The fire location was pretty remote. And then I had to take Luis—my coworker—back to his hotel."

"Whatever. The food's almost ready." Walker shut the door behind Tucker harder than necessary, still not smiling.

"Hey." Tucker tried to grab Walker, but forgot that he wasn't nine anymore, not so easy to wrap up in a hug. Walker neatly dodged his hand. "What's your problem? Did you need me for something today?"

"Nah. I'm fine. Everything's fine." Walker's heavy sigh said exactly the opposite.

After coming down the stairs, Wade had a fist bump for Tucker, which he supposed was better than Walker's unexpected surly turn.

"He's just freaking out because he took another SAT practice exam and did worse, not better," Wade offered, ruffling his brother's hair.

"Well, I'm here now. And I'm here for you, specifically." He tried to meet Walker's eyes, let him know how deeply he meant that. Had he missed something important this week? They were in the final month before senior year started, and time seemed to be rushing toward Labor Day faster than he would like. Was something going on with Walker? Guilt made his back muscles tense. "Do we need to make a study plan? How can I help?"

"I don't need a *plan*." Walker stalked off toward the bathroom.

"Well, that went *fine*." Wade did a fair imitation of Walker's sigh and his slightly slower speech. They might be identical, but Tucker was rarely fooled for more than a second or two as to who was whom.

"What went how? What's with Walker?" Heidi came breezing in from the back patio where Isaac was grilling. The picnic table was already set, and the plantings that Tucker had helped with caught the evening breeze. It would be way more inviting, however, if Walker wasn't acting strange. And if part of Tucker's brain wasn't still back with Luis. He did want more kisses, but not if it meant missing something crucial with Walker.

"Oh, nothing." Wade made a dismissive gesture. "He's pissy about his test scores. And Dad's new boyfriend."

"Dad's new *what*?" Heidi and Tucker spoke at the same time, and he was pretty sure his eyes were popping out even more than hers.

"He has this new coworker." Tone dismissive, Wade headed toward the kitchen. "Walker said he was even at the house Friday. Drinking a beer."

"Was he now?" Heidi stared Tucker down as she picked up a bowl of salad from the counter.

"It's nothing. We were just…catching up. That's all."

"I think Luis needs to join us for dinner on Wednesday," Heidi mused, voice more thoughtful than teasing, but her suggestion still stole the air out of Tucker's lungs.

"He most certainly does not." God, that was all they needed. Yes, he did want more time alone with Luis. *Alone.* Not introducing him to the chaos circus that was family dinner nights, and not risking making Walker even more unhappy.

"Yeah, he does. Let's freak Walker out." Wade, however, had no such reservations.

"There's nothing for Walker—or you—to get worked up over. It's a friend. That's all."

"Whatever you say." Grabbing a pitcher of water, Wade headed to the patio, leaving Tucker and Heidi behind.

"Yeah, Tucker. Whatever you say. Bring that." Heidi laughed and pointed toward a bowl of rice. "And now he's a friend? I thought you were both bitter and sad about the past. What changed?"

"We talked. But it's not—"

"Dinner!" Isaac called from the patio, setting a large platter of meat on the table.

"Bring him," Heidi insisted. "I want to see him again too. We can all catch up."

"Walker's mad. Not sure if it's this or something else, but I don't have time for…anything right now."

"You've got time for a friend." Heidi set the salad down and squeezed his arm. "And like I said, I want to see him too. Revisit some good high school memories."

"Yeah," he reluctantly agreed.

"I mean, don't go falling in love with the guy again or something crazy, but you're entitled to a friend. Walker can deal. And whatever he's got going on, there's more

than just you on the case—we'll get to the bottom of it.
Promise."

Don't go falling in love. Yeah, Tucker already knew
that. Luis was leaving, had no interest in a serious relationship, and might well still be grieving his late boyfriend. Tucker might be interested in exploring their
chemistry together, but it was like finding the perfect
restaurant while on vacation. He could indulge now, enjoy
it while he had it, and still understand that it wasn't going
to become a staple in his diet. As long as he didn't go
catching feelings, it wouldn't be the worst thing to…
sample the menu a little more so to speak. On that note,
he headed outside, Walker catching the door right before
it shut and brushing by Tucker.

"Food ready?" Walker slumped down next to Wade.

Damn it. No matter what Heidi said, he was still worried about Walker. It didn't matter how he justified it,
no amount of more time with Luis was worth alienat-
ing his kid over.

"Yep." He passed the rice, then leaned in, lowering
his voice. "Do you need a break? Want to sleep at my
place tonight? I won't bug you or try to hang out, but I
did notice that new superhero movie is streaming now."

"*Dad.* I'm not twelve."

"I know." Oh, how he knew, even if his heart kept trying to forget how fast the years had gone.

"And…maybe." Walker frowned and kept his voice
down. "I do need to think. It's hard to do that with so
many people around."

"Don't I know it." He and Walker were alike in that
they both enjoyed being around other people but craved
quiet to reset. "Thinking about anything in particular?"

He sent up a quick prayer that Walker's reply would

have nothing to do with Tucker's social life. He couldn't stand it if he were the reason for Walker's recent bad attitude.

"Stuff. Colleges. Everyone acts like senior year is supposed to be magical or some crap like that, but it hasn't even started and so far it sucks."

"Give it time. All you've had so far is football practice and the SAT classes. Things may change when school starts back up after Labor Day. You don't have to have all the answers right now. You've got time to figure it out. And I meant what I said inside. I'm here to help you figure it out."

"Thanks. Some things I have to sort out for myself, though." Walker snagged a roll out of the bread basket coming around. "But...sorry I was rude earlier."

"Sounds like you have a lot on your mind. I know you can handle yourself, but I'm here if you need to talk through anything, okay?"

"I don't." Then seeming to realize that he'd snapped again, Walker frowned. "Sorry."

"It's okay," Tucker said, even though it wasn't. He wanted Walker to confide in him, the way he had when the boys were little, and it sucked to think that there might be something wrong that he couldn't fix. The food was delicious, as always, but he couldn't shake the sense of foreboding that settled over him even after Walker went back to teasing Wade and Angelica, same as always.

Next to Tucker, Angelica jostled his chair as she reached for a roll.

"Here, sweetie." He grabbed one for her and buttered it as well. For a moment, only an instant really, he let himself imagine sitting next to Luis. It might not be such a terrible idea to invite him. He was a friend, and Tucker had brought other friends around the family, chaos and all. Heidi's suggestion kept poking at his brain, making him want things he shouldn't, making him try to rationalize those urges. Luis would probably turn down the offer in any event, but if he didn't…

"Butthead. See if I help you later." Wade threatened Walker over some minor tiff, and whatever cozy scenario he'd been about to imagine disappeared in a flurry of reminders about language and tone.

He managed to sidestep Heidi's continued questions about Luis while they made quick work of the dishes after dinner. Right as he was about to leave, Walker came bounding down the stairs, backpack over one shoulder.

"You were right. I do need the quiet. Okay if I walk back with you?"

"Always." Relief surged through him that Walker wasn't shutting him out entirely. He was quiet on the stroll back to Tucker's house, but merely his presence had Tucker's tight jaw relaxing at least a little.

When they reached the house, Walker stopped by the stairs, turning back toward Tucker. "Dad?"

"Yeah?"

"Invite your friend." Something unreadable crossed his face, resignation maybe or apology. Tucker still wasn't convinced that would be the right call, but Walker's effort made his chest warm.

"Thanks. And you can ignore Wade. I'm not looking for a relationship, promise."

"Whatever." Walker sounded less flip than earlier, but there was still a certain unhappiness there that wasn't his usual.

"Are you sure you don't need to talk?"

Walker's phone went off before he could reply. "Sorry. It's Mary Anne. I'll take it upstairs."

And with that, he was gone, leaving Tucker even more muddled. Despite everything, including his worries about Walker, his mind returned to Luis as he got ready for bed, replaying their car kiss. His body hummed with unfamiliar energy. Even though he knew he was risking complications, he still wanted more.

"Heidi wants you to come to dinner on Wednesday." Holding a reusable bag in one hand, Tucker entered Luis's office like they had some prearranged lunch date, shutting the door behind him.

"Hello to you too, Tucker. Come in, won't you? To what do I owe the pleasure?" Luis made a sweeping gesture at his guest chair. It was a busy Monday, getting ready for the controlled burn, reviewing evidence from yesterday's fire, and Luis had lost track of time, still hadn't eaten his own lunch. Hunger might be making him cranky, but also Tucker's seeming ease at putting aside their heated kisses wasn't helping.

"Sorry. I was intending to simply bring you food, but then Heidi texted a reminder, and I wanted to get the invitation out before I forgot."

"You brought me food?" He lightly kicked his own ankle under the desk, trying to make sure he wasn't dreaming up this bizarre encounter.

"Those premade protein boxes you like aren't enough food, and I figured you might be getting tired of the limited options around here. Made an extra sandwich this morning in case you wanted it." Tucker dug a pair of sandwiches out of his bag.

"You made me a sandwich?" Heart swelling, he accepted the foil-wrapped package. Damn it. He wanted Tucker's body, not his sweetness. Tucker caring might be more than he could take.

"With some of Wade's spicy mayo," Tucker confirmed.

"Thanks. Now what's this about dinner?" It said something about his mental state that he'd be happier to have a lunchtime quickie with Tucker than face his kid again.

"We do the twice a week family thing. Casual. But Isaac's cooking is worth it."

"You've mentioned. Still not sure how this involves me."

"Heidi—"

"What did you tell her?" Even though they were alone in his office, he kept his voice low. He didn't think Tucker was the type to run right out and give his ex a kiss-by-kiss report, but maybe he didn't know this Tucker as well as he thought.

"Nothing." Tucker held up his hands, but Luis merely raised an eyebrow. "Okay, okay. Maybe I said that we were catching up, but that's all. Walker was acting weird about seeing you at my place, so I was trying to make it no big deal."

"And bringing me for dinner is how you want to make it less of a deal?"

"I'm allowed friends. And we're friends, right?" Tucker's crooked grin did nothing to reassure Luis.

"You make a habit of tangling tonsils with friends?" He gave Tucker a pointed look, liking his blush a little too much.

"No. You know that."

"I do." Luis gentled his voice, because he did get that Tucker didn't do this sort of thing regularly, possibly ever. "I'm just saying there are far less complicated ways to invite me over to make out. We both know this isn't truly a meet-the-family sort of arrangement, right? Not saying that we can't be..."

"Tonsil-tangling friends with benefits?"

"That works." He laughed along with Tucker before sobering again. "But dinner... I'm not so sure."

"It doesn't have to be that complicated. Heidi was your friend too, back in high school. She'd like to say hello. And maybe it will defuse Walker. He said to ask you, so I think he's...trying. Not sure what's going on with him."

"Do the boys know?" He tried to hide how curious he was by taking a bite of the sandwich, which was very good, crusty sourdough with good quality turkey, cheese, and spicy mayo. If Tucker was trying to win him over, there were far worse ways to go about it than plying him with food.

"About my sexuality? Yeah. Heidi and I talked it over, and after my rift with my family, we didn't want them hearing secondhand rumors from cousins, didn't want to send the message that I was ashamed."

"Smart. And brave. That can't have been an easy conversation." Not that he'd expected Tucker to shy away from it—he'd already proven himself to be honest and caring, especially where his kids were concerned.

"Actually, it wasn't too bad. Kids understand way more than we give them credit for. And they were getting to that age... I wanted them to know that whatever identity they had, no matter where they landed on the sexuality spectrum, that it was okay and that they would be loved no matter what."

"You're a good dad." Luis's chest expanded with an emotion he refused to name. Damn. Tucker wasn't just a good dad but a great one. And Luis had had a pretty awesome one himself, so he knew exactly how lucky Tucker's kids were. He'd had too many friends with disastrous coming-out stories to not know how blessed he was that his dad had had a beloved brother who happened to be gay and that Luis's parents' support had never been an issue for him.

"Thanks. It was important to me that they know that not everyone shares my family's narrow-minded views and to create an environment where they could tell us anything. Which is why this thing with Walker is so troubling. Something's going on, but if he won't tell me what, I can't fix it." Tucker frowned, and Luis reached across the desk to pat his arm.

"Hate to tell you, Papi, but you're a dad, not a magician. You're not going to be able to fix everything. All you can do is love him and be there. He'll talk eventually." He was probably not the best person to be giving parenting advice, but he'd put his own parents through the ringer enough times, holding back some hurt until he was ready to voice it.

"I hope you're right." Tucker studied his lunch like it might have the answers he needed. And damn it, there went Luis's chest again, trying not to feel things for this man.

"I'll think about dinner, okay? The one thing I don't like about work travel is how slow the evenings are unless there's a crisis."

"Well, we don't want a crisis. And let me be your distraction?" Brightening, Tucker waggled his eyebrows.

And okay, if dinner got him more of the kissing that Tucker seemed on board with, then it might not be such a terrible idea. "Deal. Speaking of my boredom, you don't have to wait until Wednesday to distract me. I know tomorrow's going to be long day, but you want to watch a movie tonight or something?" He put heavy emphasis on the "or something" part. Movie might be nice, but if Tucker wanted to skip it in favor of Luis's hotel room, he wasn't turning that down either.

"Football booster meeting." Groaning, Tucker pushed his sandwich aside. "And I'd blow it off to hang out with you, but with Walker acting strange…"

"You better go be a dad. I get it. I can wait until Wednesday."

"Good." That apparently settled, Tucker leaned back in his chair, easy as if they had lunch together on the regular, conversation bumping between work stuff and his worries about Walker. It would be too damn easy to get used to moments like this. He could handle craving Tucker's kisses, but he had no clue what to do with all these softer urges he inspired.

Chapter Ten

By Wednesday, Luis still had no clue what he was doing pursuing anything with Tucker, let alone something that required dinner with the family. Tuesday had been a long, grueling day of supervising the burn, providing data and guidance to help make determinations about personnel and resources needed. Wednesday was mop-up crews and debriefings, and by the time he reached Tucker's driveway, he was both tired and antsy, a combo he could do without.

"I brought cookies from a bakery I found in Bend." Luis held up a box. "I wasn't sure whether Heidi or Isaac drinks wine. And then I was thinking coffee, but—"

"You're adorable nervous. And yes, there will likely be wine, which it sounds like you could use." Tucker had the audacity to laugh at Luis's hostess gift dilemma.

He'd hoped that Tucker telling him to park at his place meant that he would get some stolen pre-dinner kisses, but apparently not, as Tucker was already locking his front door and joining Luis on his narrow porch.

"I'm not nervous." Cranky with the lack of kisses, Luis couldn't keep the defiant edge out of his voice.

"Really?" Tucker gave him a pointed look as he backed Luis behind a planter on the porch for a lightning-fast kiss that wasn't nearly enough but did defuse his mood at least a little.

"Okay, maybe a little unsettled. Not nervous." He'd spent all day telling himself that he didn't care what impression he made on Tucker's kids and ex, but that wasn't precisely true. Damn it. He did want the kids to like him or at least not dislike him to the point of being a major roadblock on his quest to get more kisses before he had to leave.

"It'll be fine." Tucker led the way off the porch, long strides eating up sidewalk as they passed other smallish houses in similar style to Tucker's, then rounded the corner to a street with bigger homes, spaced farther apart to allow for larger yards. Like Tucker's, Heidi's place had modern craftsman styling and muted northwest colors.

"Hi, Tucker!" The door swung open to reveal a pint-sized curly-haired princess, complete with tiara. "You brought your friend! Mommy says I'm not supposed to ask questions, but—"

"Angelica. How about you go find your brothers?" Heidi strode up behind Angelica to usher them into the house. No longer the skinny high school girl with messy hair Luis remembered, she wore her red hair in a sleek knot, curls tamed with an elegant clip that matched her navy dress. There were still little flashes of her younger self though—bare feet like she hadn't been able to get rid of her heels fast enough, blue toenail polish, and same sparkling green eyes. "Come in, come in."

"Heidi!" Luis let himself be swept up into a hug that smelled like expensive perfume but felt like a memory. "I brought cookies."

"Fabulous. I'm so glad to see you again. I want to hear

all about you now. Isaac's making smothered pork chops and some sort of fancy potatoes."

"Smells great," he offered as they followed her into the great room, where she introduced him to her husband who was bustling around the kitchen. Slightly older than Heidi, he had a closely cropped fade, neatly groomed goatee, a Pistons T-shirt under an apron, and a quiet but welcoming demeanor that went a long way to putting Luis at ease. They chatted about NBA free agency and the ongoing baseball season as he finished cooking, leaving Heidi to supervise Angelica setting the table and Tucker to greet the identical teens, who made their way downstairs in a cloud of cheap aftershave and post-football-practice energy.

Weird, thinking about Tucker having kids old enough to shave and drive. They both shook his hand, and Luis quickly memorized who was wearing which color to keep them straight.

"How is the SAT review going?" Tucker asked the boys.

"Fine." Walker, who was in a gray shirt and was the kid Tucker had been worried about, had a predictably clipped response, while his far more dramatic brother did an exaggerated shoulder roll and groan.

"Terrible. I don't see why I should have to take it anyway. Schools should care more about what I can do on the field."

"There's that whole *student* part of student athlete," Isaac dryly pointed out as he plated the pork chops on a large platter.

"I know. I'm just saying that Walker needs these prep classes more. Glad I'm not the one trying to get into some picky marine biology program." Wade carried a big bowl of potatoes to the table.

"Marine biology?" Luis turned toward Walker. "That's a nice ambition. Where are you looking? I've always heard great things about the Florida colleges. And I've had friends in some of the California programs. Those always seem to rank high in national surveys."

"I *know*." Walker shot him a withering glance. "And I'm still thinking."

"More like Mary Anne is still thinking." Looking back over his shoulder, Wade rolled his eyes. "You were all Long Beach this and Long Beach that until she asked you to the spring formal."

"You wait until you get someone. You'll see. It's not all—"

"Guys." Heidi held up a hand. "The food is ready."

Luis tried to catch Tucker's eye because he'd put money on girl problems being at least part of Walker's recent issues, but he wasn't sure whether the message got through in the flurry of everyone grabbing seats at the large oval table. He and Tucker ended up opposite from the boys, with Angelica squeezed in between Walker and Isaac.

Heidi kept conversation moving, asking Luis about his job and deftly quashing more arguments between the boys. Initial nerves aside, Luis found himself enjoying the meal—Tucker hadn't been lying about the food being proposal-worthy, and the chatty company was a major step up from Blaze's disdain.

"Hey, Mom? Can you get off work early on Friday?" Wade did such good puppy-dog eyes that Luis had no trouble believing he was probably used to getting his way.

"Maybe. Why?" Heidi idly twirled her wineglass. Dinner was winding down, the boys having packed away an astonishing amount of food, and everyone else full on the generous portions.

"Intra-squad scrimmage at four thirty," Wade explained, leaning forward. "First chance for the parents to see us in action for the year!"

Walker made a sour face. "Which you'd know if you'd made the booster meeting—"

"Walker." Isaac's quiet voice packed a fair punch and immediately had Walker sitting up straighter.

"Sorry, Mom."

"If I go in early, I can be there, assuming there's no callout for a fire," Tucker quickly offered.

"And I'll try too," Heidi added.

"I'm gonna cheer!" Angelica narrowly avoided knocking over her milk.

"You can come with Dad." Wade gestured at Luis, involving him when he'd been perfectly happy observing the family dynamics from afar.

"Oh, I don't think—"

"That's a fabulous idea," Heidi enthused. "That way if I'm late, you still have an extra person to root for you."

"Exactly. We need all the crowd we can get." Wade's eyes lit up, and Luis couldn't tell whether he was playing matchmaker or trying to bug his brother, who looked decidedly chilly about the prospect of Luis coming.

Luis wasn't sure about how he felt about either option. He didn't want anyone getting invested in him and Tucker as anything other than a friendship. The fleeting fling part could and should stay private, and he wasn't here to be used as a pawn in some sort of brotherly one-upmanship.

"We'll see," Tucker said firmly before Luis could concoct an excuse. "And how about not bugging our guest?"

"I'm not." Wade was the picture of innocence. "In fact, we were in the middle of a video game earlier. Walker and I are going to stick around here after dinner, finish our level."

"We are? *Ouch.*" Walker went from skeptical to pained as his brother did something to him under the table. "Yeah, I guess we are. Prepare to die, f—"

"Language," all three parents chorused before he could finish.

Luis's back tightened as his jaw flexed. He was both grateful to Wade for ensuring he might get some time alone with Tucker and irritated at his continued obvious matchmaking for the sake of making his brother squirm. If Luis were sticking around, which he wasn't, he'd prefer to win over the more subdued Walker slowly and not with Wade forcing the issue. It was clear that both boys loved Tucker a lot, and the last thing Luis wanted to do, even temporarily, was come between them.

"I should be getting back to my hotel pretty soon," he said, trying to beam *I'm not horning in on your dad* messages to Walker. Yeah, he wanted to make out with Tucker, the urge to be alone with him again only increasing since Sunday's hasty but heated kisses, but he also didn't want the kid pissed at them.

"It's okay. You can talk to Dad. We'll clear." Walker sounded more resigned than enthusiastic, but Luis supposed it was something. "And if you come Friday, I'm number thirty-one and Wade's thirteen. Make sure you yell the right name when I have the ball."

"You? Have the ball?" Wade scoffed and then the boys were off bickering about sports again as they took away the dirty dishes and returned with the cookies Luis had brought.

"Way too full," Tucker groaned.

"Me too." Luis passed the box along.

"More for me." Wade helped himself to three.

"Shall I walk you back to your car?" Tucker asked as Walker too took a handful of cookies and headed up the stairs.

"Sure." He did what he thought was a good job of not sounding too eager as they made their way to the door amid a flurry of goodbyes.

"So…was it horrible?" Tucker asked once they were back out on the sidewalk. The day was finally starting to cool off a little, but still a dry heat lingered in the air. "Never to be repeated?"

"Nah. It was fine. Slightly weird, seeing you and Heidi as parents, but Isaac seems nice. If anything, you under-sold his cooking. Those pork chops were more than worth sitting through the Walker and Wade show."

"Wade…" Tucker shook his head. "He's something. And not subtle either. Sorry."

"It's okay. He's fun. But I don't want Walker mad at you over anything relating to me, Wade's antics in-cluded."

"I'm going to try to talk to him again. I honestly don't think it's you, but something's going on. He's always been quieter than Wade, but not this sullen."

"Girl trouble." Luis finally got the chance to share his theory as they rounded the corner onto Tucker's street.

"Yeah. Could be. She's generally nice, though. Quieter than Walker even and sweet. She asked him to a dance on a dare, and they've been inseparable ever since. But

I'll try to find a new way through to him, get him to talk. Ice cream and video games have stopped working."

"I'm not a parent, but my mom always got me to talk by doing chores together. Somehow her kitchen always needed a deep clean right when I was in a funk. Papi was the opposite—he'd take me out of the house. Long drive on some pretext like a piece of baseball memorabilia, and somehow somewhere in backed-up traffic on the two-ten I'd start talking."

"Those are both good ideas. Thanks." Tucker was more somber as they reached his driveway, but his head tilted as Luis headed for his car. "You're not coming in?"

"You're inviting me? It's okay if you want to focus on your kid issues—"

"He's busy with his brother on that video game, which honestly may be the better distraction for him right now. And as for me, well, I believe I promised *you* a distraction."

"You did." Luis let himself grin as he stepped back closer to Tucker. "But what about you? What do you want?"

"You." Tucker's answer was so ready, so firm, and so decisive that it made a shiver race down Luis's spine, all the way to his toes.

"Good answer." Only the fact that it was still light out with a few neighbors still out and about stopped him from kissing Tucker right there. Congratulating himself on his restraint, he bounded up to the porch. "Distract away."

Tucker's hand shook as he unlocked his front door. Luis was right behind him, close enough to feel his warmth and smell his intriguing aftershave, and he wanted him more than he'd ever wanted anything. He waited until the door shut quietly behind them to pounce on Luis, but it was a near thing.

"I was this close to kissing you on my front lawn," he confessed as he backed Luis against the wall.

"Me too." Luis's grin was feral as he tugged Tucker forward with hands on his waist. "But you had a neighbor out watering."

"True." Flipping on the lights, he brushed a kiss against Luis's temple, heart hammering, every muscle ready to dive headfirst into losing himself in this man.

"Don't want to end up the talk of the neighborhood social media group." Grinning, Luis seemed to sense both his urgency and his contrasting need to go slowly, savor this.

"Can't have that. But the whole dinner I kept thinking about this." Forcing himself to not rush, he claimed Luis's mouth with a gentleness that surprised even himself. Luis tasted sweet, like the half glass of wine he'd sipped at dinner, and Tucker mimicked that lazy pace, little tastes and sips. But even with the caution, he still was rapidly getting drunk on Luis's taste, on his nearness and warmth.

"Mmm. Those are some nice thoughts." Luis stretched against him as he pulled back to let his heart rate decrease. "I never thought of family dinner as foreplay before, but it kind of was for you, wasn't it? You seem more...relaxed somehow."

"Yeah." The back of Tucker's neck heated. "It's hard to describe, but I like feeling connected to you, almost as much as I like kissing you. And having you with me at dinner, yeah, I liked that."

"Tucker." Luis's voice had a warning note to it, a pained edge.

"I know, I know. You're leaving." He didn't need the reminder. Time was slipping away, even now. That feeling at dinner, like they were something solid and real, was fleeting at best. But he also wasn't going to lie about how it made him feel. "And I'm not going to stop you. All I mean is that I like the connection part while I have it. It enhances everything else, and I'm not going to apologize for enjoying that."

"I don't want you to." Blessing him with a soft kiss, Luis stroked his jaw. "I like it too. Probably too much."

"Same. But I don't want to stop, not when it feels so good."

"Then don't." This time it was Luis claiming the kiss, harsh and desperate. It was lusty, sure, the same urges ricocheting through Tucker, yet there was something else too. A message of sorts that Tucker wasn't alone in being over his head here, that this was more than physical for Luis too, even if he didn't want there to be. And it said something that the more time they spent together, lunches and dinners and working together, the more Tucker wanted him. He welcomed every bit of Luis's ferocity, met him kiss for kiss, clutch for clutch, moan for moan.

Deftly reversing their positions, Luis steered Tucker away from the entry wall. They stumbled their way to the couch, an oversize leather model he'd chosen to withstand the kids, but he was grateful for its study construction as they tumbled onto it. Luis landed on top of Tucker, peering down at him with an intensity that made Tucker need to swallow hard.

"Damn. You...want you. So bad." He stroked Tucker's face, fingers pushing through his hair.

"Same." Unable to wait another second, he stretched up to catch Luis's mouth in a kiss that started gentle but quickly caught back up to where they'd been by the door, both of them breathing hard as they traded deep forays.

"Tell me what's okay with you." Pulling back, Luis stroked Tucker's arms. He was hard against Tucker's hip, and simply that coupled with his warm weight had Tucker's own cock throbbing. There was no way Luis could miss that he was as turned on as him.

A frustrated noise escaped his throat. "I don't need… training wheels or something. Not gonna freak out on you." At least he didn't *think* he was. Part of his frustration was in not knowing exactly what it was he liked, not having go-to suggestions for Luis. All he knew was that he wanted *more*. "Need you."

"You've got me." Luis's smile was almost more tender than Tucker could bear.

"Kiss me again," he demanded.

"Like this?" Moving slowly, like they had decades to get this right, Luis proceeded to make a study of Tucker's mouth, showing even more finesse than earlier with little nips and sucks and flicks of his devious tongue. Tucker's heels dug into the sofa and his back arched.

"Yeah." His eyes fluttered shut as Luis started a devastating combo of delving deep with his tongue while his hips moved insistently against Tucker's. He felt the rhythm everywhere in his body, like someone had turned the bass up to eleven and each small movement was enough to have him shuddering. "Fuck. That."

"Damn. I like making you curse."

"Then do that again." Moving restlessly against Luis, he tried to goad him into more of those kisses.

"This?" Luis gave him fluttering light kisses on his lips, cheeks, chin, lips again. Torture. "Or this?"

Right when Tucker was about to demand he stop teasing, he captured his mouth for real, owning his lips completely as they rocked together. Tucker was starting to get a feel for how to follow Luis's movements, and each thrust and retreat had his cock demanding more and more until he was breathless with want.

"That. Definitely that."

"Love how damn responsive you are." Luis snaked a hand between them, pulling Tucker's shirt loose from his pants. "Can't wait to see you lose it when I suck you."

"So you keep threatening." It was hard to think with Luis's warm hand resting against his bare abs, fingers idly moving but nowhere close to where Tucker wanted him most.

"Not a threat. A promise." Before Tucker could even register what he was after, Luis scooted back, arranging them so that Tucker's feet were on the ground again and he was kneeling next to Tucker. Instinctively, Tucker sat up more so he could watch as Luis made quick work of his belt. He was slower with Tucker's fly, blunt fingertips teasing him through his pants, taking his sweet time lowering the zipper.

"Oh." He breathed out as Luis finally withdrew his cock, featherlight touches all along the shaft followed by his hot breath, so close but not close enough. "Damn. You…"

"Want something?" Luis's voice was innocent, but his eyes were molten, all sinful promises in the soft light spilling in from the entryway.

"This. Just this." Yeah, he wanted to come, but then this would be over, and he wasn't ready for that. And he wanted to see exactly what Luis had planned. "You're killing me, but it's worth it."

"Right answer." Luis rewarded him by licking all

along the underside of his cock, little flicks that wreaked havoc with his resolution to simply go along with whatever Luis wanted to do.

"That. Do that. More." Licking his suddenly parched lips, he reached for Luis's shoulder, then retreated, not wanting to be too demanding. He jammed his ass into the couch cushions, stilling the urge to thrust toward Luis's exploring mouth.

"It's okay. You can touch me." Grabbing Tucker's hand, Luis returned it to his shoulder before tapping Luis's thigh. "And move. Turns me on when you lose control."

He punctuated his words by swallowing Tucker's cock, sucking him into all that wet heat, active tongue making Tucker groan. "Oh, *fuck.*"

"That's it." Pulling back long enough to grin, Luis resumed his efforts, taking Tucker deep. So deep. Tucker could feel Luis swallow, and simply that subtle flutter and pressure was enough to have his balls tightening.

"Close. Too close." His voice shook, tone almost panicky because he wasn't ready for this to end, wanted the good feelings to go on indefinitely. But his body seemed to have another agenda, hurtling closer as Luis quickened his pace.

"Do it. Let go," he urged, voice rough, almost like he needed this as much as Tucker, and that need spiraled inside him, everything tensing as his body tried to follow Luis's orders. Sucking harder, Luis took him even deeper, more of that irresistible pressure, and there was simply no way to hold back. Years of waiting and wanting and wondering, and he was coming in waves so intense his fingers dug into Luis's shoulder. His hips lifted, almost like his body was trying to levitate with the pleasure coursing through it.

"Wow. That…wow." He slumped back against the couch, barely enough energy left to haul Luis up next to him. Luis licked his now-shiny lips, and Tucker's cock gave a valiant last twitch.

"Wow indeed." Laughing, Luis kissed his cheek before reaching for his own fly. "Damn. It okay if I…"

"Of course, but I want to help." Feeling bold, he traced a finger of the ridge of Luis's erection. "Show me what you like?"

"You." Luis chuckled as he echoed Tucker from earlier. "Here, let me…"

Undoing his zipper, he withdrew his cock, which was maybe slightly longer than Tucker's with a wider, more oval head. Unlike Tucker, he was uncut, and watching him slowly jack himself was mesmerizing. Meeting Tucker's gaze, Luis moved his hand away, making room for Tucker to touch. He trailed a finger down the silky length, memorizing the contours and veins.

"More." Luis moaned, hips moving impatiently, and Tucker got the message, wrapping his hand around the shaft and trying to duplicate Luis's grip and pace.

"This?"

"Yeah. Faster. Little…exactly that. Yeah." Luis's breath came in harsh pants, head falling back enough that Tucker could lick the straining cords of his neck muscles. Moving his hand back, he covered Tucker's fist, urging him on.

"Close?" he whispered, pulse surging, cock stirring back to life simply watching Luis's reactions.

"Fuck yes. Gonna get me off." Luis tightened their

shared grip, quickening the pace, and the eroticism of the moment had Tucker moaning too, right along with Luis.

"Yes." He wasn't sure which of them said it, maybe both of them, groaning in concert as Luis shot creamy fluid all over both their hands.

"Damn." Opening his eyes, Luis stretched, head falling against Tucker's. "You sounded like you came too."

"Almost felt like that." He was still dazed, not precisely sure what had happened there at the end, only knowing that he wanted more of it. "It was okay?"

"More than. You've never...that was a first for you?"

"Kind of. With a guy, yeah, pretty much." Cheeks heating, he looked away. "There was this guy a couple of years back. Smoke jumper in town for the season. There was a kiss, but he got transferred to Idaho before anything else happened."

"I'm not sure whether to feel bad for taking advantage of you, puffed up because you wanted that with me, or high on everything else I'd like to show you."

"That last one, please." Even now, Tucker's pulse still galloped, body more than eager to try for seconds. There was little he didn't want to try with Luis and not nearly enough time.

"Damn. You're dangerous."

"Good." Tentatively, Tucker moved in for a kiss. He could taste himself, but the earthy hint was far from unpleasant, a familiar saltiness combined with the reminder of what Luis had done for him, turning him on all over again.

Groaning, Luis pulled back. "Seriously, though, I should go before your kids come barging in and find us all messy."

"Yeah. They're probably going to end up sleeping at

Heidi's, but you have a point. Here." Since he wasn't the one who had to drive, he pulled off the cotton polo he'd changed into after work and handed it to Luis, who laughed as he used it on both their hands.

"Such a gentleman."

"I try. You sure you're okay to drive back?"

"Yeah. Orgasm did me in more than the half glass of wine, but I'll be fine. Want me to text you when I get in?"

"Please." It wasn't simply wanting to know that Luis reached his hotel safely. He wanted that last contact with him, that little reminder that he was still thinking about Tucker. And damn. Fanciful thoughts like that were going to do him in.

"I will then." Smiling, Luis looped an arm around Tucker's bare shoulders, pulled him in for another slow, sweet kiss. "Damn, Tucker. You make me want..."

Everything. Swallowing, he met Luis's gaze. "I know. Now go on before I end up dragging you off to my shower and keeping you here."

"Promises..." Looking playfully to the stairs, Luis nonetheless stood and straightened his clothes. Tucker walked him to the door where they killed another few minutes trading kisses like they were teenagers again, delaying the inevitable.

"Drive safe," he said at last.

"I'll text." Luis headed to his car, taking more of Tucker's heart with him than Tucker wanted to admit.

Chapter Eleven

"We're going to code red. Damn it." Tucker stuck his head into Luis's office, frown creasing his handsome face. No sandwich break for two today as he'd been in meetings all morning. It had been a busy two days at work for both of them, and this news wasn't going to help. Like most in wildfire fighting, Luis might as well get the warning system tattooed on his wrist. The low green and blue days of winter and spring were long gone, and as they entered the real dog days of late summer, it wasn't unusual for a high alert to transition to these extreme danger warnings.

"Yeah. They're posting warnings at all the campgrounds. About to be a lot of unhappy people this weekend." Code red meant no campfires at all, only approved vehicles on unpaved roads, no chainsaws or mowers for dry grass, and the tourists tended to protest the loudest about the restrictions.

"They can live without their s'mores. And at least the restaurants and sale of portable stoves should do booming business." Having been through this many times, he matched Tucker's concerned but pragmatic tone. The highest level of precautions was taken because the risk of quick-starting, fast-spreading fire had reached a critical point. It also meant more work for everyone, Luis especially as predicting fire behavior became essential in keeping situations manageable. Even small fires needed to be treated with an abundance of care. "What do you need from me to help?"

"There's a fire to the north we're monitoring. Ignition is unclear—reports of some dry lightning last night, but we could be looking at another arson incident. Regardless, Fred wants us to head out. I'm going to talk to the crew supervisor as we decide whether to escalate the response, and he wants you on the scene to get better data than we have thus far. He figured you might have insights as to how it started as well."

"I'm on it. You want to go sign out the vehicle?" Luis came around his desk to grab his boots and gear from the corner where he'd left it. Taking a minute to stretch his tight back, he switched from his lighter shoes to sturdy boots while Tucker darted down the hall to get keys to a Jeep. They hadn't had much time to talk since dinner and their heated make-out session Wednesday.

And talk about code red—Luis's libido hadn't been at these levels in years. All getting a taste of sex with Tucker did was make him want more. And not simply sex either. He craved all sorts of impossible things, and for that reason he'd forced himself back to the hotel and Blaze last night instead of trying to sneak in some more Tucker time. He wanted more of those kisses, but he also didn't want to hurt Tucker. Either of them, when it came right down it. They were headed for an inevitable crash, and if he was smart, he'd keep his distance.

That was easier said than done, though, when work kept tossing them together like this. Like him, Tucker seemed both cautious about the personal and all business about the fire risk, heading right out of town, no coffee stops or reminiscing about Wednesday's kisses. Heck, maybe Luis was the one making more of this than he needed to. But every time he replayed the sex in his head, Tucker's intensity was there, his grasping hands and the look in his eyes, the sort of *need* that was hard to fake. Tucker cared, of that he was sure. And thus, he wanted to tread cautiously.

"Did you bring food?" he asked when Tucker yawned, unable to shut his own caring off, even with the internal lecture. They were in Tucker's SUV because there hadn't been a Jeep readily available for them with so much of the office out dealing with the increase to the red danger levels. "If you skipped lunch, I can unwrap something for you."

"That would be good. Thanks. There's a protein bar and some chips in the bag behind you. I'll start there. I had intentions of convincing you to get lunch out today, but the fire risk stuff took care of those plans."

"A date?" Damn it. He was not supposed to find that thought sweet. Fetching the food, he unwrapped a bar for Tucker and held it out. Their eyes connected, and yup, he wasn't the only one thinking about those kisses.

"Something like that." Smiling shyly, Tucker took the food from Luis. "My plan was to butter you up with lunch, then convince you to go to the scrimmage with me tonight."

"You don't really want me at the football thing." Groaning, he let his head conk back against the seat.

"Sure I do. I like spending time with you." Another small grin, this one that Luis felt all the way to his toes before Tucker sighed. "And not that it matters now— doubt we're done in time."

"Let's see how it goes. I'll try to work fast—not cutting corners, but I can try to speed things along."

"Thanks. I appreciate it."

Out at the site, they found a flurry of activity—hand crew digging fireline, a more experienced hotshot outfit battling the frontline and dealing with flare-ups stemming from efforts to control the initial blaze. A dry, hot wind wasn't helping matters, and it wasn't long before he too was sweating. His adrenaline surged, gathering energy from all the activity as he collected the weather and other fire data he needed to make more accurate predictions. He was also carefully looking for signs of possible arson or, alternatively, evidence of a lightning strike or other natural ignition source.

Meanwhile, Tucker was busy talking to leadership, and at one point, Luis lost track of where he was. His pulse sped up, the smoke hanging in the air seeming to thicken by the second, heat increasing until for a second he was back in California, working that terrible blaze, and Mike...

Damn it. He wasn't supposed to care about Tucker or anyone else like this ever again. Tucker was a professional and could handle himself in the field and didn't need Luis hovering. Not that his expertise guaranteed his safety, though. Plenty of firefighters each year saw devastating injuries and worse, and not simply hotshot personnel and smoke jumpers on the front lines either. Simply being out here was a risk. *So is driving*, he reminded himself, but that didn't help his churning gut any.

He forced his mind back to work, but it kept wandering. What if he never got another chance to kiss Tucker? To hold him and hang out with him and listen to him talk...

Fuck it. He had it bad. And unlike when they'd been teens with the world stretching out in front of them, he'd lived enough years to know that a connection like theirs was precious and rare. And time was finite, always. Circumstances and choices made for a reality where people never had as much time as they wanted together. He hadn't pushed for meeting up after work yesterday, and now he was mentally shoving his own shoulder. *Idiot.* At this point, leaving was going to suck no matter what, and avoiding Tucker only meant fewer memories and more regrets for later.

"Almost done?" Tucker appeared back at his side. "This appears fairly contained. I don't think we need to scramble additional crews at this point, and I updated Fred with your latest insights as well."

"Yeah. Just finishing up." He was stupidly happy to see Tucker, dusty and sweaty but otherwise in one piece. "Does Fred need to see you back at the office?"

"Nah. It's Friday night. He's already on his way to the grandkids. If we get another callout, he'll come in, but otherwise I think we're good." Tucker glanced down at his watch. "I'll drop you at your car, then hustle back up to Painter's Ridge, see if I can get the second half of the scrimmage at least."

"Or we can go straight from here, get you there sooner. We're closer to Painter's Ridge than to my car, that's for sure."

"You're coming?" Tucker's smile held nothing back. He'd genuinely wanted Luis to come, and that desire was…humbling. More even than the ego boost of being wanted, it was humbling how Tucker wasn't afraid to show him what his heart needed. And Luis might not be able to give him everything, but he wasn't about to walk away with nothing either.

"Yeah, I'm in." He wanted more of Tucker, however he could get him, even if that meant braving another family thing. He needed more good memories for his stockpile.

Bringing a date to a school function was a first for Tucker, but then he couldn't say that he'd brought a date much of anywhere before. Thus, it was maybe slightly significant that he'd arrived at the scrimmage directly from the field, hot and sweaty, with Luis in tow.

"You came!" Heidi, who was also still in her work clothes and heels, scooted over on the bleachers to make room for them. Angelica was already waving homemade pom-poms, and Isaac had a hot dog from the concession stand. It might simply be an inter-squad thing, but the booster club wasn't going to turn down a chance to make money from food sales.

"Are you hungry?" he asked Luis. "It's mainly fair-type food like hot dogs and barbecue beef, but they do have funnel cakes, which are worth the splurge."

"To you, maybe." Luis gave him an indulgent smile. "You're the one who had to skimp on lunch. How about I go get you one? I'll see if there's anything else there I might eat."

"Sure." Tired after all the walking around the fire site, Tucker was okay with letting Luis be the one to get food. "But you have to have a taste of mine."

"Twist my arm." Luis's heated look contained a reminder of all the *tasting* they had done the other night and made Tucker temporarily forget they weren't alone in the stands. "Back soon."

"Hmm." Heidi made a thoughtful noise after Luis was

out of hearing distance. "I sure hope you know what you're doing."

"What?" Playing dumb seemed like the smarter option as he did not want to get into a discussion on the state of his and Luis's friendship right there, especially with an audience.

"What indeed." She arched an elegant eyebrow. "I'm just worried—"

"Don't be." Making a dismissive gesture, he gave her what he hoped was a firm look.

She crossed her arms. "I just don't want you hurt."

"Let me worry about that." He couldn't lie and tell her he wasn't going to be hurt. That much was already a given. Luis leaving was going to suck, but he'd lived a lot of years without the sort of connection he felt with Luis. He'd make it through. And unlike when Luis left before, he was an adult who could see this coming and could brace for its impact. At least he hoped.

However, that conviction wavered as the game progressed. Luis returned with food, and their fingers kept brushing as they shared the flaky sweet treat along with some fries. That one look aside, they weren't particularly flirty, but there was something about having Luis there that fed him on a deep, almost cellular level. It was cozy, but more than that, it was something he'd been yearning for without even realizing how much. They simply fit. And Luis fit here too, joking with Isaac and cheering with Angelica and sneaking more bites from Tucker's plate. He seemed far from miserable, relaxed even with plenty of easy smiles.

Maybe... Tucker's brain knew better, but his heart still painted a pretty picture where this was a regular occurrence, where summer turned fall and fire season gave way to football and Luis was still here. A few years ago, he could have scarcely imagined such a universe, but if Rain and Garrick were managing to make a life here, then maybe… It wasn't like relations with Tucker's family could get more frosty. *We could be…*

"Go Wade!" Heidi and Luis yelled in concert, Angelica and Isaac whooping as Wade ran with the ball. Not a touchdown, but close and the crowd roared.

A partnership. That was what he wanted, his most private desire, the one he didn't let himself look at very often. But wanting that, seeing the potential here, wasn't the same as getting it. Even if Luis wasn't leaving, there was still the not-so-small matter of his heart not necessarily being up for grabs. He was still grieving his losses, and Tucker couldn't blame him for being wary of a new relationship.

Not happening. Enjoy what you've got, he lectured himself as Wade's team finally delivered that touchdown. The game stayed close, fun to watch and a good sign for the upcoming season, the way the kids worked together.

"Do you worry?" Luis asked him as Walker's team completed a particularly vicious tackle.

"About?" It took Tucker a moment to realize Luis probably meant football, not all the questions and wants churning through him. A better question would be what he didn't worry about.

"The risks… I mean, it's a dangerous sport." Luis frowned as the tackled kid's teammates helped him up.

"We work in a dangerous occupation," Tucker pointed out. "But, yeah, I know what you mean. My heart stops every time one of them hits the grass."

"I can imagine. Makes me glad my brothers were more into baseball."

"We had those years too. Wade took a ball to the helmet in little league. Talk about worry. Anyway, we had a long talk when they first started to play football, but they both wanted to make the team so badly. Not gonna lie, it's hard as a parent though."

"Yeah." Luis discreetly tapped his foot against Tucker's. "I feel you."

"But at a certain point, I realized I wasn't going to be able to keep them safe forever. And that sucks. Watching them drive away the first time...football tackles... it's all hell on my nerves but they're going to fly whether I'm ready or not."

"Truth." Gaze still intent, Luis studied the game, thoughts somewhere Tucker couldn't follow.

He wasn't going to sugarcoat it. Worry about the kids was the hardest part of parenting, but he wouldn't trade all the sleepless nights and trembling hands for anything. Love was worth it, and he wished he had an easy way of sharing that certainty with Luis. Loss undoubtedly changed things, tinged the way Luis saw the world, and Tucker would do anything to shoulder even a small part of his burdens.

The game came down to the final play, Tucker back to holding his breath as Wade caught the ball and made a mad dash for the end zone.

"Run!" he yelled. Narrowly avoiding being tackled, Wade dove for the end zone. Whistles bleated as a flurry of bodies followed him.

Get up. Get up. Be okay.

Triumphant, Wade stood up, accepting the frenzied congrats of his team.

"He did it!" Luis gave him a slap on the back as the

scoreboard lit up to reflect the touchdown. "Man, you weren't kidding about the nerves."

"Yup. Never gets any easier, sad to say." A beat of understanding passed between them, an acknowledgment of the ways love and pain and risk tangled together. Caring wasn't ever simple, but hell if Tucker could turn it off. And he'd bet that Luis couldn't either. He might not want to care, but he did. It was there in the way his fingers dug into Tucker's shoulder before releasing him and in the way he didn't break Tucker's gaze until the crush of people leaving the stands jostled them apart.

"Dad! Did you see?" Wade broke free from a crowd of excited kids to come over to their part of the bleachers.

"I saw. Well done." His voice came out thick and scratchy, another casualty of caring so damn much. "I'm proud of you."

"And you brought Luis! Cool." Wade's smile shifted to something more mischievous, and Tucker tried to send him a warning look to not make his brother, who had also joined them, uncomfortable.

"You did good too, Walker. Excellent tackle right before the half," Luis praised.

"It was nothing." Expression unreadable, Walker shrugged.

"FYI we got invited to a party at Mitch Goodwin's. Don't wait up." Wade waggled his eyebrows, either not getting Tucker's message or not caring to back off the teasing.

"Are the parents going to be home? And no bonfires, right?" Tucker slid right into the concerned-dad mode that Luis liked to tease him about.

"Yes. The mom is the one who invited everyone over.

They have a pool, a strict no-alcohol policy, and no fire pit. We'll be good."

"Mary Anne and I are going too." Walker sounded more resigned than excited, but this wasn't the moment for a deep dive into possible sources of his unhappiness. But come tomorrow, he was dragging him out to their favorite trail and taking Luis's advice to get him talking.

"Be safe. I have to run Luis back to his car, but you can text me at any point for a ride. And curfew is still a thing."

"Me too. Text away." Heidi had a hug for both boys, brushing the dust they left behind off her dress.

"Me three." Isaac laughed. "No wacky diving board tricks, okay?"

"That was one time," Wade protested.

"That resulted in an emergency room trip and stitches," Tucker reminded him.

"Okay, okay. No diving board, and Walker can drive, and we'll be home by curfew." Wade jogged away to rejoin his friends and teammates, leaving Walker to trail behind him after giving them a last wave.

"You drive carefully too," Heidi told him as she and Isaac collected Angelica from where she'd been chasing some other little kids. "And text if you get a fire callout."

"Will do." After a few more goodbyes, he and Luis made their way back to his car.

"You want some actual food?" Luis asked once they were underway. "After that heavy snack, I just want something light, but I've got eggs and could make us some breakfast-as-dinner if you wanted to follow me back to my hotel. You can meet the cat."

"Well, in that case, I better accept." Anticipation thrummed through his body, making his fingers drum against the steering wheel. He had a feeling Luis was offering more than some scrambled eggs and a look at his cat, but he wasn't being pushy about it, which Tucker appreciated. As wonderfully aggressive as he could be while kissing, he seemed content to let Tucker decide when and how they got to that point of getting physical.

His respectfulness for Tucker's needs was another sign that Luis cared about more than simply getting laid while he was in town. Tucker's chest expanded, all his wishes from earlier returning full force. And while he might not get those, he did get tonight, and he was absolutely going to make the most of it.

Chapter Twelve

"I think you're right. The cat has it in for you." Tucker looked up from his eggs.

Luis had scrambled them with spinach and queso fresca, then topped his own with chorizo, cilantro, and salsa macha while Tucker got extra of the cheese and some avocado. Luis had been pleased to discover the same tiny Mexican grocer that his mother had frequented was still in business, still stocking decent brands of some of his family's favorites like the tortillas he'd heated up to go alongside. It was a cozy little late dinner at the small table in his room. Well, it *would* be cozy if the cat would stop glaring at both of them from her perch on top of the fridge.

"See? Watch." Luis held out a piece of chorizo, but all Blaze did was sniff the air mightily. Selfishly, he was glad that at least she hadn't immediately taken to Tucker, who tried the same gesture but with egg, and got a swish of her majestic tail for his efforts.

"Maybe it's simply humanity in general she's not impressed with," Tucker suggested as he used a piece of tortilla to scoop up more eggs.

"No, she adored Mike. In his lap every chance she got, eating from his hand, acting like a spoiled princess getting a massage when he brushed her…so it's not all humans. Just most."

"Well, maybe not everyone can be as special as that." There was something guarded about Tucker's expression and a certain cautiousness in his tone. "Maybe Mike was just one of a kind?"

"He was. Big blond bear of a guy but exceptionally gentle with little kids and small animals. But despite Blaze's devotion, he wasn't a saint." He didn't want Tucker thinking that like the cat he'd put Mike on a pedestal where no other guy could ever reach. "He could be moody, and we fought about stupid stuff enough that I used to tease him that if I was a cat I'd win more arguments with his stubborn ass."

Tucker laughed at that, but it was muted as were his eyes. "And still you miss him. I get that. You don't see yourself ever having another serious relationship?"

Move to California and we'll see. The flirty response was right there on his tongue, but that wouldn't be fair. Tucker wasn't leaving this place, no matter what had gone down with his family. Everyone at the game had known him and the boys. He had Heidi and Isaac and his job and a house and a whole life here. A fling with an old friend wasn't ever going to be enough incentive to pull up stakes.

"Maybe someday," he said instead, because he *could* see that for the first time in a very long time, but when he closed his eyes it was Tucker he saw, Tucker he wanted, not some faceless future partner. He hadn't thought his heart would ever come back online after Mike, but Tucker had a way of wiggling past his sternest resolve.

"I don't begrudge Heidi any of her happiness with Isaac, but there are times when I miss having an adult person to come home to, someone to watch TV with when the kids are in bed, someone to fuss over, a reason to not eat cereal for dinner, that sort of thing."

"I hear you. I miss having someone to cook for the most. Eating alone with a cat giving me the evil eye isn't the same."

"And I imagine other alone stuff sucks for you, too?" More of that careful tone from Tucker like there was something deeper he wanted to know but wasn't sure how to dig for it.

"You asking if I miss regular sex?" Luis laughed.

"Yeah." Tucker's cheeks pinked up, and he busied himself with the last of his eggs. "Sometimes I miss touch like hugging. And kissing, especially like what we had when we were younger. But, honestly, I haven't had enough experience with truly memorable sex for it to be the number one thing I miss when I think about relationships, about sharing that connection with someone. But I imagine it's way higher on your list."

"Well…" Luis drew the word out, trying to feel his way toward the right response because he sensed Tucker needed some sort of reassurance. "Sex is awesome and yeah, I miss it, but it isn't the most important thing to me in a relationship by any means."

"No?" Tucker's tone stayed cautiously curious.

"Maybe when I was younger, but having been in a couple of long-term relationships now, I can say that quantity tends to vary wildly over time, ebbs and flows. I've never really been one for juggling multiple partners at the same time, so I've always had a very robust relationship with my right hand."

"It's a nice hand." Tucker's blush darkened. "And, uh, me too."

"Ha. I might not be demisexual, but like you, I really value connection, especially now that I'm older. Quality over quantity every time for me. I can dish out orgasms on my own, but I can't duplicate that connection." After clearing the plates, he came to stand next to Tucker and put a hand on his shoulder.

"That was what I liked most the other night." Tucker leaned into Luis's touch. "How close I felt to you. It surprised me, how good it felt."

"Do you want to feel good like that again?" He tried to make his voice as low pressure as possible, idly rubbing Tucker's shoulder as he crouched next to his chair. "It's okay if you're not in the mood or distracted by kid stuff or whatever."

Meow. Blaze yodeled from her perch on the fridge, and they both laughed.

Tucker shook his head. "I'm not sure if that's an objection to us getting naked or if she's warming up to my presence. Seems more likely that she's planning my demise as soon as we're...distracted."

"I'd offer to put her in her carrier, but she's likely to get louder if I do. But ignore her for now. What do you want?"

"You." Tucker pulled him closer, giving him a soft and sweet kiss full of promise before he groaned low.

Too late, Luis remembered his spicy add-ins to the food. "Oops. Forgot about the salsa. Hope you didn't burn your lips."

"You're cute. Turns out I don't mind spicy as much when it's you."

"Nice. Still, let me do this." Skin heating, Luis fished a mint out of his pocket and quickly chomped it.

"And let me do this." Tucker found his mouth for another kiss, this one deeper and more purposeful. Tucker was such an intriguing blend of tentative and assertive, cautious and unrestrained. And Luis was perfectly happy to find out what he wanted, where this would lead. As it turned out, that meant several long minutes of trading kisses, awkward position forgotten in the rush of how good Tucker's lips and tongue and teeth could make him feel.

"Damn." Breathing hard as Tucker let him up for air, he rolled his shoulders, trying to not let his back stiffen up.

"Hey, off the floor with you." Tucker offered him a hand up, then gave him a long, considering look that had Luis's toes curving into the carpet. "Can I see your tattoo?"

"Which one?" Fingers already going to his shirt buttons, he winked at Tucker, loving how his eyes went wide and lips fell open.

"All of them," he breathed with all the reverence of a kid presented with a tray of cookies.

Shrugging out of his shirt, Luis preened under his obvious admiration. In addition to the stylized flames ringing his biceps, he had a baseball mitt on his left pec with his dad's name on it, and a small version of Mike's fire helmet on his back. His other biceps had his first tat, a fire department badge he'd gotten on a dare at his first firehouse assignment. It was fun to watch Tucker's eyes rove over his various tats, but two could play at this little game.

"Do I get to see you too? Don't worry, I'll protect you from any cat claws."

"Well, in that case…"

As Tucker unbuttoned his work shirt, Luis wasn't sure

who would be protecting *him* and his heart from Tucker, from his soft little grin. And Tucker might be a busy guy, but he clearly made some time for weights with nicely defined arms and a chiseled chest that was unexpectedly and delightfully fuzzy.

"Damn, you're sexy."

"Right back at you." Tucker laughed self-consciously as he kept going, removing his pants as well and setting them by the boots he'd taken off earlier. Like Luis, he had various scars including a long one on one calf. Such battle marks were almost a given in their line of work, and if anything only added to Tucker's rugged appeal. "Sorry that I don't have any impressive ink like yours."

"No, you've got an impressive *you*." Luis took Tucker stripping down to his boxer briefs as permission to do the same before he put his hands on Tucker's bare shoulders.

"Flattery will get you everywhere." Leaning in, Tucker gave him a playful kiss, nipping at Luis's lips until he couldn't stand the teasing a moment longer and had to capture Tucker's mouth for a thorough exploration that left them both breathless.

"Flattery enough to get me here?" Gently, he steered Tucker toward the bed, stopping short of tumbling him onto it.

"That and more of those kisses." Tucker took the hint and stretched out, patting the spot next to him. Joining him, Luis was only too happy to indulge him in long minutes of kissing, hands lightly skimming Tucker's arms and back as they lay on their sides. Tucker's intense appreciation of even the smallest gestures made kissing that much more fun, discovering what made him shiver and what made him groan. He seemed to like it most when Luis took control, moaning softly when Luis sucked at his lower lip and clutching his shoulders when their tongues met.

"Good?" Luis retreated far enough to study Tucker's face, trying hard to follow his signals for where he might want this to go.

"Very." Stroking Luis's jaw, Tucker met his gaze. "What do you like? You're so concerned about what I need and want, and that's appreciated, truly. But I want to know about you too and what turns you on."

"You turn me on." He laughed, but Tucker made a frustrated noise. "Seriously, I'm pretty easy. Getting you off turns me on, however that happens, but simply kissing is great as well. I want you comfortable."

"I am." Tucker bumped his hips forward, letting his cotton-covered cock graze Luis's thigh. "Well, most of me at least. Now, tell me what you like."

"You wanting specifics?" He didn't want to push Tucker into fucking or give him a step-by-step plan to follow, not when letting things evolve on their own was so much fun. But if Tucker wanted a little direction, that he could manage. Tugging Tucker closer, he nuzzled his neck, loving the rub of the stubble there and on his jaw as he kissed his way up from Tucker's shoulder. "This turns me on, right here."

"Me too." Tucker shuddered and rolled to his back, taking Luis with him.

"And this absolutely turns me on." He grinned down at Tucker, adjusting their position so that he was straddling Tucker's hips. Moving slow enough that he could gauge Tucker's reactions, he rocked forward, letting their cocks rub together through their boxers. "And most definitely this."

Bucking up to meet Luis's slow grind, Tucker gave a breathy moan. "Definitely that."

"Want to feel it with skin?"

"Yes." Tucker joined him in wiggling out of their boxers, groaning low when their bare cocks touched for the first time.

"See? Another turn-on for me. Love feeling you like this." He resumed a slow but firm rhythm, thrusting together. "You like it?"

"Uh-huh. More." Tucker's eyes fluttered shut and his hips started following Luis's motions, making their cocks drag together between their bodies even more. The friction was delicious, but he also knew what would make it even better.

"How do you feel about lube?"

"Uh…" Tucker's sudden intake of air and big eyes said that Luis had been right that he wasn't quite ready to consider fucking as an option.

"Not for fucking," he reassured, trailing his fingers down Tucker's arms. "But slick can make this grinding together even sexier."

That got him a tentative smile from Tucker as he bumped his pelvis up against Luis's. "Bring on the sexy then."

"You've got it." He made quick work of getting the bottle from the nightstand where he'd stashed it. "This is what I use when I'm jerking off."

Squeezing a little into his palm he slicked up both of their cocks, loving how Tucker moaned and bucked into Luis's hand.

"Ahhh. Yeah. That's good. Damn." Tucker bit his upper lip as Luis aligned their bodies so that he could jack both cocks together. "And I should have known that the King of Paint Wars would like it a little messy."

"Messy is good." Taking away his hand, he dipped his head so that they could kiss while he rocked against Tucker, their cocks slipping past each other in a way that had them both moaning.

"Too good," Tucker panted, body following Luis's lead as easily as if they were dancing, movements perfectly in sync.

"No such thing." Taking advantage of the way Tucker's head had tipped back, Luis licked and sucked along his collarbones.

"Says you." Tucker gave a laugh that ended on another moan.

When they'd kissed as teens, he'd always been so careful to never mark Tucker, never leave evidence of their secret passion. But now some primal urge made him drop a light love bite there, below where Tucker's shirt would cover but something for him to know about nonetheless. Looking at his handiwork, he growled softly, hips picking up speed on their own.

"Damn. Hard to...hold back." Eyes squishing shut, Tucker held Luis tighter as their bodies surged together.

"Don't. Want you to feel good." Hand on Tucker's hip, he urged him faster. "Want to hear it and see it and feel it when you let go."

"Soon. God. Luis." Each of Tucker's words was practically a whimper, and every sound had Luis right there on the edge too.

"That's it. Damn, you are so sexy." He tried to memorize all the little details—the sounds, the expression on Tucker's face, the way his back arched, whole body tensing under Luis, the restless movements of his legs, one of which he hooked around Luis's calf. Even the scent of sex thick in the air was sexy, ramping his desire up further. "You wanted to know what turns me on? This right here, you coming apart for me."

"Want you to go too." Tucker managed to sound demanding even as his body strained.

"Oh, I will." He chuckled darkly because that much was a given, and trying to hold back wasn't any easier for him than for Tucker.

"Good." Drawing the word out on a moan, Tucker arched his body again. "Feel so close to you."

"Me too." So many emotions were swirling through him beyond the obvious physical pleasure. He could feel Tucker's heart hammering against his chest, each intake of breath, every tensing muscle contributing to this sensation like they were…linked somehow. One in that moment. And knowing Tucker was feeling it too made it all so much better. Deeper.

"Yeah. Fuck. Want…" Trailing off as his body shuddered, Tucker moaned as his cock pulsed against Luis's. In that instant, Luis would have promised him any damn thing he wanted.

"Do it. Come for me."

"Luis." Clutching Luis like they were in a raging hurricane, Tucker came with a strangled sound, and the way everything suddenly got slicker and slipperier was all Luis needed for his hips to pump harder, thrusting fast against Tucker until he too was coming.

"*Yes.* Fuck." Felt like he'd hurled himself off a cliff, intense endorphin rush as he slowly floated back to earth with smaller surges of pleasure.

Laughing and panting at the same time, Tucker peppered Luis's shoulder with kisses as he stroked his back.

His tenderness was almost better than the orgasm, another wave of sweet pleasure. "I didn't think it could get better...but it did. Wow."

"That was something alright." God, what was Luis going to do without Tucker? How was he supposed to let something this good go? His mind spun, questions crowding out the last waves of satisfaction. His body might be exhausted, but his mind spun.

"And now we're a mess." Apparently not suffering from the same affliction, Tucker playfully pushed at Luis until he rolled off to flop next to him on his back. He was still trying to make sense of how deeply Tucker made him feel, the sort of rare connection that scared him senseless. He didn't *want* to feel these things. Not now.

Breathing deeply, he tried for a normal tone, one that matched Tucker's good mood. "Hotel bathroom is super tiny, so I can't show you all the fun of sharing a shower, but give me a minute to remember I've got legs and I'll help you clean up."

"I have a big shower." Tucker's smile was almost shy, an invitation there for more than just another round of sex.

"Filing that away for future reference." Luis's chest hurt with wanting more encounters, more memories, an endless string of them, not a few stolen minutes here and there.

"Good." Breath whistling out softly, Tucker let his head fall on Luis's shoulder and went quiet for long minutes. Luis tried again to drink it all in, bottle it up, do everything in his power to save this moment and these feelings.

"I can't sleep here," Tucker said at last, yawning.

"I know." And he did. Tucker had a life. The boys

would be done with their party soon, and he had a curfew to enforce. Much as he wanted to, Luis was going to be good, not tease him into going for seconds.

"I wish though…" Tucker's eyes were as serious as Luis had ever seen them. Not sad precisely, but intense. And all the longing Luis felt in every muscle fiber in his body was there too, all his wants and secret dreams, right there reflected back to him.

"Me too." Neither of them were going to voice that longing, give a name to those wants, and that was for the best. But for now they could lie there, bodies touching, breath still in sync, *wishing*.

Chapter Thirteen

"You were out late last night." Wade wandered into the kitchen Saturday morning, itching his stomach and blinking the sleep out of his eyes before heading to the cereal cabinet. Tucker hurried up pouring his coffee before Wade could help himself to half the pot.

"And you were back early." He'd lingered over goodbye with Luis in the hotel parking lot far longer than necessary. As a result, Tucker had pulled into the driveway minutes before the twins, Walker dropping Wade off before taking Mary Anne on home.

"Party was boring." Shrugging, Wade reached for a mixing bowl. Moving quickly, Tucker plucked it from his fingers and replaced it with a normal-size bowl before Wade could pour in the cereal.

"You don't need the whole box and a gallon of milk. And sorry to hear that about the party." He served himself his own average portion of cornflakes, wishing they were some of Luis's eggs. It had been simple food but perfectly made, and he'd fallen asleep dreaming about spicy kisses. And not worrying about the kids, which in retrospect, maybe he should have done more of. "Everything go okay?"

"Yeah, it's fine. Scrimmage was awesome, so that

made up for the boring. And on the way home, we stopped for food and I got you this." Wade slid a small box across the island countertop to him. It might have been a few years but he knew instantly what the small square box with gold foil held.

"What the—"

"Language." Wade did a fair job of imitating Tucker's deeper voice while laughing. "And I'm just saying the same thing you say to us. Be safe and have fun."

He stared down at the box like it might explode any second. And honestly, it might be easier if it did. Easier than this conversation at least. "Why are you pushing so hard for me to..."

"Get laid?" Wade wiggled his eyebrows.

"I was going to say *date*."

"You're funny when you're all flustered." He claimed the seat next to Tucker at the breakfast bar end of the island. "And somehow you were way more chill when giving Walker and I the talk than when talking about your own sex life."

With good reason. Tucker sputtered around his next bite of food. "My... I don't have..."

"Seriously?" Tilting his head, Wade gave him a long look. "You never lie to me. Ever."

Well, he had Tucker there. Damn it. "Okay, maybe I do have...a personal life, but not one I'm discussing with you."

"Trust me, I'm not asking for details." He held up his spoon.

"And yet here you are, offering me condoms and giving safe sex advice."

"Because I want you to have fun." Wade patted him on the shoulder before returning to his breakfast.

"I have plenty of fun." Like last night. All of it—the scrimmage, the food, the sex, the cuddling afterward and the goodnight kisses—had been the most fun he'd had in years. Not that he was confessing that to Wade, and not that he'd admit that Wade might have a point about the other 99 percent of his life.

"No, you don't. And soon we're going to be gone and you're going to be all alone—"

"Trying not to think about that, thanks." Appetite way less now, he turned to his coffee instead of the cornflakes. *All alone.* No Luis, no kids, no fun…

Wade looked away from him, gazing out at Tucker's little backyard oasis, recently watered plants glistening in the morning sunshine. Drawing in a deep breath, Wade rolled his shoulders back and Tucker instinctively braced for whatever was coming next.

"There was a scout from a college in Idaho there last night. He was mainly there to see Mitch, but we talked a little too. My chances of going to a Division One program are pretty slim, even if I get my grades up, but at a good smaller school, I could see a lot of playing time."

"That's…that's good." Idaho might as well be the moon for how quickly Tucker's stomach sank at this news. But Wade didn't need him shooting down his new prospect just because Tucker wasn't ready for any of this. "We'll find the right program for you, wherever that ends up being."

"Thanks. And in the meantime, you should have some fun. Then maybe I won't feel so bad about leaving you and Walker and everyone else."

Ah. It made sense now. Wade wanted Luis to fill a gap, but unfortunately Tucker had to admit the truth to him. "I get that, but Luis isn't staying around. So even if there was something going on there, it's not going to last."

"It could." Wade clapped him on the shoulder, tone encouraging. "You never know. And it could be the start of your grand dating adventure. Lots of…people."

"I'm demisexual. Remember?" Explaining ace spectrum identities to the kids had been a challenge, right up there with coming out, but it had been important to him. "We talked about what that means. I'm not looking to sleep around."

"Then don't." Wade's tone said that Tucker was making this harder than he needed to. And maybe he was. "But you can have fun regardless of whether you're having sex."

"It's not that simple."

"It could be." Wade's chin took on a familiar stubborn tilt, the same kid who refused to accept defeat at board games and family arguments.

"Wade…" He started stern, then gentled his tone because the kid did mean well even if his objectives were less than realistic. "Maybe lay off the matchmaking, okay? I don't think Walker likes it either."

"Don't think Walker likes what?" Walker clomped down the stairs and into the kitchen, heading straight for the cereal Wade had left out.

"Dad's not thrilled with our condom present." Rolling his eyes, Wade made a dismissive gesture.

"Oh *that*." Walker didn't even look up from pouring himself some of the coffee.

"You were in on this?" He expected this sort of stunt from Wade, but Walker was a different matter altogether. Not to mention, he was still under the impression that Walker wasn't the keenest on Luis.

However, Walker merely shrugged. "I wasn't *out* on it. You bought some for me."

"Well. Thanks. Both of you." Blinking hard, Tucker struggled for a response. "But I can handle my own social life."

"Not very well," Wade muttered into his cereal, but Tucker decided to ignore him and get to his real plan for the day.

"But speaking of social, who wants to tackle the Cline Butte trail with me this morning before it gets super hot?"

Groaning, Wade made a show of stretching. "I'm out. Still sore from the game. But that's Walker's favorite. You should go, bro."

"Will we be back by lunch?" Eyes conflicted, Walker pursed his mouth.

"Absolutely." With any luck it wouldn't take that long for Luis's plan to work.

While the boys finished up breakfast, Tucker collected water bottles, sunscreen, and hiking snacks. The drive to the trailhead was quiet with him trying to give Walker the sort of space that might induce him into opening up. The first part of the trail was steep with a number of switchbacks, but even after the trail leveled out some, Walker stayed quiet. Even the increasingly epic view of the rock formations wasn't enough to perk him up.

Finally, though, right as Tucker was about to give in and start asking questions, Walker slowed down and his shoulders slumped. "Mary Anne doesn't want to go away to college. Like at all, not even U of O over in Eugene. She wants to stay here, go to school in Bend, get a teaching degree."

"I see. You were planning to apply to places together?"

Tucker worked to keep his tone conversational, easy, wanting to keep Walker talking.

"Well, yeah. Of course." Walker picked his way over some rocks, not looking back at Tucker.

"But central Oregon doesn't have Marine Biology as an option—"

That got Walker to whirl around, eyes steely. *"I know."*

"Sorry." Tucker held up his hands, then tried again. Damn, this was hard, figuring out what to say. He wanted to insist that Walker not give up his dreams for this girl, even as nice and sweet as she seemed to be. And Tucker did get her perspective too—he'd never wanted to leave this area himself, and Mary Anne came from a big, close-knit family that went back to the pioneer days. "Plenty of couples do long-distance relationships for college…"

Walker made a scoffing noise. "And how many of those break up?"

"Probably some." Tucker couldn't lie. Hell, he was proof that distance and young couples didn't work out well, and he knew plenty of other stories of high school couples who couldn't make it past a freshman year apart. The trail looped around, starting the descent that would carry them back to the trailhead parking lot. And maybe he needed the reminder that distance didn't work for seasoned adults either. Whatever delightful dreams he'd had last night where Luis developed a burning urge to visit more often were about as realistic as Walker finding an ocean in their county.

"Distance never works." Slowing down again, Walker kicked at a rock. "And especially not when Mary Anne has it all planned out *now*. Live together for college, get married—"

Tucker made a strangled noise and tripped over some roots. *"Married?"*

"Don't sound so shocked." Walker stuck out an arm to keep Tucker from falling. "You were younger than she's planning on being."

"Yeah, but that was different." Looking away, he adjusted the straps on his backpack.

"Not that different."

"Please tell me she's not…" Tucker couldn't even finish the thought.

"No. Your safe sex lectures paid off, so you can stop looking like you just ate a live frog."

"Thank you." Wiping his suddenly clammy forehead, Tucker wasn't even going to pretend to not be relieved.

"She wants to teach a few years, then have two kids, two years apart, boy and girl."

Lord help us. Tucker was back to having to work to keep a nonjudgmental tone. "She has some rather specific plans."

"Yup." Mouth thinning out to a tight line, Walker gave a sharp nod.

He started to reach for Walker's shoulder, then thought the better of it. "Do you think your plans match hers?"

Walker rolled his shoulders. "She's kind of planning enough for both of us. She says if I get a business degree, I can work for her dad or something."

Tucker could barely keep back a groan. Mary Anne had ranching grandparents and various family members in businesses all around the area, but her father and uncle owned an insurance agency that specialized in farms and ranches.

"I'm absolutely not knocking insurance work, but you've talked about being a marine biologist for *years.*"

"And this is why I haven't brought it up before now. I *knew* you'd be all against me switching plans."

He wasn't wrong, so Tucker did some deep breathing before replying, trying to find his calm and objective voice again.

"People swap majors all the time. You're not going to let me down if you go to college and pick another path on your own." This time he did touch Walker, a brief pat on the shoulder that he predictably shrugged off. "But swapping plans should be your idea."

"Maybe when you love someone, their idea can be your idea?" Walker brightened like this new philosophy had just come to him.

Tucker had to take a minute to mull this concept over, try to find a way to explain nuance to a seventeen-year-old in over his head. "Sometimes. I'm not going to lie and say that love never requires sacrifices, but if you do something you truly hate or give up something you wanted more than anything, you might have some serious regrets."

"Like you?" Face stormy, Walker looked back over his shoulder as his steps got heavier.

Ah. Maybe this was some of why he'd seemed rather conflicted about Tucker's friendship with Luis. "You mean having you guys? No. Never. Raising you has been my life's greatest success."

"See?" Walker's tone had all the self-righteousness of an investigative reporter calling out an inconsistency. "You had to do something you weren't crazy about like getting married young to get something that makes you really happy now. Maybe a family with Mary Anne will make me happy too."

Damn it. Tucker didn't have an easy answer for that.

He wouldn't wish the struggles he and Heidi had had on him, but he also couldn't live with himself if he gave Walker the impression that he resented having had the boys. And his perspective that he wouldn't change the way things had turned out had taken years to fully achieve. "Maybe you're too young to know right now."

"I knew you'd say that too." The trailhead was in sight now, but Walker slowed to a stop, bitter disappointment in his voice that Tucker would do anything to take away.

"What would you like me to say?" He moved so that he could meet Walker's eyes. "What could help?"

"Tell me that you trust me to make a good choice."

"I do." They were among the hardest words he'd ever had to utter, but he knew not saying them could do permanent damage. "But I also want you to truly think about what it is you want. Really imagine your options."

Surprisingly, Walker's eyes actually fluttered shut, like he was doing that right then. "I try and then I can't imagine not having Mary Anne."

"Okay. Take your time. You still have all of senior year—"

"I get that. But some things are simply reality. Like long distance not working and there not being any oceans near here."

Oh, how Tucker knew the truth of those words. Some things were reality for him and Luis too. He couldn't magically make the kind of culture Luis loved appear here, the live music and plays and endless variety of eateries, and he couldn't make the miles between them disappear any more than he could remove Luis's past hurts. He was the last person able to argue with Walker. "I wish I had answers for you."

"I know." This time it was Walker patting him, and

Tucker's throat tightened. "And hey, if I do stay here, at least Wade can stop worrying about you being all alone and puttering around missing us."

"That should be the least of your concerns." Being stern didn't work out so well when he was fighting against rising emotions.

"What is it you like to say? 'I'm always going to worry about you. It's my job.'"

He managed a laugh at that. "True, but—"

His cell trilled with a familiar tone, cutting him off. He groaned even as Walker made a "go ahead" gesture with his hand.

"That's your work number, isn't it?"

"Damn it, yes." A few minutes later, he had all the details and a growing sense of foreboding. Hanging up, he turned back to Walker. "There's a fire. I have to go after I drop you at home. I'll call your mom on the way so she knows I may be busy a few days. They're setting up a fire camp about an hour and a half east."

"Understood. And worry about that, not me."

No way was Tucker going to be able to follow that advice. His talk with Walker had only raised his level of concern for his son, but also illuminated some stark truths for himself too. And now he had to go and turn his attention toward work, but those worries were going to dog him the whole time. What he needed was life to slow down and stop throwing him curveballs, but he might be better off wishing for an August ice storm.

Chapter Fourteen

A weird mix of anticipation and restlessness coursed through Luis as he and Tucker loaded up his SUV at headquarters. The official vehicles were all already underway, with more personnel coming in private vehicles like them. Time was of the essence, and Luis could have caught a ride with some others heading to the fire site, but he'd chosen to wait for Tucker for reasons he didn't want to examine closely.

"Thanks for waiting for me." Tucker slammed the back of the SUV shut.

"Yeah, figured you might want some company on the drive." Luis tried to play it casual, like him wanting to see Tucker alone before the chaos of the fire camp wasn't a big part of his motivation for waiting. "You sure you don't want me taking a turn behind the wheel? You look exhausted."

Tucker wiped some sweat from his forehead. He was in forest service clothes, but his face was dusty and hair messier than normal. "Sorry. I barely had enough time to change, let alone shower or recover. I was out hiking with Walker. Took your advice and got him out of the house."

Warmth spread though Luis's midsection. He liked

knowing he'd been able to help Tucker, liked being listened to. "Good. Did it work?"

"Sort of. He talked, but it's not something I can fix. Big life direction and college questions." Sighing heavily, Tucker leaned against the SUV, not making a move to head to the driver's side. Luis took the opportunity to reach for the keys dangling from Tucker's fingers.

"That sucks. And it looks like it wore you out in more ways than one. How about you set the GPS? That way you can shut your eyes, try to rest while I drive. I promise to take good care of your baby."

"It's just a car," Tucker said with the weary wisdom of a guy who had actual kids and a perspective on his priorities. Pushing away from the SUV, he let Luis go ahead and take the keys. "Yeah, that sounds good. Wake me up if calls start coming in that need my response."

"Probably not a ton we can do until we're on site." Luis opened the driver's side door. He liked that Tucker was willing to let him drive, wasn't such a control freak that he couldn't turn it off when needed, unlike some guys Luis had known. And taking care of Tucker simply felt good. Right.

The fire was on federal lands east of Prineville, a small ranching town enough distance from the fire to not need evacuation, unlike the popular national forest campgrounds closer in. Traffic going away from the fire was heavy, lots of RVs and campers leaving the forest area. The quick spread of this fire situation was why the code red and extreme warning level they'd escalated to yesterday was so important. The plentiful dry brush surrounding the scenic vistas coupled with many unpaved roads at risk of sparks from passing vehicles could be a recipe for disaster, which was why the interagency fire management had made the decision to respond aggressively, setting up a fire camp for the many crews en route.

Smoke was visible over the mountains even when they were still more than twenty miles out. The steep terrain, some of which had dead timber from prior fires, would be an extra challenge. Aircraft had already been sent in with water and retardant, but last Luis had heard they were holding ground crews at the staging area due to concerns about snags, those dead trees that could cause sudden, deadly flare-ups. That was where he could make a difference—predicting fire movement including the effect of the snags.

Somehow Tucker managed to doze even through the changing terrain. Luis hoped he hadn't worn him out too much the night before. It had been late when they'd parted, and while Luis had slept in, it sounded like Tucker hadn't been so lucky. Unexpected tenderness swept over him each time he glanced over at his sleeping face.

"We're getting close," he murmured as he turned off the main road.

"'M Awake," Tucker lied adorably, blinking and stretching like he'd been deeply dreaming.

"You're cute when you nap."

"I wasn't really asleep," Tucker protested, stretching again.

"Ha. You snored. You sure last night isn't to blame?"

"Not a chance." Tucker gave him a surprisingly heated look. "I enjoyed every minute. I hope you know that."

"I do."

"I've got no idea how long we'll be on site here, but after we're done, I'll show you how not exhausted I am." Tucker winked as the sound of aircraft overhead increased, traffic picking up too, trucks from the various agencies heading to the makeshift fire camp base.

"Ha. More like you'll be ready to sleep for a week." Luis had to stop glancing at Tucker and focus on navigating the tightly curving road.

"Not ruling that out either, but I do have that big master shower…"

"Tempting." Luis liked that Tucker had been thinking about them showering together. He was trying to be careful and not let Tucker think he expected sex in a given situation. He wanted to make sure that Tucker had the emotional connection he needed, but there was also no denying that Tucker was sexy as fuck and Luis enjoyed the hell out of spending time with him in that way. Making Tucker feel good was a rush whether feeding him or giving him an orgasm. Maybe if the stars aligned, in a few days he'd have a chance to do both.

But first there was work to do. Within minutes of their arrival, they were pulled into a trailer for an administrative meeting dealing with logistics. There was a push for moving ground crews in, but concerns about safety persisted as leadership worked together to come up with a plan. Luis had more than enough to occupy him, but every so often he was struck by how damn good Tucker was at his job, juggling multiple variables to make insightful recommendations in a way that commanded respect. His competence increased his appeal and made Luis quietly proud. There had been glimpses of Tucker's potential when he was younger—on the football field, in group projects, settling friend disputes—but seeing him as the capable man he was now was satisfying in a way Luis wasn't prepared for.

He also was pleasantly surprised by how people he'd

known less than two weeks listened to him too, the leadership team coming together in a way that made the job that much easier and smooth. Luis ended up on a team headed close to the fire to collect better data, and as he left, his eyes met Tucker's.

Be careful. Tucker's unspoken concern was right there. His furrowed forehead reflected all Luis's worry from the day before, and it was both humbling and reassuring to know that Tucker cared as deeply as he did.

Always am. Luis tried to reassure him with a nod as he held his gaze. He enjoyed being out in the field, loved the adrenaline rush that reminded him of his years on the line, but for the first time in a long time, he had an added reason to return safely.

It was hours before they saw each other again, his data and recommendations paving the way for some cautious ground crews to move in followed by tense hours of monitoring them. The snags were an ever-present concern, and he wouldn't tell Tucker how close he personally came to a few of the spot fires. Smoke singed his eyes and lungs, and his muscles burned from all the moving around.

As the light started to slip from the evening sky, he finally got a chance to stretch his back and head to the food truck. But he didn't even have to get in line because Tucker was already there, holding out a sandwich for him.

"Got you one. There's a place we can sit over here. How are you holding up?"

"Fine." Luis took a seat on a flat rock next to him, enough away from the line of hungry crew members and scattered clumps of people that they could speak freely. "Back's a bit tight and not looking forward to a tent tonight, but we need to monitor the overnight developments and get an early start."

"Yup, we'll move crews in at dawn if possible." Tucker nodded. "I grabbed an extra camping pad when I got my gear. You can have it. Maybe double the cushioning will help your back?"

"Thanks." Luis wasn't too proud to turn down the offer of assistance. "And yeah, that may help. It's holding one position too long that really gets me. That and lifting heavy loads, but that's why I moved into this job. I just couldn't deal with the gear we had to haul on the front lines."

"Wish we were alone. I'd rub it for you. You could tell me what to do," Tucker said idly.

Luis liked how that was probably a genuine desire to ease his pain and not a pretext for sex. And there was none of that macho "I know what you need" bullshit either—Tucker's willingness to take direction both on and off the job was one of his most appealing character-istics. As his earlier competence had more than demon-strated, he was capable of being the one in charge, but he also wasn't too proud to defer to others.

"I might take you up on that later."

"Good. Do that. Now, what's your early feel for how this started? Are we looking at another arson case?" Tucker leaned forward, as animated about the job as he'd been all day, with an unflagging energy level that Luis admired.

"At first glance, the fast spread would seem to go against the pattern of smaller fires, but I think this might be related. Nearby hiking trail, very early morning igni-tion, another anonymous report for the authorities to in-vestigate that I'll put money on leading to a burner phone. I'm hoping to get closer to the ignition area tomorrow, look for more of the same patterns I've seen at the other sites with the placement of fuel. I'll be reviewing the data and evidence in the coming days, see what's worth turning over to authorities to see if any leads are promising."

"Good. Glad we're keeping you busy." There was a certain wistfulness to Tucker's tone, like he was grateful Luis had reason to stay, but he knew it wouldn't last.

Glancing around quickly, Luis patted his hand. "I'm here as long as they need me." He couldn't promise to stay forever, and they were hardly at a point where he could make other sorts of promises, even if part of him wanted to do just that.

One of the administrative staff came striding toward them. "There's a meeting in five."

"On our way." Tucker shot Luis a regretful look as he stood, then offered Luis a hand up.

Luis's tight back muscles appreciated the assistance even if he did hate feeling nine hundred years old some days. If he was lucky, he might end up in a tent with Tucker later, and maybe some of his boundless energy could make its way to Luis, sustain him for what was likely to be a long day ahead tomorrow. Working together was far more satisfying than he could have predicted, having a common purpose, but also having someone at his side, looking out for him, bringing him sandwiches and extra bedding and listening to him bounce theories around. He'd been prepared to miss Tucker on a personal level, but now he saw that he'd miss him professionally as well, and he needed to figure out how to cope with that added layer of emotions.

Three days. It was hardly the longest fire Tucker had been involved with, but by the time Monday night rolled around, he was beyond grateful that personnel were being dismissed. On-site admin needs were lessened to the point that Tucker and Luis were free to go home and get some rest. Then they could gear up for the cleanup efforts that would take far longer than the initial blaze.

"I'm starving," Luis said as they loaded up. "No more sandwiches. I need something hot, and for once, you won't have to talk me into fast food."

"There's a local burger place in Prineville with amazing fries if you're indulging." Tucker slammed the back of the SUV shut and headed to the driver's side. This time it was Luis's turn to rest as he looked like crap after two nights in a tent with a bad back. Tucker was going to do his best to take care of him, make those dark circles under his eyes disappear and his smile come back out. "And then after dinner, you're coming back with me. Boys are with Heidi tonight, and you, my friend, have a date with my shower."

"Too exhausted to argue too loudly with that." Giving him a tired smile, Luis buckled up. Tucker didn't miss his wince as he shifted in the seat either.

"What else can we do for you? Meds? Heating pad?" Tucker started the slow trek back to the main road, following a line of other vehicles leaving the fire camp.

"I took a dose of an over-the-counter anti-inflammatory a while ago. I don't like taking the stronger stuff unless the pain is way worse than this. This is just how chronic issues tend to go—flaring up when it's least convenient. I know I look a little worse for the wear, but a good night's sleep on a decent mattress will go a long way to getting me back to normal."

"I splurged on a quality orthopedic mattress when

I bought the house. And my offer of a back rub still stands."

"Sounds tempting." Groaning, Luis stretched again. His flexing triceps made Tucker remember how his cat had stretched on top of the fridge when he'd visited.

"And how about Blaze? Do we need to stop by your hotel, pick up her and a change of clothes for you?"

"She's generally good on her own—I left multiple bowls of water in case anything spills, the automatic dry food dispenser, and a second litter box, and let the front desk know the situation. But even though it's out of the way, I'd probably feel better checking on her. And clean clothes sound great."

"It's a plan then. Food, your place, then my shower."

"Tucker?" Luis's voice dropped lower and softer, and a quick glance revealed that his face had gone decidedly more tender.

"Yeah?"

"You're a nice guy. I was about to give you crap for going into dad mode on me, trying to fix everything, but then I realized you've always been like this. Caring about me. Taking care of little details."

"I try." The back of Tucker's neck heated. "I mean, I know I didn't always do the best job of thinking about your needs—"

"We were kids. There were things we both could have done differently. I meant what I said last week. I own my part in what happened. Quit beating yourself up for the past, because I'm sure as heck not dwelling on it, not when the here and now is so enjoyable. And I mean it. You're a good guy."

"Thanks." He let a few more miles tick by, absorbing Luis's praise, and during that time, Luis shut his eyes.

Tucker let him rest until their stop for food. Giant piping-hot burgers and a basket of fries to share had seldom tasted so satisfying. They were far from the only forest service people who had stopped for food there, making for a lively atmosphere but not particularly date-like, making Tucker all the more eager to be alone again.

"Okay, that was worth the food splurge." Luis's smile was at least a little wider as they resumed their drive, heading south to Blaze, who greeted them with the full force of her disapproval, meowing loudly as they entered the suite, then turning her back on them and stalking off.

"I'm going to change her water and such, but I'm not going to bring her to your place." Luis made quick work of his tasks. "In this mood, she's likely to climb your blinds or scratch the sofa before settling in to ignoring us again."

"Makes sense. I don't mind taking the risk though, if you'd feel better bringing her." Tucker tried to pet the cat, but she swished her tail and jumped out of reach onto the counter. Simply the prospect of spending the night with Luis had him more energetic despite the days of little sleep, and he'd put up with the cat if it made Luis more likely to stay.

"No, I think she's fine here." Grabbing clothes out of his dresser, Luis quickly filled his backpack with essentials.

"You can bring…" Tucker nodded at the nightstand, hoping Luis could read his mind without him needing to spell this out.

"Yeah?" Luis got the hint, retrieving the bottle of lube and putting it in the bag's front pocket. "Not too tired?"

"Apparently not." He had to laugh at his own eagerness, which honestly delighted him. Being this interested in sex with a specific person was still unfamiliar to him, and the arousal Luis inspired felt good, like champagne bubbles in his veins or like sampling a dessert he only rarely got to have. "Wade brought me condoms the other day."

"Wade did what now?" Luis gave a slow blink as he zipped up the bag.

"I think it was supposed to be his seal of approval or something, but anyway, I now own condoms. But not lube."

"I see." Luis rubbed his chin.

"My main priority though is getting you feeling better. Hot shower. Back rub if that helps. I'm not saying we have to have sex of any kind, but I also figured you might be feeling better by morning..."

"Oh, I'm feeling better right *now*, simply knowing that you're thinking about sex." Chuckling, Luis started to heft his backpack, but Tucker grabbed it from him.

"Let me save your back." He pointed at the door. "And if the cat is squared away, you can think more about sex in the car."

"Aye, Captain." Luis gave him a tired-but-still-wolfish smile. "Tell me you're joining me in this magical shower you keep promising me."

"If you want." Tucker led the way back to the SUV, and Luis waited until they were both buckled up to speak again.

"You do know that just because Wade gave you condoms, we don't need to do anything that requires them, right? I'm perfectly fine with what we've done so far, and I've been in long-term relationships where anal wasn't on the table for a variety of reasons. I don't want you feeling pressured by me or anything else."

"I want to." The very tips of Tucker's ears were on fire as he headed toward Painter's Ridge. "I've never... I've been curious before, but there's never been anyone I felt comfortable with enough to go there with. Not sure when the opportunity will arise again, honestly, so yeah I'd like to try that with you, if it's something you enjoy."

"I enjoy." Luis's laugh had a tight edge to it, and Tucker couldn't tell if he was turned on or if his back was bothering him again. Then their eyes met at a stoplight, and the heat there stole his breath for a second. Turned on it was. "Can you get a little more specific with what it is you want? I'm rather vers, so I'm happy to be your...*experiment* either direction."

"I didn't mean that you were convenient," Tucker was hasty to explain. "More like I feel so close with you, and I really want to know what it's like to get fucked by someone I care about, but also very specifically *you*."

"I get it." Laughing more readily now, Luis gave him a quick pat. "I appreciate that. A lot. And my back is feeling better by the second, thinking about fucking you through that mattress of yours."

"Don't make me tempted to speed. And only if your back is truly up for it. I've waited this many years. I can wait until you're able."

"Trust me that my cock is doing everything it can to make that happen."

"Don't exhaust it before I have a chance to." Chuckling, Tucker began counting down the miles to home, to having Luis in his shower and in his bed at last. It was strange how very *right* it all felt, like they'd been destined to end up here all along.

Chapter Fifteen

"And here we are." Tucker flipped on the light to the bathroom after Luis set his bag near Tucker's bed. The rest of the drive back and the race upstairs made him feel like a teen again, desperate to be alone with Luis, willing to trade an awful lot for a room with a door that locked. And now they had that, and despite his tiredness, time stretched deliciously in front of him, a whole night with Luis. Unable to resist, he wrapped Luis up in a hug from behind.

"Okay, now that's a shower." Luis sagged against him, gesturing at the shower, which occupied most of the far wall. The bathroom itself was a bit much for a single guy—sage-colored walls, double vanity, walk-in closet, separate toilet stall, but the glass-and-tile shower was definitely the star. He'd agreed to double showerheads for resale value, then added a rain-type upper shower for his own indulgence.

"Told you. Choice was a big walk-in like this or a soaking tub, and I'm not really the tub type. But I did upgrade the fixtures in here." Releasing Luis, he busied himself with fetching towels for them.

"I love it. I may move in tomorrow." Chuckling, Luis started removing his clothes.

Please. Do. But somehow he managed to snort, not reveal that private wish.

"Seriously, this is gorgeous." Still moving stiffly enough that Tucker felt for him, Luis finished stripping, revealing his muscled body. It was a working man's body with several scars—upper back, arms, and one across his thigh. However, to Tucker, he was more gorgeous than any airbrushed model. He liked everything from the gleaming tats to his already half-hard cock, and all of it made his own blood hum.

Sliding back behind Luis, he dropped a kiss on his shoulder. "So are you."

"Flatterer. I'm a dusty mess."

"But a cute one." He managed to sneak in a neck kiss before Luis wiggled away.

"Less compliments, more naked." Luis flipped the shower on while gesturing for Tucker to get busy.

"Okay, okay." Tucker made fast work of undressing, slipping into the shower right behind Luis, who turned to give him an appreciative look.

"That's more like it." Luis tilted his head, getting his hair and body wet before he moved closer to Tucker, looping his arms around him, pulling him close for a soft kiss.

"Yeah, it is." Not ready to let him go, Tucker held him tighter, bestowing a kiss of his own. This one started like kindling catching a spark in winter, soft glow, gradually increasing in warmth until there was a powerful blaze, heating him from the inside out. They went from trading little sips and nips to Luis backing him against the wall, all out claiming his mouth. The tile was cool against his back while Luis was warm and urgent against his front, and the contrast was enough to make his cock pulse.

"Damn." Breathing hard, Luis moved so that their hard

cocks brushed, making them both moan. "You're going to distract me from my plan to soap you up."

"Me first." Tucker grabbed a bottle of body wash and squirted some in his hand, gleefully lathering up Luis's chest and arms, reveling in his smooth, slippery skin. Laughing, Luis retaliated by getting his own palm full of soap and rubbing it all over Tucker as he continued his mission to touch as much of Luis as possible.

"I'm not sure we're supposed to have this much fun." Still grinning, Luis moved so that they could both rinse off.

"Sure we are." Tucker pulled him back into his embrace for a quick kiss.

Luis's eyes danced. "Maybe you're right."

"Of course I am...*fuck*." His voice went from boast to groan as Luis fisted his cock, stroking slowly. "You're too good at that."

"Mmm. Just you wait." Licking his lips, Luis raised his eyebrows.

Unfamiliar need unspooled in Tucker's gut. He *wanted*. His body wasn't entirely sure what yet, but simply that look was enough to unleash a powerful urgency. Behind the need was a tremor of nerves, worry that Luis had way more experience in this sort of thing. "That confident?"

"Take pride in your skills." Luis shrugged, adjusting his position so that the spray rained down on his back. "That's what my abuela was always saying."

"Somehow I doubt she meant *that*." Tucker moved so that even more water could massage Luis's back.

"Point. But I still stand by my claim. It's not bragging when it's true." Arching into the spray, he briefly closed his eyes.

Not even Tucker's dreams had ever conjured up such an arousing sight, and again he worried that maybe he'd be the one letting Luis down. He exuded sex appeal while Tucker...well, he was *Tucker*.

"Now I'm the one worried I won't live up to your lofty standards," he finally admitted as he took a minute to actually shampoo and wash instead of simply finding more excuses for making out. "I haven't... I'm not sure of all the moves and rules."

"There're no rules. Only what feels good." Luis punctuated his words by pulling Tucker close again and giving him a lengthy kiss that went a long way to chasing out Tucker's nerves. Luis's eyes were tender, like he knew something of Tucker's unease. "And it's *you*. It's going to be good, even if you change your mind about the fucking part."

"Not changing my mind. I want this with you. For exactly that reason. It's *you*." Not releasing Luis, he gave him a firm but fast kiss.

"It's *us*." And with that, they were kissing again in earnest, Luis backing him into the corner until they were rocking together, lips and tongues and teeth combining to get him back to that needy, urgent place.

"Damn. I wish we could stay right here forever," he groaned when Luis finally let him up for air.

"Your water heater might have something to say about that." Luis laughed, which honestly was probably better than him taking Tucker seriously. Forever wasn't on the table, and he didn't need the burden of knowing how much part of Tucker wished it was.

"True." He echoed Luis's light tone. "And your back."

"Quit worrying about my back. The hot water was exactly what I needed. And you." He gave Tucker another lingering kiss before finishing his own washing.

"Good." When he was done, Tucker flipped off the water, which was indeed starting to cool.

"Now show me to your bed." Luis grabbed a towel and handed one to Tucker. "Shower fucking is probably not what I'd recommend for your first time."

"I gotta admit, I'm intrigued, but yeah, you've got a point." Toweling off quickly, he led the way back to his room where he turned on the gas fireplace and adjusted the dimmer. "Now, where were we?"

"Here." After grabbing the lube from his bag, Luis steered him toward the bed. Stretching out, Tucker made room for him, cuddling him close.

Luis rolled so he could peer down at Tucker, leg brushing Tucker's cock before he settled more firmly against him. The electric sensation of their skin meeting had Tucker gasping. "And maybe here?"

"Definitely there. More of that."

Indulging Tucker, Luis gave him slow kisses and even slower grinding together until Tucker was thoroughly drunk on every single thing about this.

"I could kiss you all night." He stroked Luis's cheek, running his finger down his bristly jaw. Neither of them had shaved, but Tucker found he loved the contrast.

"We might fall asleep in the middle." Luis gave him a playful kiss on the nose. "I think we're still running on adrenaline."

"Always so practical. But true. We better hurry before one of us starts snoring."

"Now that's romantic." Dipping his head, Luis licked Tucker's neck.

"I'll show you romantic." Tucker tugged him back up for a thorough kiss.

"Yup. That works." Smiling, Luis wiggled backward, sending more friction against Tucker's aching cock. He moved until he was low enough to nip at Tucker's chest. "But my turn now."

"Mmm. I like your turn already." Stretching, he arched into Tucker's roving mouth, groaning more when Luis sucked at one of his nipples. It wasn't electric, like his cock, but still arousing.

"You'll like this even more." Holding eye contact, Luis continued his trek south pausing with his lips millimeters from Tucker's cock.

"Fuck. Yes. That." He made a rather undignified whimper until Luis took pity on him and flicked his tongue all along his shaft. Then, right when Tucker was about to really start begging, he sucked him in deep.

"I want to finger you open while I suck you, okay?" Luis reached for the lube. "Want you nice and warmed up."

"Oh, I'm warm. Burning." Tucker took the opportunity to grab a condom from the nightstand where he'd stashed them. He tossed it next to Luis.

"This? You're barely at code yellow. I want you all the way to red. Spontaneous combustion."

"Sounds messy." Tucker had to laugh with him. Joking like this, even this turned on, felt wonderful, another layer of something to share. And he was pretty sure the only extreme warning level risk was to his heart, not his body.

Not that Luis's efforts to turn him on more were in vain though. Once Luis began teasing him with slick fingers, his nerve endings all jangled even louder, that need he'd felt in the shower back now, stronger.

"Yes. That." He tried to be encouraging even as speech was rapidly failing him.

Rubbing little circles around his rim, Luis resumed a slow rhythm of taking Tucker's cock deep with his mouth, holding his cock there, and gradually getting firmer with his touches at the same time. It felt…good. Powerful. Alive, even, like a whole new part of his body was coming online. He'd experimented some on his own, but it had never felt this intense.

Gasping a little, he bit his lip as Luis pressed a finger in. "Okay…"

"Still with me?" Luis licked idly at Tucker's cockhead.

"Uh…" Tucker opened his mouth to say that maybe it was too much, but then Luis moved his hand, finger delving deeper, curving, and all he could do in the end was moan. He knew perfectly well what a prostate was, but he hadn't realized that his was apparently hardwired to his cock, which pulsed with every caress from Luis. In fact, he'd assumed much of what he'd heard was exaggeration, but there was no mistaking how hard even the slightest contact made him.

"More," he groaned because he wanted to know *now* what else could feel this good. If one finger lit him up like a Christmas tree, then two or even Luis's cock might be like a whole bodily carnival, might do something about this rising urgency inside of him.

"That's it," Luis encouraged as Tucker started rocking his hips, chasing more from Luis's fingers and mouth. He'd been right about two feeling even better, but it wasn't enough.

"Fuck me," he whispered, crass words so unfamiliar on his tongue and yet so very *right*.

"Say it again." Luis's eyes went dark and hot as he reached for the condom.

"Fuck me."

"Hell, yes." Withdrawing his fingers gently, Luis wiped them off, then put on the condom with quick, efficient movements that still managed to be highly erotic.

"Doing okay?" Applying a generous amount of lube, Luis jacked himself slowly while holding Tucker's gaze.

"More than. Please. Now." He wasn't above begging if it got him Luis inside him that much faster.

"Can you roll? My back muscles will thank me later if we try this on your side and that might be easier on you too."

"Whatever you need." Tucker scrambled to comply, groaning softly as Luis fit himself along his side. Luis kissed the back of Tucker's neck and shoulders as his hand guided Tucker's upper leg more open.

It was like kinky yoga, and he had to suppress a grin as he let Luis arrange their bodies to his satisfaction. His torso pressed against Tucker's back and his hard cock was right there against his ass.

"Want it." He tipped his head against Luis's shoulder, loving it when Luis snaked one arm around his chest while his other hand guided his cock—

"Oh." His voice dipped to a whole new pitch. This was way more intense than fingers. The blunt head of Luis's cock felt like it might as well have been a widow maker tree branch for all the yielding Tucker's body wanted to do.

"Breathe." Luis kissed his neck again.

"Trying." He tried some slow inhales, focusing on relaxing his ass.

"Want me to stop?" Luis's eyes narrowed, concern apparent there and in how he stroked Tucker's chest and arms.

"No way." He pushed back to make his point, and Luis slid deeper. Still not the most comfortable, but better than the initial tightness. Earlier had been so good that he wanted to give this a fair chance. And judging by Luis's soft moans and curses as he pressed forward more, it was at least good for him. Knowing that made it easier to relax a little more, the satisfaction of pleasing him at least something even if the earlier fireworks weren't happening.

But then Luis grabbed Tucker's thigh and pressed it forward as he thrust deeper, pressure switching from not-so-great to glorious as his cock connected with Tucker's prostate for the first time.

"That. Do that again."

"This?" Luis did a soft, glancing variation of the previous thrust, a movement that seemed tailored to driving Tucker out of his mind with want.

"More," he demanded.

"If you insist…" Lightly biting Tucker's ear, Luis finally started the sort of deep, hard pace Tucker's body had apparently been waiting its whole life to feel. Forget a tree. He could power a whole damn city on this energy. Instinctively, he reached for his cock, making even more sparks radiate throughout his body, abs tensing.

"Yeah, that's it. Touch yourself." Luis pulled him tighter, and his arm anchoring Tucker felt so good too. Secure. Warm. Being held like this made every sensation that much more intense. He moved with Luis, finding it easy to follow his rhythm, and Luis's low moans of approval spurred him on too.

He'd never felt closer to another human being, and that more than anything happening physically made him that much closer to coming. Seeming to sense that, Luis picked up speed and intensity, thrusts hammering against that spot that made Tucker feel like a generator switched on inside of him.

"Fuck. Tucker. This is too good." Luis kissed his neck and shoulders before tilting Tucker's head so they could kiss.

"I know. Close. Can't…"

"Don't hold back. It's okay. Come for me." Luis's mouth found his again, possessive and greedy.

The kissing was what did it, that extra bit of connection making his hand move faster and tighter while Luis fucked harder into him. They both moaned but didn't stop kissing, even as Luis's thrusts became more erratic and Tucker's whole body stiffened. His free hand landed over Luis's and then he was coming, big body-shaking spurts that stole his breath.

"Coming. Me too." Luis buried his moans in Tucker's shoulder, hips slamming deep one final time before they collapsed in a sweaty, sticky heap. A sweaty, sticky, *happy*, heap, laughing softly as they traded sweet kisses. Slowly, they untangled their bodies, but Tucker still felt floaty, as high as he'd ever been, veins humming with whatever magic Luis had unleashed.

"How fast does your water heater refill?" Luis asked, nipping at Tucker's shoulder.

"Faster than me. I'm old." Tucker laughed and didn't even pretend to be able to move yet. Yeah, they'd need a second shower, but right then, he simply wanted to revel in this weightless feeling.

"Speak for yourself." Luis tapped his ankle against Tucker's, but likewise didn't seem in a hurry to leave the bed. Instead, he laced their fingers together, squeezed. And that, not the shower, not the sex, not even the epic orgasm, was the moment Tucker realized he was well and truly screwed. *Stay. I want you to stay.* He wanted Luis right here every night, holding his hand, laughing at his terrible jokes and stealing all his hot water. He wanted *everything.* And now the only question was how on earth he was supposed to get it.

Chapter Sixteen

Despite being told by the higher-ups to come in late that morning after the nonstop action of the prior few days, Luis still woke up early, before Tucker even. The sun was peeking through the blinds in Tucker's bedroom, slats of light dancing across the carpet and walls, adding to the peaceful, homey vibe. The walls were a mossy green, a few shades darker than the bathroom, and they contrasted nicely with the light linens and framed nature prints. It was a grown-up, adult space, nothing like Tucker's superhero-and-hand-me-down-laden childhood bedroom, but it fit him just the same. Woodsy without being cliché, and a sort of understated sexy, the sort of room Luis could see spending a lot of time in. *If only...*

Trying not to wake Tucker, he carefully stretched, testing his back muscles. Fucking when he'd already been fighting a flare-up was probably ill-advised, but damn had it been worth it. Tucker in bed was everything Luis had ever imagined and so much more. In fact, the effect on his already rattled emotions was almost more than that on his muscles. He'd tried to mitigate the effect on his back with the position and some pillows behind his shoulders, as well as the second shower, but he was still feeling stiff enough to know he wasn't going to fall back to sleep. Creeping from the bed, he retrieved pants and his anti-inflammatory meds from his bag. Tucker snoozed on, but Luis knew from experience that he shouldn't do the pills on an empty stomach.

Maybe he could surprise Tucker with breakfast. It was the sort of small gesture he used to do all the time with Mike, but he hadn't had the urge or opportunity since then. And Tucker had a nice kitchen that put Luis's cramped galley kitchen to shame, having the sort of open arrangement that practically begged him to whip up a big meal. The fridge and pantry didn't disappoint either—plenty of eggs and milk and other staples.

He was in the middle of preparing a potato frittata and some bacon when he heard the door.

"Hey, Dad! Just grabbing a notebook—*Oh*." One of the twins strode into the living area opposite the kitchen. "Not Dad."

"Nope. Sorry." Keeping his tone matter-of-fact, Luis figured that there wasn't much he could do to alleviate the awkwardness of finding a shirtless stranger in his dad's house, but he slid the plate of bacon across the breakfast bar. "He's still asleep. Bacon?"

"I…uh…didn't mean to interrupt. Just need…" The kid—who Luis was reasonably sure was Walker—had gone bright red and his voice came in little sputters.

"It's okay, Walker." Luis held up a hand. "It's your house, too. I'm the one who should probably apologize for startling you."

"How do you know I'm Walker?" Eyes narrowing, his head tilted, his expression dared Luis to screw this up.

"Easy. You haven't cracked a joke yet and you're here for a notebook, not sports gear. Also, there hasn't been a single mention of football."

"There is that." His mouth curved like he was thinking of smiling, then straightened again. But he did step closer and swipe a piece of bacon from the plate. "Most people can't tell us apart even after years. Wade's always trying to get me to fool teachers, especially newbie ones."

"Too bad the SAT is going to require separate identification for each of you. No trying to take his for him, right?" Luis joked.

"Ha. He should take *mine.* He keeps beating me on practice scores." Exhaling hard, Walker slipped around the island to get a cup of coffee that was mainly milk and sugar, same as Tucker used to do. "Test is this weekend and I'm starting to freak out, but maybe it doesn't matter anyway."

"What do you mean?" He'd resumed his cooking, but he kept one eye on Walker, trying to encourage him to keep talking.

"The local university doesn't care about scores as much. And my grades are okay enough. Dad didn't tell you about me dropping marine biology? Figured he'd have been dying to complain to someone about me wanting to stay with Mary Anne." Walker made a sour face.

"He mentioned you were wrestling with some big choices, but honestly, we were a little busy with the forest fire for him to vent, and even then, I don't think he'd betray your trust."

"Yeah. You're right. It's… I haven't even told Mom yet. She's going to freak too, same as he did. Everyone thinks we're too young to know what we want."

Oh, how Luis remembered those years. Add in the secrecy, and he knew exactly Walker's frustration. Young and in love with no good choices sucked. "And what do you think?"

"I think she's the one. I mean how many chances do people get, really?" Walker leaned against the counter.

Tucker and Mike's images leaped to the front of Luis's brain. How many chances indeed? One? Two? Three? Could he really expect more from the universe if he left Tucker behind here? He might not agree with Walker that people only got a single soul mate for their whole lives but there also weren't infinite chances out there either.

"I don't know," he admitted at last, slipping the frittata into the oven to finish.

"Exactly. No one knows. And she has all these plans for our future…"

"It's fun to daydream." Even knowing how it ended, he still wouldn't trade all the hours spent with Tucker as teens, painting pictures of a future in California that had never come. In one letter, he'd made a list of all his favorite places he wanted to take Tucker to, experiences he wanted to share. He'd attached a picture he'd snapped at a music festival of two men holding hands. *This could be us.*

"Not just a daydream." Walker's chin took on a stubborn tilt that made him look even more like his father. "It could happen. A life here isn't the worst thing in the world."

"No, it's not," Luis gentled his voice further.

"I know Dad had to pass on whatever dreams he had for skipping town, and Mom had to turn down that college in Iowa she liked, but they need to stop acting like me doing the same thing would be this huge failure."

"Your dad wanted to leave?"

Walker shrugged. "Not that he's ever told *me*. But I've heard him and Mom talking over the years. Yeah, he wanted out. But of course, now he's all 'you're the best thing to happen to me' dad talk."

Luis had to blink a few times as he tried to figure out a response. Tucker had wanted to leave? All this time, Luis had assumed that he'd been…well, not *grateful* for his dad's health issues but maybe relieved as it had seemed to provide him an excuse to stay. Part of Luis's bitterness had been his conviction that there was no separating Tucker from this place. But maybe he'd been wrong. Maybe Tucker truly had been torn. Which meant Luis had been even more hasty with his ultimatum. Mistakes. They'd both made them. But if Tucker had been willing to leave once…

Stop. He couldn't think like that. This was here and now, not almost twenty years ago. "Kids do tend to change things."

"Exactly. Maybe I'll feel that way too." Walker gave a firm nod, again so much like his dad.

"Maybe."

"Wade can be the one to go." Walker sounded like he was trying to convince himself about this as much as Luis. "For someone who always talked about playing ball here, he's doing a ton of looking. He's already talking to places in Idaho, Colorado and Washington."

"Looking is good," Luis said mildly. "If you want—"

"I don't." Walker's face shuttered, no more confessions, only the same sort of stubborn determination his dad was famous for.

"Do I smell food?" Tucker's voice preceded his footsteps on the stairs. "Was hoping you might let me— *Walker.*"

Tucker managed to go from sleepy and seductive to dad voice in a single syllable, and Luis had to laugh.

Tucker had been naked when Luis left him in bed, but he'd managed to find some flannel pants at least.

"Forgot my notebook. But then there was bacon…" Walker's eyes shifted, casting Luis a glance that begged him not to reveal their earlier conversation.

"And now there's frittata," Luis said easily, sliding the finished dish on a trivet. "There's more than enough for you too."

"I should really get going. But thanks for the bacon and coffee." Walker turned to leave but Tucker stopped him with hand on his shoulder.

"Hey. I haven't seen you in days. Sure you can't stay?"

"Nah." Walker moved away, but he gave Tucker a pat on the hand. "Test is Saturday. I better not skip the prep class, and someone has to go wake Wade up."

"Okay, okay. Go on then." Tucker looked genuinely sad to see Walker go, which made Luis's stomach churn as he hoped he wasn't the reason Walker was jetting out of there.

"So that was…uh…something," Tucker said after Walker dashed upstairs, retrieved his notebook, and let himself out the front door.

"It wasn't *that* awkward." Luis served him some of the frittata. "At least we were both sort of dressed."

"Still." Tucker gave him a sheepish sort of smile. "I was looking forward to a more…romantic morning with you. Didn't want you to have to deal with my moody kid."

"I like your kids, moody one included." Pouring them both coffee, he passed Tucker the creamer and sugar with his. "You were right. He's got stuff on his mind, but he reminds me an awful lot of you, the way he shoulders responsibility, weighs everything over in his head."

"He talked to you?" Tucker's eyebrows went up.

"Some." Trying not to look *too* pleased, Luis took a sip of his coffee. "I think he's worried about disappointing you and Heidi."

"I'm not worried about that." Tucker made a dismissive gesture, but his eyes were thoughtful. "I'm more worried about him disappointing himself."

"I feel you on that. I'm not sure there's an easy answer for either of you."

"Yeah, I miss the part of parenting where the toughest question was whether he could have the latest Lego set or another ten minutes before bedtime." Voice going wistful, Tucker paused before he started eating his breakfast.

"My nephews are still at the Lego age. I want to keep them there forever."

"Did you ever want kids? You're good with them. And you certainly could keep them fed. This food is fabulous."

"Thanks. And I'm not sure," he admitted, giving Tucker a far more honest answer than he gave most. "Mike was adamant on no kids, so it wasn't something I thought about that much while we were together. I love my brothers' kids, though being able to send them home at the end of the day is nice too."

"I get that. There have been weeks when I've counted down to the days that Heidi has them. And other times I miss them like crazy."

"Yeah, I can imagine. But unlike you and your complaints about being old, I still feel like I've got some time to sort out whether that's a goal for me or not. Right now, the job has me traveling enough that going it on my own as a single parent would be a no-go, but who knows about the future."

"There are times when I feel like thirty-five is still

young, and other times when I see twenty-year-olds bickering and I feel ancient."

"Perspective is everything. And you seemed plenty spry last night, old man."

"Yeah. We both did." A blush crept up Tucker's chest, flushing his neck, before finally settling into his cheeks. "That was... *Thanks* feels inadequate somehow but thank you. I had no idea...didn't expect...any of this, really."

"Good. And I know the feeling." Boy, did he ever. He liked sex fine, had had plenty of it, but he too had not been prepared for sex with Tucker, specifically, for how emotional the experience would be. And now that he knew how good they were together, he couldn't bear the thought of leaving it all behind him. But he refused to think about that right then. "Whatever this is, we've got it now. We should make the most of it."

"I know." Tucker's tone was solemn but then he brightened, almost as if like Luis he was forcing himself to live in the here and now. "Are you suggesting shower number three before we have to be at work?"

"If you'd like."

Tucker nodded, blush deepening, but he managed a roguish grin nonetheless.

"Soon I have to share you with the office, and then later your family will undoubtedly need you, but right now you're all mine, and I intend to enjoy every second of having you." Luis's throat felt strangely thick. *All mine.* He'd meant it as a sensual tease, but the words sprang from a deeper level too. Tucker was *his*, and forget living without the transcendental sex, how was he supposed to live without this man, period?

"Well, then by all means. Let's skip dishes for now,

and see how much enjoyment we can squeeze in before we're late."

"You're on." He knew better, he truly did, but he couldn't quite seem to tamp down his suddenly rejuvenated inner optimist whispering, *maybe…*

Chapter Seventeen

"There. See? Not late." Luis was all smiles as he exited Tucker's SUV at headquarters. Tucker wasn't quite as merry as him, but he had to admit that his own mood was rather good, thanks to a long, steamy shower and mad-dash race of dressing and driving to work. He'd parked in the back of the lot, and he wasn't too worried about being seen arriving with Luis—plenty of other people had carpooled due to the fire and shortage of department vehicles.

"Yup." His body was still humming with the after-effects from the shower as they walked toward the building. They'd kissed and kissed, stroking each other off like they had decades, not minutes, and when he'd finally climaxed, his knees had barely held him with the force of the pleasure. "Back to the grind now."

No more flirting, no more tender glances, and definitely no touching. For a few hours at least. "You want to come over tonight? Boys are probably both at Heidi's. You could see to Blaze, come over later…"

Luis's mouth quirked like he was thinking about turning Tucker down, his eyes distant but thoughtful. "Maybe."

"You were the one who said we should make the most

of the time we have." He didn't want to have to beg, but he also wasn't squandering another opportunity to spend off-duty time together.

"Yeah. Good point. But—"

"Tucker! And Luis! Glad you made it in." Christine came up the sidewalk from the other direction. "Fred wants an admin meeting in ten."

"Got it." Tucker nodded, back tensing because somehow he knew Luis wasn't going to finish his thought even once Christine moved on. He'd undoubtedly wanted to remind them both how much parting was going to hurt and how they were in over their heads. Which Tucker knew. He knew and he still wanted.

Tonight, he mouthed at Luis right before they entered the building. Hesitating, Luis held his gaze for a second, then gave a subtle nod.

Good. At least Tucker had that to look forward to. The meeting ended up being a long debriefing of the fire management efforts, and his mind started to wander, but then he perked up as the talk turned to the arson investigation.

"Rivera, you seem convinced that this fire was connected to our arsonist. You want to explain your theory?" Fred leaned back in his chair in the conference room.

"Happy to." Luis in professional mode never failed to inspire Tucker. "First, the hiking trails link the fires. They're all backcountry trails, designed for experienced hikers, so this is a fit individual, but they're cautious too. Ignition is less than half a mile from a trail in most of the cases. And the fires are slow starters without outside fuels as far as we can tell—no gasoline or other accelerants like that."

"I'm still not convinced that this fire is connected to

the others," Adams interrupted, tone more curious than accusatory.

"Yes, most have stayed contained with early response, which leads me to think that this weekend's fire was something of a fluke. The code red conditions took the arsonist's signature small fire and led to a larger-scale event, but I still think it's connected."

"So it's an experienced hiker, good at traditional fire starting, not some kids with a gas can?" Garrick asked. "That describes half the county, though, in terms of fitness levels and abilities."

"Well, yes, but the investigation has other ways of narrowing in on suspects. Since arsonists often have a connection to the fire community, I've been working with both the air base and the rural fire stations, looking at disgruntled former employees and candidates. I've also been working with the law enforcement authorities on building a profile of the arsonist based on the specific fire characteristics. I'm pretty confident our forensic evidence will help lead to a conviction."

Tucker had known Luis was working on all this but was still impressed nonetheless. It was one thing to get to spend time alone with Luis, reconnect with him on a personal level, and another to admire the professional he'd become.

"Will you have to come back to testify if there's a trial?" Christine looked up from the notes she'd been taking.

"Yes, that's likely." Luis gave a quick nod, never even glancing in Tucker's direction.

Come back. Tucker hadn't thought that far ahead with the arson investigation. If Luis had to come back, maybe this didn't have to end like Tucker feared. And if he came back once, perhaps there was a chance…

Tucker knew better than to let himself get bolstered by such thoughts, yet there he was, spinning fantasies for the fall out of nothing more than the possibility of a professional obligation. It spoke how desperate his brain was for any evidence that this thing between them wasn't headed for a mighty crash.

He tried to get his head back to worrying about the arson investigation for the remainder of the meeting. Luis was headed out to the field to meet with mop-up crews and others from the investigation. For once Tucker wasn't asked to take him, and he couldn't exactly volunteer, not with a stack of his own work to handle.

Finally, the meeting broke up, and hoping to catch Luis before he left, Tucker hustled to the conference room door. However, Garrick stopped him before he could complete his getaway.

"Hey, Tucker. Was hoping to catch you. If we don't get another callout this weekend, Rain and I were thinking of having some folks over, firing up the grill. You busy Saturday?"

"The boys have SATs in the morning," he hedged. Assuming Luis was still in town, that along with the boys was his priority, but he couldn't exactly confess that to Garrick.

"This would be late afternoon, early evening." Garrick was undeterred, wide, easy smile firmly in place. "Linc and Jacob, my dad, couple of people Rain works with. Small but fun. Figured we'd ask the new guy too."

"The new guy?" Tucker's pulse sped up. What had Garrick discovered? He'd thought they'd done a good job keeping things purely professional at the office, but maybe not.

"Yeah, I noticed you guys have been spending a fair bit of time together."

Tucker blinked. Garrick's tone was conversational, but he still felt called out and had no clue how to respond. "Uh..."

"He's been working most closely with you, right?" Garrick pressed, and okay, maybe he did simply mean his observation on a professional level.

"Yeah, guess so," he said carefully.

"If you come, it'll give him someone to talk to. But I know firsthand from smoke-jumping assignments out of the area how boring a weekend in a new place can be when there's no emergency. He might jump at the chance to socialize, eat some home cooking."

"Yeah." Tucker couldn't argue with that. And that whisper of *maybe* he'd had during the meeting was back. Maybe if Luis saw that times had changed some in the area, that other same-sex couples were living and thriving here, maybe then he might look more forward if he had—or *wanted*—to come back.

"So how about it? Think you can come?" Stretching, Garrick leaned back in his wheelchair.

"Let me make sure the boys don't need me that evening, and I'll see. And...uh...yeah, ask Luis. Good idea." He glanced back at the now-empty conference room.

"Tucker?" Garrick tilted his head and lowered his voice.

"Yeah?"

"You do know that it wouldn't bug me if you were... *social* with anyone, right?" Holding Tucker's gaze, Garrick kept his expression neutral, but sincere as he echoed back Tucker's own word for dancing around Garrick's relationship with Rain last year. They were friends, more so now that they worked together daily, and he knew he could trust him.

"I know. And I appreciate that." This wasn't like coming out to his family—Garrick would be supportive, and it was entirely possible he or Rain had already guessed something. Tucker was still somewhat reluctant to be openly dating a coworker, but if it meant Luis being more comfortable around here, he would at least consider taking that step for him. "If my kids don't need me, I'll try to come. Let me know what I can bring."

"It's the SATs. They're going to want to come home and collapse. And then because they're seventeen, they're going to recover enough to go out with their friends that night." Garrick laughed, but his eyes remained serious, trying to reassure Tucker about his earlier comments, making Tucker even more grateful for his friendship.

"True. And thanks again. I owe you."

"I'm the one who owes you. All those rides last year. You've saved my ass more than once too. You ever need… anything, my door's open."

"Appreciated." He was saved from more conversation by a stream of coworkers exiting another conference room further down the hall. But no one, not even Garrick, was going to be able to save him from his own churning thoughts, from the glimmer of hope competing with the growing sense of doom, the little voice that kept telling him to *try.* If last night had shown him anything, it was that what they had was worth fighting for.

"You want us to go where?" Luis turned to face Tucker, stomach pleasantly full of the grilled cheese Tucker had plied him with. They were nominally reclined on his couch to watch TV, but neither were in a hurry to find a show. Instead, Luis had been enjoying the rub of their shoulders and legs and some lazy conversation while they watched Blaze explore. Feeling bad for leaving the cat so much, not that she particularly seemed to care, he'd packed her and some supplies up for the drive to Tucker's. She'd been her usual good traveler and aloof self upon arrival, and watching her stalk around Tucker's living room was fun. But then Tucker had dropped this invite. "A party?"

"You don't have to sound so shocked that I might have a social life." Tucker stared right back, expression as unflappable as Blaze's, tone mild. "Garrick's a great guy. You should remember him from school. Didn't exactly run with your and Heidi's theater friends, but he's a real one."

"Yeah, I remember him a little, and he's fine to work with. Not complaining about him, just surprised."

"Well, how about making it a pleasant kind of surprised?" Tucker suggested, bumping shoulders with him. "And his guy, Rain, is nice. Helpful. Garrick pretty much thinks he manufactures the sunrise every morning, and I have a feeling this get-together is both to keep Rain from missing his Portland contacts and because Garrick seems to think you might be bored. He's worried you have nothing to do with your evenings."

"Not a thing. Poor me." Giving Tucker a meaningful look, he ran a bare foot up Tucker's jeans-covered calf. "And that's kind of my point. It's one thing to keep professional at work, but in a social situation…it's highly likely that someone will guess we're more than coworkers."

"Maybe let them." Tucker gave a maddeningly casual shrug. "Garrick's not a gossip, and I doubt any of his friends are either, but it's not like we're breaking any regs or that I'm your supervisor. So we're…social. People can deal."

"Tucker…" Luis struggled with how to respond. On the one hand, Tucker had come thousands of miles from the shy kid who didn't want anyone knowing he held Luis's hand in public. On the other, though, Luis felt oddly protective of him. "If you come out to work contacts, you can't take that back. Even after I'm gone, you'll still be out. I don't want you regretting that."

"It's not like I'm deeply closeted. I'm not sixteen anymore, afraid my parents will disown me. The kids know and seem to like you." Tucker squeezed his hand. "That matters more to me than who might guess at work. I mean I'm not suggesting we start kissing in the break room, but I'll be fine. And I thought it might be fun for you, getting out of your hotel room."

"Yeah, it might be. But I don't want you thinking I need this." Across the room, Blaze coolly regarded him from her perch on Tucker's built-in bookshelf. She knew Luis was lying a little—he had been bored prior to spending more time with Tucker, and he did generally prefer getting out over staying in with the royal feline pain in the butt, but he also wasn't going to let Tucker make a choice he'd later regret.

"I don't." Tucker sounded confident, but Luis wasn't sure he believed him. "And I think it will be fun. Don't make me use my superior powers of persuasion."

"Oh? And what might those be?" Despite his misgivings, Luis let himself drift back into the flirty place they'd been in since his arrival. The boys were gone, deep in some gaming tournament at Heidi's, so it was only the two of them. Tucker had had food waiting for Luis, and it was nice, being taken care of. And Tucker in a seductive mood was new and fun and very welcome.

"This." Leaning in, Tucker gave him a soft kiss, sipping at Luis's lips, and right when Luis was about to deepen the kiss, he slithered lower, licking Luis's jaw and neck. He toyed with Luis's shirt buttons with his nimble fingers. "I want to try something…"

"To get me to go to the party? I'll go. You don't have to blow me to get a yes, promise." Much as he liked this playful side of Tucker, he didn't want him feeling obligated to be sexual.

"Maybe I want to blow you for the same reason I want to go—it'll be fun and different." Venturing lower, he plucked at Luis's belt. "At work this afternoon I kept thinking about how you got to taste me, but I haven't had a chance to do the same yet."

"I take being interrupted by fantasies is something uncommon for you?" Laughing, Luis stretched so Tucker could have more access to his clothes. He might want to make certain that Tucker was into this, but once assured, he wasn't about to turn down his explorations.

"Yes. Rather. Both annoying in that it made work harder and nice in that it meant I was thinking about you. Weird to miss you even though you were just a few hours away."

"I missed you too." Reaching out, Luis tilted Tucker's chin up so he could brush another kiss across his mouth. And he had missed him. Being out in the field always relaxed and energized him, reminded him why he loved this line of work so much, but he'd also been weirdly antsy, ready to get back to Tucker and the plans for the evening that he'd initially been reluctant about. Which was silly, really, thinking he could stay away.

"Good." Wiggling loose, Tucker finished unbuttoning Luis's shirt and made quick work of his buckle next.

"You sure the boys are gone all night?" Luis was all for whatever sexy plan Tucker had in mind but he also didn't need another awkward interruption.

"I'm sure. The newest expansion pack for their game just launched. They'll be lucky to sleep tonight. Tell me if I do this wrong. Porn's not my usual thing, so I'm afraid I haven't studied up…"

"There's not an exam. Have fun with it. Do what feels good for you, and I promise it'll feel good for me."

"And no teeth. I know that part." Chuckling, Tucker withdrew Luis's cock, which was already hard and more than a little interested in this discussion. He jacked it slowly, watching Luis's eyes the whole time. The way he used eye contact as another point of connection was rapidly becoming a favorite turn-on for Luis.

Tucker stretched out next to him, head resting on Luis's thigh while Luis sat in the corner of the couch. "God bless your extra big couch."

"Uh-huh. Busy." Tucker tentatively licked at the shaft, little flicks that sent sparks zipping up Luis's spine.

"Feels good, especially on the underside," he encouraged.

Tucker took the hint, focusing his attention there, more licking and openmouthed kisses and more driving Luis out of his mind with want. He was determined to let Tucker set the pace, figure out what he enjoyed doing, but all that patience might do him in. However, Tucker was a fast study, quickly figuring out how to use his hand on the base while his mouth did devilish things.

"See? This *is* fun." Tucker flicked at Luis's foreskin with the tip of his tongue. "More to play with."

"Glad...to be...fun," Luis groaned. For someone inexperienced, Tucker was rather intuitive, teasing all around the crown, gently playing with the foreskin. He had Luis on edge, and he hadn't even really sucked in earnest yet. In fact, his playfulness was almost more of a turn-on than had he shown off deep throating skills. Using his free hand, he stroked Luis's stomach and chest, which only ramped him up further.

"Is this good?" Tucker asked before he focused his attention on the frenulum, the bundle of nerves right there on the underside of Luis's cockhead, which all started singing at the first touch of Tucker's tongue.

"And how. I can come if you keep that up long enough."

"Really?" Tucker smiled widely before doubling down on the motion, using his thumb along the shaft for added friction that had Luis groaning.

"Oh, you like that idea, don't you?" Luis somehow still had the power of complete sentences, but it was a near thing, his breath coming faster now. "Want to get me off?"

"Yes. Please." The breathy *please* turned Luis's pleasure dial up even further, especially when Tucker started alternating the licking and flicking with shallow sucks, little bobs of his head to meet his stroking hand. Already, he knew exactly how firmly Luis liked to be held, how fast to jack him to get him close without letting him tumble over.

Tucker's shoulder wiggled, making Luis glance down. Instead of continuing to play with Luis's chest, Tucker had worked his other hand under himself. From the way he was moving, he was at least putting pressure on his cock if not outright jerking off.

"That's so hot, you touching yourself. You like sucking me?"

"Mmmm." Tucker made a happy noise around Luis's cock. And those small, sexy movements of his body against the couch were as arousing as any blatantly explicit display. Knowing he was turned on by what he was doing made Luis's own enjoyment that much more. He loved being something other than merely a curiosity for Tucker.

"Think you can come when I do?"

Not stopping what he was doing, Tucker made a desperate sound in the back of his throat that made Luis's cock pulse.

"Fuck. You're so sexy. If you don't come, I'm going to suck you too. Make you feel so good…"

Tucker moaned as he pulled back enough to do more flicking with his tongue. That combined with the fast friction from his fist had Luis panting, no more sexy boasts.

"Close," he warned.

"Good. Want it." Tucker dove back down, sucking harder. His body moved faster too, his shoulders tensing against Luis. Fuck. Somehow every sex act with him felt brand-new, sexier than ever, imbued with a new level of meaning that had Luis burning bright.

Moaning, he skated along that edge of soon-but-not-yet for a few blissful moments. His thigh muscles ached with the effort of keeping still, not thrusting, and his hands dug hard into the arm of the couch. Then Tucker discovered how to use his tongue on the underside of

Luis's cock while sucking, and the edge evaporated, tumbling him into a powerful orgasm.

"That's it. Coming."

Tucker swallowed the first spurt then pulled back, moaning and still stroking Luis through the rest of his climax. Still groaning, Luis sank back the couch, little more than rumpled clothing and still pulsating muscles. Pleasure had taken over every cell, and he wasn't sure when he'd last been this relaxed.

"Oh, *wow*." Tucker rolled slightly, head still on Luis. He was a sticky mess, and Luis swiped at the come dripping from his cheek.

"Wow, indeed. Not bad, rookie." With his other hand, Luis brushed at some of his disheveled hair. "Did you…"

"Uh-huh. Pray for my couch cushions, but I couldn't hold back."

"Damn. Knowing that is almost enough to get me off all over again. You seriously liked doing that?"

"Yeah. It surprised me too, honestly. But making you feel good makes me feel good too, in ways I never expected."

"I get that. It's why I love doing that to you. There's a connection there—a power trip, but it's also kind of humbling, being trusted that much."

"Exactly." Tucker gave an adorably happy sigh.

"Soon as I can brave the stairs, we're heading for that magic shower of yours. You're more than a little bit of a mess." He spared a glance for Blaze, who hadn't moved from her position as a feline bookend, casting her judgment over all their ridiculous human behaviors.

"But you like mess." Tucker grinned up at him.

"That I do." Luis had to laugh along with him.

"Maybe I'm *your* mess." Tucker's dancing eyes said

he meant it as a silly tease, post-orgasm fooling around, but Luis felt the words in his soul. *Yours.* Tucker was. He was all Luis's, and hell if he wanted to ever let him go.

"You are." He couldn't even make it to the laugh he'd planned when he had to exhale hard and whisper, "What am I going to do with you?"

Instead of the flip response Luis expected, Tucker went more somber, his playful expression buttoning back up. "*I know.* God. Is it so wrong that I want the arson case to drag on and on?"

Oh, Tucker. Any estimates Luis had made on the size and scope of the damage this was likely to do to his heart were woefully inadequate. And he was a guy who prided himself on such calculations, both professionally and personally. And unfortunately, the professional part of him had had a pretty kick-ass day apart from the whole missing-Tucker thing.

"Investigators working the human side of the case found a pretty good lead today, actually, one that dovetails with my theories and analysis." The little clues were starting to add up, and while on site earlier, they'd lucked into a rare piece of physical evidence, a metal disc, that might match evidence from another site's possible ignition point. They should have enough to tie the fires together, and the suspect list was coming together too, according to those investigators.

"Oh." Just like that Tucker deflated, and Luis felt like his too-full heart might do the same.

"But you know how these things go." He was quick to backtrack. First time ever he wanted to be wrong. "Investigations are unpredictable. The lead could dead-end, and we could get another huge callout before the season's done."

"One way or another though, it *is* going to end."
Tucker dropped his head back to Luis's thigh.

"Yeah," he quietly agreed, stroking Tucker's messy
jaw, "But we don't have to think about that right now."

"True. Let's not." Tucker still sounded sad and far
away though, and Luis would have given a lot to be able
to take that hurt away.

"Maybe—"

"You said we don't have to talk about it." Tucker's
expression took on the same stubbornness Walker dis-
played so well.

"But—"

"Come on. My magic shower and bed await you."
Sitting up, Tucker hefted himself off the couch, subject effectively closed. Even Blaze nodded like she was
dismissing the topic. But he couldn't let it go. He was
painfully aware that while he might be able to move his
body, make himself follow Tucker up the stairs, there
were plenty of immovable facts and realities standing
between him and Tucker and anything resembling what
their hearts might both want.

Chapter Eighteen

Luis needed time to slow down. But as always, the universe refused to listen to him, sending him rushing from one task to another.

Wednesday, Tucker dragged him to another family dinner. Not that Luis was complaining—Isaac made his famous macaroni and cheese, which was every bit as good as advertised. The company was good too, fun kid antics and interesting conversation that beat eating alone. And somehow, he and Blaze kept right on staying over, even when that meant enduring some teasing from Wade.

Walker, meanwhile, continued his grumpy mood, but had the rare distinction of being a human Blaze actually tolerated, something that seemed to please the kid. Tucker joked that no way could Luis take the cat away from her newfound buddy, and Luis didn't exactly put up much of a fight when it came to where he slept.

And apparently Saturday he was going to the gathering at Garrick's house. It was all very…couple-y, very fast, but then again there was little point in moving slowly, not when time kept right on ticking away.

Friday seemed to appear out of nowhere, tumbling after long workdays in the middle of the week. Luis came out of one meeting at headquarters and rushed to another.

Proving his point, Adams opened the meeting with an acknowledgment of how quickly the week had gone by and how many hours people were racking up.

"Rivera, we're sure working you hard too. Making the most of our loan, at least. Tell me about the latest from the arson investigation."

"Oh, I don't mind the work. Burn pattern analysis is continuing to show links between the fires, and in addition to circumstantial evidence of similarities, we now have some forensic evidence from a few of the sites. Small metal coin, kind of a lucky charm medal sort of thing, and that feels like a calling card to those on the investigation team. Law enforcement is focusing on connections to the fire community, and they have some strong leads. I wouldn't be surprised if next week we see some suspects brought in for questioning."

"Good, good. Any chance of predicting where the next spot fire might be?"

"I'm working on that, actually. We're making a list of possible sites to keep heavier surveillance on. I'm pretty confident in my calculations."

Across the table, Tucker's eyebrows went up, admiration clear in his eyes. Impressing him was fun. It was one thing to show him something new in bed or to cook for him, but this professional recognition was another thing altogether, a certain respect that passed between them, that Luis liked a lot. Mike had always been the sort of guy who was one hundred percent convinced he was the smartest person in the room and the hardest worker, so it was refreshing to have a…whatever Tucker was these days, who didn't mind Luis getting some recognition too.

"Excellent. We're going to miss that mind of yours

when Angeles gets you back. You can tell you worked the front lines—your kind of fire savvy is hard to teach."

"Well, you've got me for a while longer at least."

"Not sure about that. There's been a new rash of California fires too, and word is the hiring freeze might get lifted next week. They'll probably let us keep you through next week, depending on how the investigation goes and if we get any callouts, but after that, your guess is as good as mine. Wouldn't be surprised if they send you back, which has to be good news for you, right?"

"Right," Luis echoed weakly. He was supposed to want to go home, to his tiny apartment with his few scraggly houseplants that had inevitably died in his absence, and not supposed to care about leaving Tucker's open kitchen and backyard oasis and *Tucker*.

Tucker, who had looked stricken for the instant their eyes met, was looking down at his notepad now, expression shuttered. He'd been hoping for more time, that much was clear, and Luis's neck tensed with the realization that so had he. He wasn't ready for talk of his work here winding down.

"They'll probably still need me if they go to trial, so I might not be completely out of your hair either way," he joked to Adams, carefully not glancing again at Tucker, even as the tension spread from his neck to his upper back.

"Or you could save me a job hunt, put in for the position if the hiring freeze lifts." Adams laughed jovially. "But I know you Californian guys. No way are you trading your winters for ours."

"Or the beaches and things to do," Christine added, typing away on her laptop. "We're taking the kids to Disney at Christmas break. I'm already looking forward to it, and the rainy season hasn't even hit yet, let alone the snow."

"Have a great trip," Luis said, grateful for the chance to ignore the remark about putting in for a job here, which Adams had clearly meant mostly in jest, a way to say he appreciated the job Luis was doing. He didn't really expect him to stay. Tucker on the other hand...

Well, that might be a whole different story, especially judging by how the thundercloud over Tucker's head only darkened, unhappiness radiating off him when they passed in the hall a few minutes later as the meeting broke up.

"Hey," Luis said in a low voice. "You got a minute? Have you eaten lunch yet?"

"I've got a hand crew to check in on. Was planning on grabbing something on the way there." Tucker's frown didn't waver.

"Oh." Hell, Luis didn't know what to say, especially not in the hall like this where anyone could walk by. "We should talk later—"

"Thought we weren't doing that," Tucker said in a near-whisper. "Not gonna think about next week or what comes after that. Live in the moment."

"Yeah, but—"

"It is what it is." Tucker rolled his shoulders, still not meeting Luis's eyes. "I better get on with my day. Should be in the field most of the afternoon."

"Ah. We still on for tomorrow?"

Tucker's gaze darted down the empty hall. "And tonight. Your cat is currently busy terrorizing dust bunnies at my place. She'll want to see you."

"And you?" Head tilting, Luis studied him, trying to decipher all the things Tucker wasn't saying.

"Figured that much was a given." Tucker gave him half a smile that didn't reach his eyes.

"Maybe not. You seem in a mood."

Tucker blew out a breath, then softened his tone. "Not enough of one to not want you around."

"Not exactly a denial." For whatever reason, Luis didn't want to let this go, didn't want tension simmering between them, hurts and resentments building up, not when they'd done such a good job of moving past the old ones.

"What do you want me to say? Like I said, it is what it is. Us talking about it will only make things worse."

"You're probably right." This was hardly the place to unpack complicated feelings, and even if they were in a more private locale, Tucker had a point. Talking might simply make the pain more stark, underscore realities they couldn't change. He might not want tension between them, but he wanted an argument even less. If they were down to days, he didn't want to waste them.

"I know I am. Listen, I'll text on my way back from the field. You can help me figure out dinner."

Luis's chest hurt as he laughed at that. So domestic. If only everything could be so easy. "That I can do."

But there was so much he couldn't do. So much he couldn't control. The future was rushing up to meet both of them, and there wasn't a damn thing he could do about it.

"You seem to have acquired a cat." Heidi arched an elegant eyebrow at the cat, who was currently on her favorite bookshelf, the one that caught some of the morning light. Every so often the cat's whiskers twitched, and she glanced toward the stairs, undoubtedly waiting for

Walker. Or possibly looking for an opportunity to do Tucker in. With Blaze, he could never be too sure.

"I'm borrowing her," Tucker said lightly, not looking for a deep conversation with Heidi, especially not this early in the morning. The boys were due to leave soon for the SAT, and Heidi had arrived with breakfast muffins from Isaac.

"And the cat's owner?" Heidi broke off a piece of muffin, apparently in no great hurry to leave.

"Borrowing him too." Tucker couldn't keep the sadness that had plagued him the last twenty-four hours or so out of his voice. The inevitable was coming, and he remained sure that talking about it would only make things worse, ruin what little time they did have. However, living in the moment was also complicated by the very real emotions that kept bubbling to the surface. Like now.

"Aw. Tucker—"

"Don't say it." The last thing he needed was pity.

"I warned you." She might be his best friend, but she wasn't Tucker's keeper, something she sometimes forgot. She'd warned him about other things too—coming out to his family sprang first to mind. But much as Tucker appreciated her in his life, he'd always had to go his own way, learn his own lessons.

"Since when has that ever stopped me?"

"Good point." She sighed and leaned against the counter. "You could *try* listening to me."

"I'm not looking for advice."

"You're more stubborn than Walker, you know that?"

"Guess he had to get it from somewhere." Keeping his voice mild, he gave her a pointed look because she too had a tenacious streak.

"Did I hear my name?" Walker stumbled down the

stairs, carrying his prep book. Tucker hoped he'd gotten at least some sleep. For someone determined to stay local, he sure was taking the test seriously, which again made Tucker wonder what was truly in the kid's heart.

"Your mom brought you and Wade muffins because apparently cornflakes won't cut it this morning."

"Did...uh...*she* bake them?" Walker eyed the muffins warily.

Hand over her heart, Heidi sighed dramatically. "Isaac made them, and we all had to suffer a test batch on Thursday to make sure that the protein-packed recipe he found was actually tasty. So you get muffins version two-point-oh, and I swear I'm just the delivery lady. I figured I'd let Isaac sleep in, just like your dad is letting—"

"Okay, how about we save some muffins for Wade?" Tucker cut Heidi off before she could tease him more about Luis, who was indeed sleeping upstairs, although Tucker thought it was also highly possible he was hiding out reading on his phone rather than join the chaos down here.

"Okay, okay." Muffin in each hand, Walker put one back. "I don't know why you guys are making such a big deal over this either. Dad packed us snacks."

"Actually, I suggested snacks, but Luis did the chopping." Tucker tried to give credit where it was due. And it had been fun last night, making little baggies of veggies and a homemade dip for the boys together. They'd cooked a shrimp and rice dish for dinner that Tucker had remembered Luis's mom making, one of her favorites from growing up in Baja, and Luis's version was almost as good. The boys had certainly scarfed it down at least.

Far peppier than Walker, Wade bounded in wearing his lucky football jersey and immediately scooped up two muffins. "I'm all about the free food. I'll take the stupid test again if it means more snacks. Then tonight, *party!* Mitch's mom is making celebratory lasagna and then we're marathoning all our favorite car chase movies."

"I thought you had a boring time last time you hung out with them?" Tucker asked.

"And then I met his sister." Wade gave a dreamy smile.

"She's in college, doofus." Walker jostled his shoulder. "She's only visiting, and just because she's willing to watch movies with you and Mitch means—"

"*Everything.* True love is built on compromises. Don't you listen to Mom about anything?" Wade rolled his eyes.

Compromise. Tucker tested the word out in his brain. He still wasn't asking Heidi for love life advice, nor was he going to take Wade's crush-of-the-week as evidence either, but maybe his current avoidance tactics weren't the only way of coping with the next week either.

And he kept thinking even after the boys—and Heidi—finally departed. Shutting the door behind them, he snagged the last two muffins and some coffee and headed upstairs to Luis, who somehow had managed to sleep through all that noise.

He set the food on the nightstand and stretched out next to Luis on the bed, watching him sleep. Geez. One would think *he* was the lovesick teen around here, but there was something compelling about how peaceful Luis looked. Tucker's heart wasn't entirely sure what to do with itself either. He'd given up hope of finding anything that made him feel like this, and now he had, and life simply wasn't fair.

Compromise. Damn it. Maybe they were going to have to talk after all.

"Hey." Luis blinked his eyes open, stretching into Tucker. "Did I miss the big send-off?"

"I'm not sure how you slept through it, honestly." Tucker laughed.

"Enough travel and time trying to sleep in hotels, and toss in a few boyfriends whose snores almost rattled the house apart, and I could sleep through anything." Luis nuzzled Tucker's neck. "Is that coffee I smell?"

"Yup. Left yours black. And Heidi brought muffins by. I saved you some."

"Mmm. Breakfast in bed brought by the hottest guy in the county. Not sure what I did to deserve that."

"You didn't have to *do* anything. Just be you." It was a simple truth but a deep one, one that had defined so much of their friendship. Yes, Luis was attractive and smart and funny, all the sorts of things that made him a popular friend, but there was something more there, always had been. Just him, just whatever unique glow made him Luis was enough to inspire devotion from Tucker.

"Sweet talker." Luis pulled him in for a kiss, and Tucker's toes curled against the sheets. He was even more sure that they needed to talk. But not now. Not quite yet. Not when everything was this perfect and good and he could pretend a little longer.

Chapter Nineteen

"This feels weirdly like high school," Luis grumbled as
they looked for parking on Garrick's street. He'd made
noises about whether they should arrive separately, but
Tucker's points about tight parking had won out over trying to be discreet about their friendship. "Hoping the cool
kids won't notice us crashing their party."

"High school didn't have this quality of food." Tucker
gestured at the crudité platter they'd made—sliced
vegetables, homemade dip, olives, artichokes.

"True. And unlike the two bottomless pits you call
kids, we're actually in a position to slow down and enjoy
the eating part." Luis tried to pump himself up. He wasn't
usually this grumpy about being around people and generally liked getting out, but like Tucker, he'd been in
a mood ever since yesterday. He wanted to hide away
with Tucker, pretend the real world and all its obliga-
tions didn't exist.

"The socializing part will go fine too. No one here is
going to try to get us to play that stupid five-minutes-
in-heaven game."

"I don't know." He made an effort to laugh, give
Tucker a grin as he finished parking. "I'd play that with
you."

"Wait till later." Tucker's look could melt an entire ice cream stand. "I've got more than five minutes in me, guaranteed."

"Counting on it." Luis congratulated himself on not suggesting they skip the party and go right to the sex. The boys were both out of the house, and anticipation for later made his pulse thrum. Last night, the twins had been up late, prepping for the test, and neither he nor Tucker had been confident enough in their ability to stay quiet enough to have sneaky sex. So they'd ended up cuddling in bed with a movie, which had been its own sort of cozy, and their morning make-out session had more than made up for any lack of sex, but he still wanted more.

He was fast coming to the conclusion that he was always going to want Tucker, wasn't ever going to get enough of him. This wasn't some random itch to scratch and get out of his system. No, this was the sort of desire that didn't have an easy cure, and what was worse was that Luis wasn't even sure he wanted one. Being turned on by every little thing Tucker did felt too damn good, this permanent state of arousal and appreciation.

"Come on. Promise I'm not throwing you into the tiger pit." Tucker led the way up the walkway and short ramp to Garrick's front door.

"Tucker. You made it! And you brought the new guy from work Garrick mentioned." A younger man answered the door in a lavender shirt decorated with the cartoon ponies Luis's nieces loved so much. Luis recognized him as Rain thanks to all the photos on Garrick's desk.

"Yup." Tucker was matter-of-fact as introductions were made, and after that, Rain escorted them outside. The house was a smaller remodeled ranch with a living area that opened to an expansive backyard patio with hardy plantings and a couple of seating areas, including one with a picnic table loaded with food.

"This is Garrick's dad." Rain introduced them to a big guy manning two grills.

"You're the Californian, right?" the older guy asked, gesturing with a pair of tongs.

"Yeah," Luis said warily, not sure where this was going. Many locals had decided opinions on transplants from other states moving in, as he'd found out as a kid. They were all about the tourist dollars, but not so much about Californians and New Yorkers and such taking up residence.

"Vegetarian? Half your state seems to be, I found. I've got mushroom caps and veggie kabobs, but also plenty of steak."

Oh. That was easy. "Can I have a little of both? I'm not vegetarian, but I do love grilled vegetables."

"Sure thing." And with that, Garrick's dad went back to his grill duties and Rain continued introducing them to different people, including a couple of coworkers from his hand crew. Garrick was in conversation with Lincoln Reid and his boyfriend, which was still such a strange sentence that Luis couldn't help but smile.

Speaking of smiling, Rain and Garrick kept grinning at each other across the patio, and as best Luis could tell, the gathering was actually an excuse for them to engage in repeated eye-fucking, the sort of easy courtship where they weren't afraid to show their feelings. Seemed like they each knew they had a good thing and weren't about to waste it. It was the sort of established couple behavior that Luis had tried hard to convince himself that he didn't miss, but even this short amount of time with Tucker had shown him otherwise. And now, watching the other couples, bitterness rose in his throat. Damn it. He needed more time.

After Rain left them to mingle, they headed back to the food table. He was fixing himself a plate when his phone buzzed in his pocket.

"Excuse me. Better make sure they aren't about to call us out." Not wanting to be rude, he ducked into the house to check his messages. But it wasn't a work emergency. Instead, the message was from his mom, sad kitten emoji included.

You haven't messaged your mami in a few days! We're planning Josefina's birthday in two weeks. Any chance you'll be back? Everyone misses you so much, mijo.

Slumping against the kitchen wall, he took a breath while typing out a fast reply that he didn't know a return date and would call soon. He missed the family a lot and didn't want to miss little Josefina's birthday, had picked out the perfect junior scientist kit for her weeks ago, but hell, he was going to miss here too. No easy way out of any of this.

"They calling you back to California?" A coworker of Rain's, an older retired smoke jumper they'd been introduced to earlier, helped himself to some water from the fridge dispenser. He'd made some small talk about a brother on a hotshot crew near Los Angeles. Luis didn't know him, but apparently the California connection had stuck in this guy's head.

"No. Just my mom missing me." He pocketed his phone.

"Ah. Surprised they haven't sent for you. You heard the latest on the fires?"

"No, sorry, I haven't." Guilt snaked up his spine. He'd been so wrapped up in Tucker the last few days that he hadn't paid much attention to out-of-the-area news.

"It's bad." The man, whose name escaped Luis, pulled out his own oversize phone and showed Luis a news story about all the acres burning in several different fires due to a rash of dry lightning.

"Hell." That was his territory, the area he'd worked so hard to protect over the years, and his friends and coworkers on the line. He should have been paying more attention, and that was the truth. And if these fires continued, the chances were even higher that Rosalind or someone above her would call for him—he had the expertise they'd need, and as much as he wanted more time here, he hated the thought of his coworkers shouldering this big burden shorthanded.

"Yep. It's a mess all right." The other guy unknowingly summed up Luis's entire last few weeks. A mess. He couldn't be in two places at once, but oh how he wanted.

Eventually, he drifted back to his abandoned plate and Tucker, who had found a seat on a bench near the group that included Garrick.

"Everything okay?" Tucker patted the place next to him.

"Yeah." He sighed as he sat down because he couldn't lie to Tucker. "Well, nothing dire at least. Mami misses me and the fires in CA are getting worse, but no imminent callout here."

"Of course your mom misses you. Tell her we enjoyed her recipe last night." Tucker took on a wistful expression, eyes distant, undoubtedly because he knew Mami would like him a lot better if Oregon was around the corner from her suburban neighborhood.

"Will do. She always did enjoy feeding you, even if most of your appetite tended to come out at dessert."

"That it did." Tucker laughed, but it sounded forced. "Loved her chimangos. Way better than any ordinary donut."

"If you're nice, I'll make them for you."

"Deal." Tucker bumped his shoulder, but the tight line of his mouth said he knew as well as Luis that the opportunity might not materialize.

Time. Ticking away, making Luis's chest ache and his food turn to wood pulp, bland and heavy and about as appetizing. Around them, conversation swirled, people playing with Garrick's dog and sharing funny pet stories, but Luis's attention kept drifting. This was a nice, welcoming crowd, showing how far the area had come in the years since Luis had left. Garrick's big rancher father managed a teasing relationship with Rain that even a cynic would call fond. Meanwhile, Lincoln and Jacob were sharing a glider, and their feet kept overlapping, little casual touches that showed how comfortable they were here. And yet Luis couldn't shake the feeling that any fitting in was to be short-lived, a sense of doom rolling in like a wind from the west.

"You sure you're okay?" Tucker asked Luis as they walked back into his dark house together. The twins were still out, Wade texting that they'd started another movie at Mitch's and Walker still at Mary Anne's, and both adding that they were likely to sleep at Heidi's, a move that had aspiring matchmaker Wade's fingerprints all over it. He flipped on the hall light while Luis hung close beside him.

"No. Not okay." Luis shrugged, weary half-smile on his lips. "You?"

"Nope." At least they could be honest together. Being with Luis at the party had been bittersweet—sweet because for the first time, Tucker could truly see how it *could* work here. Good food, good friends, no one there who cared whether he and Luis were more than coworkers, and good inspiration in the form of other couples making a long-term go of things. Hell, simply the way Rain and Garrick looked at each other was sugar overload. And sitting next to Luis, who wasn't so bad at heated looks himself, definitely qualified as sweet. But also bitter because everyone kept talking about the California fires, and Tucker could practically feel the space-time continuum conspiring to zap Luis back there, body and mind, like one of the old sci-fi movies they'd enjoyed so much as kids.

"Sorry." Eyes serious like he was apologizing for more than a bleak mood, Luis touched Tucker's sleeve.

"You think we should talk about it?" Tucker gestured at the couch, but Luis tugged him toward the stairs instead.

"Not yet."

"No?" Tucker truly was in no great hurry to have this conversation either, but the *yet*, now that was different. And ominous.

"Later. Right now, your kids are gone, my cat's asleep on your sofa, and it's okay if you don't want sex, but I want to hold you and not talk for a while."

"I feel that." He absolutely did. Escaping the world sounded perfect right then, and it wasn't like he had the words ready to explain everything in his head. Maybe if they hid out together long enough, the right words would come.

Following Luis to his room, he shut the door and fiddled with the dimmer and fireplace. They might be miserable, but at least they could be cozy and miserable. Silently, they stripped down to their underwear and climbed under the covers.

"This work?" Trying to give Luis what he needed and wanted, Tucker moved into one of his new favorite positions, head on Luis's shoulder and chest, arm and leg across him. They'd fallen asleep like this more than once, and he loved all the little details—the drag of their fuzzy legs against each other, the warmth of Luis's skin under his cheek, the sound of his heart and breathing, the secureness of Luis's arms holding him even closer.

"Perfect." Luis kissed the top of his head, and they lay there, breathing deeply for long moments. Where Luis's thoughts were, Tucker couldn't say, but for himself, he tried to block out everything other than the rise and fall of Luis's chest. He wanted to memorize Luis's scent, the way it mingled past and present with its familiar clean notes layered with his newer choices of aftershave and shampoo. Luis's strong arm around his back was a heavy, welcome weight, keeping him tightly in Luis's embrace, as if he'd even dream of escaping.

He was more than half-hard against Luis's hip, and Luis was in a similar state, but neither of them moved to make this about anything other than finding comfort together. *Not yet.* In a moment they'd kiss. In a moment their hands would roam. In a moment they'd be that much closer to the conversation neither of them wanted to have. But right now there was this and Luis was right—it was *perfect.*

Tucker's eyes burned, whether from emotion or from trying so hard not to drift off, he couldn't say. Luis moved his fingers restlessly against Tucker's back, the only clue that he too was still plenty awake.

"There's always been something so right about holding you. Always," Luis whispered.

"Yeah." He had to swallow hard. "I wish—"

"No wishes." Leaning down, Luis silenced him with a soft kiss across his mouth. "No regrets."

Tucker already knew he wouldn't be able to stick to that. So many wishes. So many regrets, past, present, and future alike. But he didn't have to voice them. *Not yet.* Not when the alternative was to kiss Luis back, matching his tenderness, soaking it all up. His heart soared with everything he wasn't able to articulate, finding all it needed in Luis's kiss. They might not be able to talk, but their lips wrote poetry together.

Eventually, those sonnets turned more urgent than sweet and sad, their bodies adding a thrum of need, underscoring everything they weren't saying. Luis rolled toward him, meeting in the middle, bodies in alignment even if nothing else was.

"What do you want?" Luis asked in a husky whisper.

Everything. But it wasn't time to talk. "This."

He didn't need anything fancy, didn't need fucking or even Luis's ridiculously talented mouth. Only this, them moving together, shared desperation.

"Need to touch you." Luis pushed Tucker's boxer briefs down the second he nodded, then wiggled out of his own. Nothing between them now, their bare cocks brushed and they both moaned. Luis swept his hands all up and down Tucker's back and sides, igniting all his nerve endings before drifting toward his cock.

"Mmm. Yes. That."

"This work?" Moving even closer, Luis lined up their cocks so he could stroke them both together.

"Oh, yeah." The friction was delicious, but he also knew how Luis liked things like this slick, so he grabbed the lube from the nightstand drawer, drizzled some onto Luis's hand. Wanting to share in the sensations even further, Tucker moved his hand to join with Luis's, creating a slick tunnel for their cocks to slide through. He felt the bond between their linked hands every bit as much as the slip and slide of their cocks.

"Kiss me again," Luis demanded as if Tucker could do anything other than that, as if he might say no.

"Always." This was all he could do, all he wanted, to kiss and stroke and feel Luis tremble against him, hear the rumble of his muffled moans. They kissed and moved, hips in perfect rhythm, legs and arms holding each other as tight as possible. Their hands had almost no room to operate, but somehow the press of their bodies made it all the sexier, let the slick friction between their cocks and the kissing be the stars of the show.

"Close." Luis moved faster, Tucker following as readily as if they were tied together with imaginary string. And he knew Luis, knew that sucking on his delving tongue made him moan and shudder, knew how much to tighten his grip. The power of that knowledge ramped his own pleasure higher.

"Want this to last forever," he panted.

"I know. Me too." Slowing down his body, Luis kissed him long and deep, but the lack of fast motion was possibly even more devastating than the quickness had been. Tucker tried to quiet his breathing, but it didn't work, muscles surging anyway until he was the one driving the tempo this time.

"Need…"

"You…"

"Yes." Their bodies were back to writing shared poetry again, hips mirroring each other's thrusts, lips equally demanding, sweat gathering on their skin as they pushed each other closer to the edge. His hand cramped and he didn't care, didn't care about anything other than making sure Luis went over first.

"Come," he urged.

"Tucker." Luis gasped his name like a prayer and curse all at once, and then they were both coming and Tucker forgot to care about who went first, hard shudders racking his body as he clung to Luis.

"Tucker." That one was a whisper as Luis stroked his face with his free hand. There was a question there, one Tucker didn't even begin to know how to answer, so he dropped his head, resting it on Luis's chest again, staying silent as their breathing returned to normal. Sticky and sweaty, they lay quiet like that, holding on to each other for a long time.

"We're a mess," Luis whispered at last.

"Yup." It was true on so very many levels that he almost had to laugh as he tugged Luis out of bed. "Shower."

"We should ta—"

"Let me do this first."

Luis might finally be ready to talk, but Tucker wasn't quite there, wanted to spend another few stolen moments in this quiet place. And Luis seemed to get it, nodding, and letting Tucker spend the whole silent shower reverently washing Luis's body, cataloging every muscle and every scar. He even washed his hair, selfishly using his own shampoo, like branding Luis with his scent could make a lick of difference. And Luis let him, trading slow, gentle kisses and ministrations of his own, lathering Tucker up with strong hands and tender eyes.

His dark, soulful eyes were what did it, the depth of emotion there echoing everything rattling around in Tucker's brain. Finally, Tucker knew the right words. The only words really. But he held back, waiting until they'd toweled off and fixed the bed, waiting for the moment when Luis turned those eyes on him again, when the words simply refused to be denied a second longer.

"I want you to stay."

Chapter Twenty

Tucker finally did it, finally said the words. Luis wasn't even that shocked. Tucker didn't bluff well, and his body had said plenty for him earlier. His sorrow at Luis's impending departure had been clear even before the sex, but it was his kiss that had said all the words that neither of them was brave enough to voice.

Except apparently Tucker was, and now he was sitting on the edge of the bed, expectant look on his face, waiting for Luis to reply. They were both in boxers, but Luis wasn't sure he would be any more ready for this talk even if he were fully dressed. Tucker stripped him bare no matter what.

"I can't," he whispered, sinking down next to Tucker, because that was as much as he could muster.

Surprisingly, Tucker's mouth didn't so much as droop, and if anything, his eyes become more resolute. "I don't mean right this second. I know you're likely needed for the fires in California."

"I am. They'll need all hands on deck if this drags on. But also—"

"And you have a life there. I get it. However, I'm asking you to think about coming back, and not simply if they ask you to testify in some court case. I don't want to be a convenient while-you're-in-the-area hookup."

"You're not." Of that Luis was certain, and he squeezed Tucker's knee to be sure he knew it too.

"Good." Tucker nodded firmly, same decisive body language he used at work when it was time to lead. "There's no sense in pretending this thing between us is only casual. We both know better."

"Yeah." His agreement came out on a huff of air. He couldn't pretend with Tucker, not even when that might make this whole thing easier.

"What I feel for you, that's real." Grabbing his hand, Tucker held it tight. And damn, did Luis ever love his hands. Luis might be slightly taller these days, but Tucker still had broader hands, rough, working man's hands as capable of passion as comfort, able to hold even heavy situations.

"It's real feelings for me too," he admitted, clinging fast to Tucker's hand as an anchor. Even that wasn't enough to settle the tsunami in his stomach. "But maybe it's also way too soon to say whether there's staying power. It's only been a couple of weeks."

Tucker gave him a pointed look, narrowed eyes calling Luis a chicken. "You know this isn't some flash in the pan. Plenty of staying power. If LA was an hour away, you know as well as me that we'd both be scrambling to make this work. And it *would*."

Oh, wasn't that a nice fantasy. He could easily imagine them living in two suburbs, side-by-side maybe. Weekends together checking out local festivals and Luis's favorite haunts drifting into weeknight dinners, a slow courtship where eventually they'd work out the little details, settle in the middle. He wanted that so much that his jaw clenched, tension radiating all the way down his neck, finding all the trouble spots in his upper back. If wishing was enough, he'd already have that future.

"Yeah, you're right. It would. But facts are facts, and the distance *is* a factor. You know it too, or else you wouldn't be asking me to stay."

"Yep." Some of the certainty left Tucker's eyes. "I mean, perhaps we could make the distance work for a short time while we figure stuff out."

"We don't have the best track record when it comes to distance."

Tucker's wounded face was punishment for Luis bringing up the hard truth they both knew. "You're going to throw that in my face *now*?"

"I'm not accusing you or blaming you. As I've said, we were kids. We both made mistakes, but it's also another fact that the distance played a huge role in why we didn't work out."

"I can't argue with that." The fading of Tucker's resolve was an almost palpable thing, and Luis felt its loss on a deep level. He didn't want to be the downer here. This was one of those times where being a realist fucking sucked.

"And it's not just us. Distance doesn't work. It's why Walker's so hell-bent on staying local. Everyone knows that either one person ends up moving or the couple breaks up. Usually badly."

"You mean someone cheats." Tucker glanced down at their still joined hands.

Luis blew out a rough breath. "You're focusing too much on the past again. You didn't cheat, Tucker, and I'm not thinking you would here either. I don't think you have that in you. I broke up with you first, remember?

However, that's more what I meant—hurt feelings and resentments seem inevitable with distance."

"You're right. I hate that you're right, but you're not wrong." Tucker's shoulders slumped before he seemed to build himself back up, vertebra by vertebra, voice firming back up. "Which is why I'm going out on a limb here, asking you to think about staying. I want to make this work, and I think deep down you do too."

"I do." Luis didn't even have to dig that far to find that truth. And maybe it was time he admitted a truth of his own. Maybe he owed Tucker that much. "And that's why I want you to *go.* Come to California with me. You know you'd be in demand for any number of fire community jobs."

"I can't do that." Tucker raked his teeth over his lower lip as he looked away.

"*I know.* Which is why I didn't bring it up first, but I still want it." Man, did he ever. Simply saying the words made his throat burn. "Every bit as much as you want me to stay, I want you to go."

"My life is here. It feels like it would be so much easier—"

For the first time, anger replaced longing, stiffening his spine and making his heels dig into the carpet. "And this is how I ended up back here in the first place. So much easier for the single guy to uproot himself. Every. Damn. Time. All I've got is a cranky cat. My preferences and connections and *life* don't count."

"I didn't mean it would be easy." Untangling himself from Luis's fingers, Tucker held up both hands. "And I'm not saying your life doesn't count. I know you're close to your family. But there's going to be a position open here.

You could put in for it, give us a trial run, see if being here permanently would be that unbearable."

How could someone so damn smart and insightful be so damn wrong? Luis's mind hissed like an overfull teakettle left on the stove too long. That Tucker wanted him to stay so badly was understandable, but his stubbornness was about to make Luis boil over.

"Tucker. Do you get what you're asking? You're not willing to even entertain the possibility of the converse, but I'm supposed to be eager to uproot my life?"

"Sorry. I'm not being fair. I get that." Tucker reached for his hand again, and fool that he was, Luis let him have it. "I don't want to lose you. I don't want to let this go."

"Me either." Fighting to keep an even tone, Luis squeezed his hand. "But I don't see a way out of this mess either. I *know* you can't leave. But I also know me, and I don't want to promise moving and then end up resenting the move."

"Or me." Tucker's voice was hollow, all his earlier conviction gone now.

"That too. Maybe especially. I like you, Tucker. I want to keep liking you." Dropping Tucker's hand, he paced away from the bed. "I wish like hell there was some way out of this, but I can't magically make LA appear next to Bend."

"I know. I want you to stay. You want me to go." Hands on his knees, Tucker leaned forward. "The alternative of occasionally meeting in the middle in the Bay Area or something isn't really that palatable to either of us."

"No. It's not." A chill seemed to sweep through the room with the finality of his words.

"Damn. This hurts." Pushing off the bed, Tucker

strode over to where Luis had ended up by the fireplace and hugged him from behind, head resting against his.

"I know. It does. Me too." He pulled Tucker tighter against him, like that might stave off what he knew in his soul was coming next. "And I know it means shit now, but I didn't intend to hurt you. Or me, for that matter. I don't think either of us intended to fall like this."

"Yeah." Tucker's exhale was warm on the back of Luis's neck. "So what now?"

He gave in to the urge to slump against Tucker. "Hell, if I know. Feels trite to say that we should try to make the most of the time we have left, but that's all I've got."

Gently settling Luis back upright, Tucker stepped away in a surprising move that made Luis mourn his nearness. He scrubbed at his hair, not meeting Luis's gaze. "I don't know if I can."

"Okay. Fair enough. I should probably go." The last thing he wanted was to make things worse or hurt Tucker more, but he hadn't realized how much he'd been counting on a few more days until that possibility was gone. However, Tucker stopped him before he could turn, hand on his arm.

"You don't have to leave. It's late."

"Be miserable together? No." Time for Luis to be the realist again, do the hard thing. "Your kids will be around tomorrow if not tonight. You don't need us making sad eyes at each other all day. And I don't want to keep hurting you, either. Prolonging the misery for either of us is simply torture at this point."

"Yeah." Tucker's mouth was a thin, hard line and his grip tightened on Luis's arm. "Damn. I hate this."

"Me too. Me too. So much." And then Tucker was pulling him into a desperate embrace. They kissed artlessly, mouths rough and needy, hands grabbing, and Luis wasn't even sure who started it, only that he couldn't be the one to end it. Breathing hard, he broke the kiss, but kept holding on to Tucker.

"See what I mean? I can't stay and make things worse."

"That wasn't worse." Tucker gave him a crooked grin that didn't change his sad eyes.

"But it wasn't better either." Digging deep for strength, he made himself step away, go to his bag, get out clothes. Next step would be rounding up his blasted cat, who might miss this place even more than him, and that was saying something because Luis was going to carry this room, this man, in his heart forever.

"Damn it, Luis. I don't want to accept that our story ends here. Again."

"Maybe we don't get a choice." Tone edging toward bitter, Luis put on a shirt. "I hate being the bad guy here, spoiling the fantasy of what might be with the reality of what *is*."

"You're not the bad guy. Never. I'm not blaming you."

"Good. I don't want you to hate me. I want… *Fuck*. I want so much." Unable to resist, he met Tucker in another hopeless kiss, falling headlong into need and regret and want and loss. But this time it was Tucker who stepped away, shaking his head.

"Go on before I drag you back to bed, which isn't going to solve a damn thing."

"Yeah. Damn it. I…" He trailed off because it wouldn't be fair to say the words, not now. Not when Tucker had said his words and Luis had said other ones and now the gulf between them was oceans big. And the words, the ones that wanted so urgently to come, wouldn't change a thing.

"Me too," Tucker whispered as their eyes met, gazes holding, moment drawing out. They both knew it. Knew what they were losing. And it fucking sucked that the only thing left to do was collect his cat, drive away from this place one more time. Once again back here in this futile place where it wasn't Tucker he was furious with but rather fate and a universe that would give him this but not a means to hold on to it.

Chapter Twenty-One

Tucker could have sworn he didn't sleep, but somehow it was morning and he was alone. Again. Big bed. Only himself and the scent of Luis on the pillow next to him. And regrets blanketing him, one after another. Not regret for starting something with Luis—he couldn't bring himself to wish that, but for all the rest of it he railed against a God he didn't talk to much these days. Clearly whatever higher power was out there either couldn't be bothered with Tucker's petty problems or simply didn't care that they were getting screwed again by inescapable realities.

Also a reality? That he had to leave this bed. He could hear clanking around downstairs, and for an instant he thought maybe Luis and Blaze had come back, but then he heard the twins' voices. He took a deep breath as he sat up and stretched. It wasn't their fault that he'd dared to hope, even for a second. They didn't deserve him grumpy this morning, so he pulled on clothes, headed downstairs, and tried not to look like he'd had his heart ripped from his chest last night.

"Thought you guys were sleeping at your mom's?" He headed straight for the coffeepot, which was almost full. God bless Walker for listening to one of his many basic cooking demos. From the looks of it, they were making pancakes, every surface covered in ingredients and bowls.

"Yeah, about that…" Wade grinned at him. "We slept there. Promise. But then I had this idea of making you and Luis breakfast."

"Not in bed." Turning pink, Walker coughed. "Figured you'd come down when you smelled food."

"Actually, I heard you rattling pots and bickering, but that was nice of you guys. Unexpected, but nice." His dad senses went on red alert because chances were high that they wanted money, privileges, forgiveness, or all three.

"Is Luis sleeping in again?" Wade was cheerfully loading up the griddle with uneven circles of batter.

"No. He uh…he's not here. Slept back at his hotel."

"You broke up?" Frowning, Wade mopped up some batter drips. "Why'd you do that?"

"It's complicated." He wasn't going to lie about breaking up, but he also wasn't getting into it with the twins. Hell, he wasn't able to unpack all these roiling emotions with *anyone*, but especially not with the kids, what with Walker dealing with his own problems with distance and all.

"I bet you can solve it. Tell me what you did, and I'll tell you how to fix it." Wade's boundless confidence was at once funny and tragic because if only it were that easy.

"Thanks, but I don't want to talk about it. Sorry."

"I get it." Walker laughed as he accepted a plate from Wade. "I wouldn't take Wade's love advice either. He'll have you spamming Luis with relevant GIFs until he gives in and talks to you again."

"Hey! I've got more game than *that*," Wade protested. "He could try a funny present or—"

"No advice." Shaking his head, Tucker had to chuckle even as his chest still felt so hollow. Bringing his coffee, he took a seat next to Walker at the breakfast bar.

"Okay, okay. I think you're both idiots, but that's not why we came over anyway." Wade smiled, but Tucker's back muscles tensed. Now they got to his ulterior motive, and lord, he hoped it wasn't too expensive.

"We?" Walker rolled his eyes. "More like you dragged me along."

"Can I help it if I'm excited?" Wade grabbed a stack of papers from over by the toaster oven. "This was in the mail at Mom's yesterday. Addressed to me with a personalized letter and everything."

"Another college?" Tucker glanced down at the glossy catalog and several loose sheets of paper, including a letter from the head of the athletics department.

"Not just any college. This place in Kansas is a Division II, yeah, but they have one of the best-ranked teacher's colleges in the country, and they've churned out guys who coach at the best high schools and colleges across the country. And they're interested in *me*."

"Kansas?" Gulping, Tucker tried not to sound too horrified.

"This would be why we're here, and not at Mom's. She's going to flip out." Walker reached for the syrup.

"Yeah, I know it would be a plane ride, not a drive for you to come to games, but you keep telling me to have some goal beyond partying and playing ball. So I've been thinking, and dude, what better life than to coach once I can't play? I'll be good at it. You know I will."

"Of that, I have no doubt." Tucker's throat was thick.

"And if I'm going to be awesome at it, well then I better go to one of the best places to learn how to coach.

And play some ball while I'm at it. Coach says he'd like to schedule a call with me and my parents. How exciting is that?" Wade bounced on the balls of his feet, almost dropping the spatula in the process.

"Very." Trying to draw from Wade's enthusiasm, Tucker figured he could at least do the phone call if it meant that much to his son.

"You're going to hate Kansas," Walker scoffed around a bite of pancake.

That earned a wild gesture with the spatula from Wade. "F—"

"Language." Tucker plucked the spatula from his grip and set it back in the spoon rest before he could bop his brother like they were toddlers again.

"I am not going to hate it." Wade stared Walker down, eyes daring either of them to object. "I looked at the pictures. There's frats and brick buildings and a big quad where they play Frisbee when the weather is good. You're just bitter because you're stuck staying here."

He was so animated that in that moment, Tucker could see it, leaves changing colors, kids scurrying from building to building, rush week for the Greek system, Wade out there catching Frisbees. He was as good as gone. If not this school, then some other one. Utterly fearless, exactly how he'd been since his first steps. He had a goal now, and the same kid who had managed to scale every obstacle in pursuit of extra cookies or some forbidden item was going to crush it. Tucker was more than a little awed by him.

Walker rolled his eyes at Wade's taunt, but a flush spread up his cheeks. "At least I'm not falling in love with every brochure that comes my way."

"Hey, I want options. Nothing wrong with that." Picking up the spatula again, Wade started in on another batch of pancakes.

"Options are good," Tucker agreed. Damn how he wished he could say the same for himself and his Luis dilemma. They seemed fresh out of options, no choices that would work and not end in more misery and heartache. Unlike Wade and his buffet of attractive alternatives, Tucker simply didn't see a way out of this for himself. It was all the more depressing in the face of such adolescent enthusiasm. For the first time in a long time, Tucker missed when the world had been that wide open and shiny.

"I figure I'll apply everywhere, see where I get the best package—"

Tucker let out a relieved laugh. "My bank account thanks you for that."

"See?" Wade whirled back to Walker. "Dad's not freaking out. He gets it. I've got to go where I've got to go."

Where I've got to go. Tucker did get it on multiple levels. Like he understood Luis had to return to California, that that was where his roots were, where he'd bloomed, where he wanted to be. And Walker would reach this same understanding with Wade—Tucker was sure of that. When you loved someone, you let them go.

Whoa. Wait. He felt deeply for Luis, no question, but was it that kind of unconditional, selfless love? Maybe so because he did want the best for Luis, even if that wasn't him, even if it meant bearing this awful emptiness in his chest that even the distraction of this conversation with the boys couldn't erase.

"I'm cheering for you," he told Wade, even though it

was hard, even though he would miss him like crazy. And Luis too. But he had to do it, had to let them go.

"I don't get why you have to *leave*." And okay, maybe Walker wasn't quite to that point yet himself. The pain in his voice made Tucker reach over, pat his shoulder.

"Because sticking around here with you and Mary Anne isn't happening." Wade punctuated his words with crisp movements as he plated some pancakes for Tucker and himself. "And U of O isn't exactly knocking on my doorstep to play Division One ball either."

"It doesn't mean he doesn't love us," Tucker interjected before Wade could make things worse. And that was another truth he knew in his bones. Luis not wanting to move didn't mean he didn't love Tucker. And maybe it meant Luis loved him *more*, not willing to give him an unhappy, bitter version of himself, resentments stacking up until eventually the whole thing toppled.

"Ha." Walker didn't sound convinced. "Just because you struck out with Mitch's sister doesn't mean you couldn't be happy here."

"Sure I could." Wade shrugged as he finally took a seat next to Tucker. "I just don't want to."

Ah. That right there was the heart of his argument with Luis. Tucker *knew* he could be happy here. If Luis would only let himself…but he simply didn't want to. And that was valid. After all, Tucker didn't want to move and uproot his family, and if he was being totally honest with himself, he hadn't even considered the possibility of going to California. Not since he'd had notebooks filled with facts about smoke jumpers and pictures from Luis of a life they could have, sunny and open, no more cold and gray days. *This could be us.* Oh, how he'd treasured that picture. And there he was back to being seventeen again himself, world full of shiny promise and California starring in all his big dreams.

"Must be nice to have options." Walker's voice was a combination of dismissal and longing.

"You could—" He started, but Walker cut him off by holding up his hand.

"No. I couldn't." Hunching over his plate, Walker stabbed his last piece of pancake. His eyes were pained, and Tucker's heart ached. He couldn't fix this. Couldn't make Walker choose differently, even if he could see the bitterness coming. All he could do was rub his shoulder and hope he figured things out before it was too late.

He might not. Tucker weighed that possibility. And just as he'd seen future Wade owning that Midwestern college, he could see Walker staying in place, always wondering what might have been.

Like me. Did he truly want to grow old here alone, watching Walker navigate through regrets, wallowing in his own? Wasn't that the real question? Did he want to be *here* missing Luis forever? And if the answer was no, why wasn't he fighting more to keep him, whatever it took?

Next to him, Wade was thumbing through the catalog again, a little smile on his face. *Risk taker.* He'd always been one. Tucker not so much. He'd stayed here once even when his dreams had pulled him elsewhere, even when he'd fallen asleep every night senior year dreaming of a different life, one full of adrenaline and sunshine. But he wasn't a risk taker, and he'd had reasons for not packing up the day after graduation. *Wade wouldn't have.* Wade would have loaded the car even before the ceremony. Wade wouldn't leave that dream unchased.

And no amount of lecture was going to sway Walker.

Nothing might, but what kind of example was Tucker setting for both of them? He needed to sit with that question, really sit with it. He'd assumed for twenty years that good men stayed, that he had no alternatives, but was that truly the case? He simply didn't know. And he needed to unearth some answers quickly before it was too late for him. For Luis. For them. Before he let his second chance slip away.

Luis had often wondered what it would be like to be one of those people who lost their appetite when feeling down. Not him. He'd lost track of how many teeny kitchens he'd attempted stress cooking in, how many times he'd tried to convince himself that making some comfort food would solve the ache in his chest. His usual healthy eating resolve went out the window when disappointment reigned supreme, all other emotions fading into a big mass of regret.

Thus, Sunday morning he was attempting to use his tiny hotel kitchenette to make chilaquiles the way his abuela always had—lots of tortillas and sauce and plenty of queso fresco. Of course, the whole time he wished he was cooking for Tucker, and when his phone buzzed, his heart leaped. Might be ill-advised, but if it were Tucker, he was going to answer. Simply going this many hours without contact was hard enough.

But the call was Mami. And further fool that he was, he answered, making it through the pleasantries on autopilot. Yes, he was fine. No, he wasn't sure of a return date. Yes, he'd heard about the fires. Yes, he wished he were there to help. All truths and yet so far from the whole story.

"Is it so bad being back in Oregon?" Mami made a

rustling noise. Chances were good that she too was cooking, something that brought him comfort, same as the way they effortlessly fell into their usual mix of Spanish and English conversation, her accent heavier as she peppered him with questions.

"Not sure," he hedged as he stirred his skillet. "Seeing some old friends here and there hasn't been *terrible*."

"Old friends?" Her tone perked up, but Luis was having none of it.

"A few. Tucker says hi and that he misses your cooking." He kept his tone deliberately casual.

"I always did like that boy." She'd never known the full story of what happened to their friendship, and he sure as heck wasn't going into it now.

"But it's still the same rural area. Nothing much open after five other than chain stores and restaurants. Waiting on tractors on country roads. Lots of belt buckles and rodeo ads."

"See, that I always liked. Give me all the cowboys." She laughed, but he made an outraged noise.

"Mami!"

"What? I like to look. You don't have to sound so scandalized. I always liked it there. So pretty. The mix of all that green and then the desert colors. The ability to go for hikes in the summer without roasting. Housing prices didn't hurt either."

Luis's view of his past tilted, old assumptions wavering in the face of her surprising enthusiasm. "Didn't you miss LA? Could have sworn I remembered you being excited about moving back."

"Of course, I was. I've always liked new adventures, and I missed family. Our neighborhood. But missing people is different from *hating* a place."

"Huh." His tangled-up emotions were becoming more knotted by the moment. As the new kid, his longing for familiar people and things had been closely tied to how he felt about the area. And now as an adult, resentment over the assignment and mixed emotions about seeing Tucker again had initially clouded his return. But he could also admit Mami had a point. The cheaper cost of living and gorgeous scenery were nice bonuses. "I guess if we had to be somewhere new, there were far worse locales the bank could have sent us."

"Exactly. I wasn't miserable in Oregon by any means. It was a great opportunity for Papi. His parents didn't work every day of their lives to send him to school to see him waste that sort of chance. And it was good for you boys too. Room to roam."

"We certainly did that." It had been a long time since he'd let himself dwell on the happy memories. Even after reconciling his friendship with Tucker, he'd kept his focus on the present. But there had been good memories. Long hikes with Mami and his brothers. The bigger house and yard, all the possibilities for hide-and-seek he and Tucker had maximized as kids. His first time river rafting. The fire explorers program. All the school plays, and the way the whole town had come out for them. He'd found his love for the outdoors in this area and his passion for fire-fighting had sprung from this place as well.

"But now your brothers have given me so many reasons to stay local, I don't even have the time to travel that I always said I would." She laughed lightly but Luis still felt the sting. Grandkids trumped everything else in her life, including apparently her urge to experience fresh adventures.

"How are the kids?" he asked, both dutifully and to

get her away from pointless walks down memory lane
that only left him more confused.

"Oh, the birthday party is going to be so fun!" She
filled him in on all the particulars before adding, "We all
hope you can make it. You're their favorite!"

"Because I bring toys." He went ahead and plated the
food he'd probably only pick at.

"You spoil them, yes, but we want you there because
we miss you. Maybe no more trips for a while?" Her voice
was softer now, less upbeat.

"I don't have much say in it, but that would be nice."
God knew he was going to be recovering from this one
for a long, long time. He'd survive the hurt because he'd
been here before, but damn, this part where the loss
seemed to come in waves was the worst.

"Yes, I'm sure your apartment misses you too."

"Not sure I miss it." He laughed but it was true. It was
still his rebound place, the place he'd found because he
couldn't stay in the old one with the memories of Mike
closing in on him. He'd literally signed the first lease
in his price range that he'd found because he'd been too
stressed to manage a long hunt. Only later, coming out
of his grief fog, had he noticed all the little things he dis-
liked about the place. Seeing Heidi's and Tucker's houses
had only underscored for him that he probably needed to
move. He seriously doubted it would help him get over
Tucker any faster though. A nicer kitchen was only going
to make him wish he was cooking for someone special.
Someone like Tucker.

"You could always move in with me. There's room."

"Thanks, Mami, but you know I need my space."
More like he needed his *life*. He loved his family, loved

spending time with them, but he needed his own life. His own...

Family. He sank into a chair at the tiny dining table. That was what was missing from his life, what he'd been in a funk over without ever naming it. Even after he ended the call, he continued to sit there, ignoring his food, rubbing his temples. He'd come close to having a family with Mike—they'd certainly cared for each other and started building a life together. But then he'd lost all that potential, lost a piece of himself too. And it had taken him time—years—to return to this place where he wanted that. His own family. Someone to come home to. Overlapping social circles. Extended family. All of it.

And the worst thing was that he could see that life with Tucker, so easily. The two of them at the center of a life rich with people and food and shared interests. They could be a family, not simply a couple. And God, he wanted that. He wanted Tucker every night, not stolen visits here and there. He wanted Tucker to...

What? Make the impossible happen? No. He knew better than to demand that from Tucker. But letting go of all the potential they had for the life he truly wanted, that was *hard.* He honestly wasn't sure he could, wasn't sure he could go back to his old life as the perpetual bachelor uncle, the single friend, the unattached coworker. And if he couldn't, then where did that leave him? Right here. Desperately wanting an answer to all his mixed-up questions, already missing Tucker more than anything.

Meow. Out of nowhere, Blaze launched herself into Luis's lap.

"What the— *Cat*, what are you doing?" He reflexively started to pet her. Years together and he could count on one hand the number of times she'd willingly snuggled with him. Maybe she sensed how down he was. Or maybe she wanted to tell him to stop being an idiot.

Probably that. She undoubtedly missed Tucker's house too, would rather be there, would rather Luis figure his stuff out. Regardless, here she was, purring in his lap. He took a deep, steadying breath. Funny enough, Blaze feeling sorry for him made him feel even more alone and hopeless. Like his last, good chance at that life he wanted was gone.

How many chances are you going to get? Fragments of his conversation with Walker kept filtering back to him as he kept petting Blaze. How many chances in life did a person get to have what they truly wanted? He had a feeling he already knew the answer, so now the real question was how to apply that knowledge.

Chapter Twenty-Two

Watching Luis at work Monday was torture for Tucker.
Their eyes had met during the morning meeting, both
of them looking away fast. Which was understandable
because no greeting or meaningful look was going to
solve this gulf between them. Tucker couldn't pretend
that he was okay, and he doubted Luis had it any easier.
The last time he'd ached this bad, he'd been kicked by a
horse out at his folks' place. Luis's tired eyes looked like
he too hadn't been sleeping much. And it wasn't like he
had a clue what to say to Luis in any event.

He'd done nothing but think for the past day, turning
everything over and over in his head, trying to find a
reason to go to Luis with something more than desperation. Now, because he still hadn't found those answers,
every interaction *hurt*. Seeing the tight lines around
Luis's eyes and mouth made his chest ache. Noticing his
tense posture while he tried to joke with Garrick as they
waited for another meeting to start made Tucker swing
his feet against his chair base, restless with a need to be
over there too, a craving for one more smile.

The meeting was an update on the arson investigation, and Luis was so damn smooth as he presented that
Tucker couldn't help but be impressed all over again. He

was so good at the job, pointing out minutiae in various clues, finding relationships where others might miss the connections.

"I'm headed over to the air base later today for an interagency meeting about the case. I'm expecting to be able to report a big break soon."

Ah. No Luis to accidentally bump into that afternoon should have been good news for Tucker's worn-down psyche, but it was simply one step closer to no Luis in the office at all, something Fred made clear when it was his turn to speak.

"Hope that break arrives soon. I know you want to see this case through, but California is getting loud about needing you back." Fred shuffled the stack of papers in front of him.

"Yeah." Luis nodded like this wasn't a surprise to him. His gaze never so much as flitted Tucker's direction. "I talked to some folks back home today. They're almost as shorthanded as you are here. The hiring freeze has affected everyone."

"Thankfully, that's about to be over, but good luck scheduling interviews at the height of fire season," Christine interjected.

"Yup. And that's where we're at." Fred drummed his thick fingers against the table. "Was hoping we'd have you through the holiday weekend, but I think this week is going to be it. See what you can do to have everything you're working on ready to hand off by Thursday."

This week. Thursday. Three days and change. Hours. He was running out of time. Luis said a bunch of other things, mainly updates on how officials were monitoring activity on some potential spots the arsonist hadn't hit yet, but Tucker's brain was still crackling like a radio station out in the desert, only intermittent signals making it through.

After the meeting, he was slow getting up, as was Luis. *Stop him. Say something. Anything.* But he didn't. Couldn't. And so their gazes met, held, air thick with an almost palpable longing as the room emptied of people. And it wasn't all him. He could swear Luis was feeling it too, and indeed, he paused near the door.

"I…" Luis licked his lips.

Please. Tucker's heart sped up. Whatever Luis wanted to say, he wanted to listen.

"Yeah. We should—"

"Luis? Do you need Jeep keys or are you taking your own vehicle to the air base?" One of the young assistants poked her head in the room, right as Tucker was about to ask…hell, he didn't even know now. Whatever he'd been about to say, the moment passed as Luis brushed by him.

"I'll take my car, thanks." He followed the assistant down the hall, away from Tucker, but spared him a last glance over his shoulder. His eyes were troubled, mouth tight, and Tucker hated the thought that he might be distracted by their falling-out at his big meeting or while driving.

Damn it. This sucked. Back in his office, he slumped in his chair, but his phone buzzed with a message before he could wallow in the awful, empty sensation taking hold of his body.

I've got a time scheduled Wednesday for a video chat with that coach from Kansas. You can do it, right? Mom is still freaking out. And a place in South Dakota sent me stuff too. Cool!

Tucker was in the middle of typing a reply to Wade when a message from Walker arrived too.

Don't let Wade choose South Dakota. Seriously. He's like a puppy with too many toys. Can I sleep at your place tonight if he won't shut up?

He hit Send on the message to Wade, then sent one to Walker. Yes, of course. Tell your mother. And having choices is a GOOD thing. Go easy on Wade.

Poor Walker. Couldn't be easy dealing with Wade, who had possibly too many options, while Walker was clearly still feeling like he had none. Exactly like Tucker. No feasible alternatives sucked.

But then he stared down at his phone at what he'd typed, at the unspoken message he was trying to convey. Walker *did* have choices. So did he. The problem was that neither of them wanted to acknowledge them, which was different than actually lacking options. And Tucker wasn't seventeen himself any longer. He drew his shoulders up, straightened his legs. He was an adult and so was Luis. They both had free will here. Specifically, Tucker did have a choice. He could choose to let Luis go or he could fight. And not just fight the universe or Luis's own reluctance, but fight himself and all the assumptions holding him back too. He needed to look at *all* the options and possibilities, remove his self-imposed limits, and do the hard work of examining what it was he truly wanted.

Because there were choices out there. He knew it. He simply needed to be brave enough to see them. And then he needed to convince Luis to dream with him.

That might be the harder thing, but he wasn't giving in to despair and bitterness. Not yet. This time he was going to *fight*.

"We're one break away from cracking this thing wide open." Luis's fire investigator colleague from the inter-agency team, a tall woman with curly hair, walked him out of the meeting room where they'd just completed several hours of intense review of all the files on the various fires suspected of being linked to the same arsonist.

"That's for sure." He'd spent most of the meeting hyper-focused on the case at hand, trying to block out any distractions. But during the boring parts, he kept drifting back to Tucker and to the haunted expression on his face earlier that day. His brain felt one missing piece away too, like if he could only come at the problem of him and Tucker from a fresh angle, he'd have the solution they so desperately needed.

"I hear they're shipping you back home at the end of the week." The investigator paused near the end of the hallway, near the break room and restrooms.

"Looks like it." The last thing Luis wanted was to think more about leaving. He was so fucking torn. Rosalind had sounded scattered—they were all spread too thin, everyone out in the field, long hours, not enough manpower, and the fires not yet fully under control. He needed to be back there. But leaving meant no more Tucker, no more time to fix this.

"Take care if we don't see you before then. Drive safe." The investigator gave him a little wave before ducking into the restroom, leaving him to walk the rest of the way out of the building. He was almost to the double glass doors when he heard his name.

"Hey, Rivera!" Lincoln Reid came striding up, in street clothes. He had a bag over one shoulder, like he too was heading out for the day. The meeting had gone long, and Luis supposed he was heading back to his hotel, but fuck, he was already dreading the hours alone.

"Reid." After the party at Garrick's, he felt like he knew the guy a little better than he had as kids, and he was happy to exchange small talk if it meant delaying the long evening ahead of him. "How's it going?"

"Eh. Did two flights today as spotter. Then a lot of meetings. How I let anyone talk me into supervision is beyond me. Damn bum knee. It'll have me in management soon enough, and I'm already dreading the paperwork."

"I know, right? For me, it's my back, and I miss frontline work still. I'd even take the weird hours, just to be back out there again." It had been his stock answer for years, but lately he wasn't as sure. He did like his work, meetings aside. Besides, if he was still on a hotshot crew, he probably never would have met back up with Tucker, wouldn't be tangled up with all these feelings right now. He shook his head, trying to stay focused on Lincoln. "Paperwork. It comes for us all, I guess."

"Yup. How are things with you?" Lincoln didn't seem any more inclined to head out than Luis.

"Not bad. We're close on the arson case."

"That's great." He slapped Luis on the upper shoulder. "I heard your theory about it being someone connected to the fire community. Gotta say I agree. Reminds me of this disgruntled rookie who flunked out of spring training back when I did some time in Idaho. He was later caught setting fire to his ex's trailer."

"Exactly." Blessedly, Luis's brain left the Tucker quan-

dary for a few moments. That was what he'd been thinking for a few weeks now. Someone had a grudge, a motive
beyond being a firebug. "I had a few cases like that in
California too. Any chance you could help me get a list
of the last few rookie classes here, focusing on people
who didn't make it through?"

"Yeah. I was one of the trainers this year. I'll see what
red tape we can cut through to get that information to
you."

"Thanks. I appreciate it."

"No problem." Lincoln turned like he was going to go
back into the offices, but Luis held up a hand.

"Tomorrow is probably soon enough. I don't want to
keep you today, especially if you were already heading out."

"Nah. It's okay." Dropping his bag by his feet, Lincoln
exhaled hard. "Jacob's on loan to a fire up near Hood
River. House is way too quiet, even with the dogs."

"You miss him." Luis had to smile at this big, badass
guy who would be as at home on a battlefield as a mo-
torcycle gang, yet who also had such a soft spot for his
man and wasn't afraid to admit he had feelings.

Lincoln sighed and rubbed at his closely cropped hair.
"That's one way to put it."

"He'll be back soon, I'm sure. Has it been hard this
year, being on different crews?" New regulations meant
that the smoke-jumping management was reluctant to
put people in a long-term relationship together on the
same small crew.

"Yeah, it has. Not gonna lie." Rolling his neck, Lincoln
stretched and looked away. "We still work together some,
but it's not the same. Weird too because I'm so fucking

proud of him advancing. Like I didn't even know it was possible to be that proud of someone else, you know?"

"I get it. I've been there." And he had. Both with Mike, being worried and proud every time he advanced or got called out, and now with Tucker, being in awe as he managed things at the fire camp. And *weird* was the right way to put it. Pride in someone else was a great, positive emotion, but it also brought with it a certain vulnerability that could be less than comfortable, especially when risk was involved.

"Yeah? You got someone back home?" Lincoln studied him carefully. "Was kind of under the impression that you and Tucker…"

"It's complicated." Luis wasn't going to lie and say it was nothing, but he also wasn't about to air any private business right here in the lobby. "And no one at home. Not for a long time now."

Knowing how the rumor mill worked in the fire community, he added that last bit so that no one would think Tucker was his piece on the side. But saying the words made certain thoughts reappear. *No one at home.* He'd been perfectly fine with that reality right up until now, when he suddenly wasn't. It was like forgetting to eat all day, then realizing he'd been starving for hours.

"Ah. Complicated sucks." Lincoln arched his eyebrows like a guy who'd been there a time or two.

"Word." Luis still wasn't giving him details, but they exchanged a sort of knowing look, an acknowledgment of past battles they'd each fought, a certain mutual respect passing between them even without words.

"Been there. Fucking sucked. But I also wouldn't change a damn thing. Sometimes complicated works out. I hope it does for you, man." This time when Lincoln clapped him on the shoulder, it was softer, less Hulk and more understanding.

"Thanks." They had another wordless conversation with their eyes, more of that understanding that made Luis's throat strangely tight.

Lincoln gave him a last commiserating look before picking up his bag. "I'll get on those names for the investigation. You have a good rest of your evening."

"Will do," Luis replied before heading to the parking lot even though he had no intention of having a *good* anything. The empty evening was merely something to be endured, a series of hours to try to avoid the urge to call Tucker. Not that he needed to call. The air base was on the outskirts of Painter's Ridge. It was getting late. Tucker was probably already on his way home. He could simply swing by, wait for him to show up after work, and…

That was where his imagination failed him. He wasn't sure what to say that wouldn't make things that much worse. And yet his car pointed itself toward town, not the rural highway back to his Bend hotel. He didn't head right to Tucker either though. Instead he wandered, past the house where his family had lived. It was older now, needing new paint, and had several vehicles out front, so he only briefly paused there. So many memories. His mom was right. It wasn't *all* bad. There was the tree he'd climbed so many times and his upstairs window that had once had a row of vinyl superhero decals. A dad-type guy emerged from the house, two small children trailing after him, and Luis moved on, same as the house had.

His meandering drive took him by the high school next, and there he parked, led by some weird pull to the empty bleachers where he'd spent so many hours talking with Tucker as kids. And then the newer memory of watching Tucker's kids play. He'd felt it then, all that potential they had, not simply from their past connection, but all the present possibilities.

We'll make it work. He'd sat right here, all those years ago, and believed that with every neuron he had. He'd known that Tucker was the one for him from that first kiss. *Maybe we're not kissing the right people.* And it had been there in every kiss, but also every conversation. All the long hours talking, both recently and back then. He couldn't walk away from that now. Somehow he'd known the second he'd turned his car toward town that he couldn't leave without seeing Tucker one more time. They *needed* to talk, even if he had no clue what words to use. Maybe he could start with the big scary ones, the three they'd left unsaid even as they glowed neon-bright between them. His pulse kicked up at the very thought.

"Luis? What are you doing here?" Coming from the direction of the school, Walker climbed up the bleachers.

"Thinking." He wasn't going to lie to the kid, but like with Lincoln Reid, he also wasn't pouring his heart out either. "You?"

"Dropping off some stuff Coach needed." To his surprise, Walker plopped down next to him. "You going to go talk to Dad?"

"Maybe." Again, he couldn't lie, especially when he'd pretty much already decided. "Probably."

"Why did you guys fight anyway?"

"It's complicated." It was the same answer he'd given Lincoln, but it came out wearier now, tinged with more frustration. They'd wasted precious days and hours.

Mouth pursing, Walker considered this for a long moment. "Is it about me?"

"You?" It hadn't even occurred to Luis that one of

the kids might blame themselves for his falling out with Tucker.

"I know I wasn't the most…enthusiastic about you at first."

"No, it's not about you. Promise." Luis looked him in the eye, making sure he knew Luis meant it. "You're a good kid. You're like Blaze. You take a while to warm up. I get it. And your dad having anyone around, that's new."

"Yeah." Hands on his knees, Walker bent forward. "It was new. But also… I want everything to stay the same. Which is stupid, I know."

"No, I get it. I've been there. Change sucks." Luis wasn't kidding. He knew that feeling. He'd had it so strongly when his parents had announced their move back to California. Why couldn't things stay the same? He'd railed against the universe for weeks then. And then later, the year his dad and Mike had died. Time marched on, whether he was ready or not, and he could feel the frustration radiating off Walker because that had been him, more times than he could count. Now as well. He hadn't wanted to take this trip, and now he didn't want it to end. Didn't particularly like everything about his life back home, but he was reluctant to change. It was a mess.

"All my friends are in such a hurry. Can't wait to get the year started, then homecoming, then prom, then graduation. And it never slows down."

"That's life. Never slows down when you want it to." Unlike Walker, he knew it was futile to try to control time, but man, how he wanted to. He'd tried to savor as much of his time with Tucker as possible, but that had only made it go faster, had made him fall that much deeper and further for the guy. And time would keep on churning, regardless of what he decided now, no matter what words he finally said to Tucker. His back tensed with the knowledge that had dogged him for days now that life only gave so many chances to maximize what little time he did have.

"Yup." Walker shook his head, eyes glassy and distant as he looked out at the mountains in the distance. "And anyway, I wanted to say that I liked having you around."

Luis had to swallow hard before he could reply. Tucker sure as hell had done something right with how he'd raised these kids. "Thanks. That means a lot."

Gaze still far off, Walker managed to laugh. "And not just because you're a good cook."

"You and your brother and food."

"Yeah. It's kinda mind blowing how much we go through in a week, especially during the season. F— *man*, I can't believe this is it. Last season."

"Last times suck." Now it was his turn to stare off into the distance. Last kiss. Last words. Last chance. But unlike Walker and the finite football schedule, Luis didn't have to accept things ending here.

"And goodbyes," Walker added softly.

"Truth." He patted the kid on the shoulder, even as his own head spun, words finally coming together. *I don't want to say goodbye.* There. That was how he could start.

"I heard Mom say you might have to come back for a court case thing. If you come back, will you come to a game?"

"I'll see what I can do." First, he had to win back Walker's dad, but he wasn't going to mention that here.

"Good." Walker gave him a tentative grin. "Wade needs the cheering section."

"I think his ego will be fine either way, but I'll try." And he'd try specifically for Walker, because maybe

Wade wouldn't even notice, but Walker would. And that mattered.

"Okay." Seemingly satisfied, Walker stood up. "I need to get over to Mary Anne's."

"Yeah. Be careful, okay?" Luis wished he could say more, wished he had the right advice since the kid was clearly still wrestling with some big things, but he could barely sort out his own life. The last thing he wanted to do was make things harder for Walker.

Walker shrugged. "I'm a good driver."

"I'm sure. I meant—"

"*I know.* And I am."

"Good." Luis sighed because he'd meant it as more than a safe-sex lecture, which he had a feeling Walker knew too, but if he didn't want to talk more, Luis wasn't going to make him. Instead, he sat there a few more minutes after Walker departed, gathering his thoughts. And courage. Because he finally did know what to say, but more importantly what to *do.* But the real trick might be getting Tucker to listen.

Chapter Twenty-Three

Tucker had grabbed his keys and was heading to his SUV when a familiar car pulled into the driveway.

"Luis? What are you doing here?" Tucker had to blink a few times, wondering if he'd somehow managed to conjure Luis up with the sheer force of wanting.

Licking his lips and seeming uncharacteristically antsy, Luis exited his car to stand in front of him. "I came to talk, but if it's not a good time…"

"No, actually I was coming to *you*. Like right now." He'd suffered through a hasty dinner with Wade, but even Wade had picked up on how much Tucker wanted to be anywhere else, and had waved him away even before cleanup. Tucker had been rehearsing what he needed to say for hours, and now he simply had to see Luis, tell him everything churning in his head. "Because, yeah, we need to talk."

Luis's eyes went wide, and they stood there in the driveway, staring at each other, awkwardness prevailing. Finally, Tucker couldn't stand it anymore and laughed, which broke the silence and got Luis smiling.

"I was going to see if you wanted to go for a ride with me." Luis gestured at his car. "But if you'd rather stay here…"

"Wade's inside devouring the last of the spaghetti." And not that Wade would care, but Tucker really didn't need an audience for this. Besides he was curious as to what Luis had in mind. "Drive sounds good."

He ducked his head into the house to tell Wade what was up so that he didn't worry when he saw Tucker's SUV still in the driveway.

"Go. I'm heading back to Mom's anyway for my tablet. I'll probably sleep there." Wade gave him a meaningful look before Tucker made his escape.

Folding his frame into Luis's little car was an adventure, and the proximity only served to make him more aware of the distance that remained between them. He wanted to touch Luis so badly, the possibility of curious neighbors and spying Wade be damned, but he didn't feel he had the right. Not yet.

"I was driving around earlier," Luis shared as he put the car in gear. "Finished up at the air base, but I couldn't seem to make myself go back to the hotel, but also couldn't find the way to you either."

"Even if you didn't, I was going to come to you. I know it's only been two days, but it feels like two years."

"Maybe we can meet somewhere in the middle." Laughing, Luis headed into town.

"Let's try." Tucker didn't laugh with him because that was exactly what he wanted to do, find some common ground to build on.

"Okay." Luis echoed Tucker's gravitas as he turned into the high school parking lot, stopping near the football field. "I know this isn't exactly the middle. But I keep coming back in my head to where it started."

"Me too. God, how many hours did we spend in those bleachers talking?" Tucker swore that if he squinted he could see the ghosts of their younger selves up there, second row from the top of the home team section.

"Exactly. And I was here earlier. Ran into Walker actually." Drumming his fingers against the steering wheel, Luis glanced over at him.

"You did?" The parking lot was mostly deserted, only another couple of vehicles. No sign of Walker and Wade's car. It was still plenty light, but the sky had taken on that warm late August evening rosiness.

"Yeah. He thought maybe he was to blame for us falling out. I set him straight." Luis gave a firm nod.

"Good." He never doubted that he could trust Luis to say the right thing with his kids. "Only fault here is mine."

"And mine," Luis added quickly, bumping shoulders with Tucker. "Let's not play the blame game."

"Good point, but—"

"No blaming yourself." Luis gave him a stern look. "Anyway, I sat in the bleachers for a long time, thinking. About us then and us now and everything in between."

"I feel that." Tucker looked out at the bleachers again, at the ghosts roaming around this campus, seeing both who they had been but also who they could be now as well. "Feels like I've done nothing but think since Saturday night."

"Same. And I don't have all the answers, but I do know that I don't want to say goodbye." Luis met his gaze, eyes dark pools of seriousness.

"Me either." Tucker inhaled sharply.

"That's why I wanted to bring you here. Remember when we would have each done *anything* to stay together?"

"Yeah." Damn. He could remember the feel of Luis's

skinny fingers against his own, the press of their sneakers under the bleachers. "We would have given a lot to not say goodbye back then, which is why—"

"—I'm willing to move," they both said at the same time.

"What? Seriously?" Tucker swiveled in his seat to better study Luis's face. "You were right. It wasn't fair of me to ask you to stay here. Especially not if I wasn't willing to consider the opposite option. And I wasn't giving enough respect to the life you've got back in California."

"I appreciate that." Luis patted Tucker's thigh. "A lot. But I wasn't being flexible either."

"You shouldn't have to be. Compromise should be on both of us, not all on you." He grabbed Luis's hand on his leg before Luis could pull it back.

"Yeah." Luis blew out a rough breath. "But the facts haven't changed. If we want to be together—"

"I do. More than anything." Conviction made his voice rough, even in a whisper.

"Me too." Luis squeezed his hand. "And if that's the goal, then one of us needs to at least think about moving. And you weren't wrong that I'm more in position to do that than you."

He hated how resigned Luis sounded and knew that a lot of that was his own fault for being so damn stubborn. But he could fix that now. "Not necessarily."

"Oh?" Luis's head tilted.

Outside, some kids drove through the parking lot, windows down and peals of laughter echoing through the evening air. But inside Luis's car, Tucker was all seriousness.

"This life I've got here…it's changing." He hadn't wanted to admit it, even to himself, but saying it aloud helped make it more real. "Another year and both boys will out of the house, one way or another. Wade's looking at colleges all over. And no matter what Walker decides, he'll move on too. And then it's me and an empty house and a lot of mixed-up thinking about what my life is and what it has to be."

Luis frowned at that. "Not sure I want to be your empty-nest fallback plan."

"That's not what I mean." Making a frustrated noise, Tucker tried to meet his gaze. "I'm not saying you're… some sort of replacement. More that you're my *future*."

"I like the idea of being your future. A lot," Luis said softly, looking down at their linked hands.

"I've put the boys first for over seventeen years now, and maybe it's okay now if I listen to what I want, at least give some thought to my own needs and wants." It had taken him days to reach that conclusion, but the more he thought on it, the less he wanted to end up thirty years from now bitter at all the chances he never took.

"I get that." Luis nodded. "However, much as I want to be your future, I also can't deny that you've built a life here. You've got deep roots."

"And I let those roots hold me back once before. I'm not going to do that again." He kept his voice steady, but some of his frustration at past regrets seeped into his tone.

"Your family—"

"Is mainly only Heidi and the boys these days. The rest of them, my parents and such, can either come around to being supportive or not. I'm not making any decisions with them in mind. I spent too many damn years caring about what they thought, and I'm not going to start again."

"Fair enough." Luis restlessly moved his fingers in Tucker's grasp, thumb sweeping along the edge of Tucker's fingers.

"And you *do* have a great family. That's not nothing. It doesn't feel fair to ask you to leave all that extended network behind simply because I've got a few connections here that I'm reluctant to leave behind."

"I appreciate that, but you've got more of a support system here than I was willing to admit as well. I was so focused on the past that I wasn't allowing myself to see a future here." Turning more in his seat, Luis added his other hand on top of their linked fingers. "You've got friends. We wouldn't be alone. The area has changed some. When I really let myself stop and think things through, I could see a life here. And more importantly, I was having a hard time seeing a life back home without you."

"That…thank you." Licking his suddenly parched lips, he swallowed hard. "And same. I mean it. I close my eyes and think about the future and it's you. The *where* matters a lot less than the *who.*"

"Same. I don't want to look back and think about lost chances, think that if I'd only been a little more flexible that we might have had it all."

"Maybe that's on both of us." Reaching out, Tucker stroked Luis's jaw. "We were thinking about distance like we were seventeen again, like a couple of months or a year is forever and not the blink of an eye."

"True. I was all up in my fears." Luis's exhale was warm against Tucker's fingertips.

"Me too. But I want to believe that we can make it this time." Staying Tucker's hand, Luis pressed a kiss to his thumb.

"I think we can." Unable to resist another second, Tucker leaned in for a soft kiss. He'd meant it to be brief, reassuring, but not particularly sexy, but as usual their bodies had their own agenda. He wasn't even sure who moved to deepen the kiss, only that one moment their lips were barely brushing and the next they were clutching at each other, tongues tangling. Needy sounds filled the car until Luis pulled back, harsh breathing echoing Tucker's.

"Wow. Enough kisses like that, and I might stop caring about who lives where." Laughing, Luis rested his head against Tucker's. "We can stay right here."

"Ha. Let's not get arrested for making out in your car all night." Tucker nudged him with his shoulder.

"I'm willing to risk it." Voice playful, Luis dramatically slumped against him. Tucker was ready to not have to tangle with the console to properly hold him.

"I know we don't have all the answers yet, or even a solid plan, but…come back with me? Maybe we don't have to settle everything right this second."

"I've missed you. So, so much. I'm willing to do whatever it takes to not feel that way again." Back to solemn, Luis's eyes shone. There was pain there, and Tucker felt it, deep inside his chest. He'd hurt Luis, and he wanted to do the work to make sure he never did that again.

"Ditto. Whatever it takes." He held Luis as close as the cramped quarters of the car allowed. And then because the moment felt almost too heavy, he added, "My bed misses you almost as much as me."

"Is that right? I suppose I can come back, get reacquainted with it." Luis gave him a fast kiss on the cheek before adjusting his position, rebuckling the seat belt he'd lost at some point. "And I don't mean sex necessarily. I want to hold you for a while and have it not be so sad this time."

"We can do that." Tucker appreciated how cautious Luis always was about not assuming that he was up for sex, but right then, they were on the same page. He wanted Luis back in his bed, in all senses of the word, wanted to hold him and never let go. He had to believe they'd figure everything else out in time.

Chapter Twenty-Four

On the way back to Tucker's house, Luis felt a thousand pounds lighter than he had earlier in the day. They still didn't have all the answers for how to make this work, but he now believed they would, which was a marked improvement.

"Okay. Dad duties done for the day." Looking up from his phone as Luis turned down his street, Tucker gave a boyish grin. "Wade's over at Heidi's playing a game on his tablet. Apparently, he ate an entire second dinner with them when Isaac cooked late."

"Somehow I'm not surprised. And the other twin?" Luis parked next to Tucker's SUV.

"Walker's on his way back from Mary Anne's, and Heidi says she'll text when he's back for the night."

"So I can race you to your bed?" Luis waggled his eyebrows at Tucker as they made their way up the walk. Joking was far easier than returning to the heavy conversation and all the surprising revelations like Tucker being willing to move. Luis simply couldn't unpack that offer right then, needed the humor to take the edge off all his roiling emotions, most of which he couldn't even name.

"You can absolutely race me to my bed." Tucker all but beamed as he unlocked the door, then right when Luis was going to drag him close for a kiss, he slipped around Luis and headed for the stairs. "But I'm going to win."

"We'll see about that." Careful to not actually knock Tucker down, Luis jostled him as they bounded up the stairs. He overtook him at the landing, but then Tucker took the remaining steps two at a time, leaving Luis to play catchup in the hallway. Both of them flat-out sprinted for the bed, diving for it and landing in a heap of limbs and laughter.

"Beat you." Tucker was breathing hard and Luis couldn't wait to make him pant for other reasons if he got the chance.

"It was a tie." Luis had ended up half on top of Tucker. Peering down at him, he gave him the softest of kisses. He didn't need sex. Just this closeness, them together blanketed by their resolve to find a solution.

Of course, his body wasn't going to turn something other than cuddling down, and when Tucker growled and kissed him back with a ferocity that made Luis's blood hum, he more than welcomed it. Tucker this kind of aggressive was exactly the vibe he was craving. He generally loved being the one calling the shots, but there was also something intoxicating and freeing about letting Tucker set the pace. He liked how Tucker meandered along, trying different ways of kissing, but slowly ramping the heat up at the same time.

Tucker paused from exploring Luis's mouth to pluck at his shirt buttons. "Too many clothes."

"At least you got a chance to change after work." Sharing the urge for skin, he pushed at Tucker's T-shirt.

"Hazard of cooking with Wade." Tucker untangled their bodies before gesturing at Luis's clothing. "Less talking, more stripping."

"Yes, sir." Luis had to laugh because bossy Tucker was the best Tucker. He got busy on his buttons before adding, "And you too."

"Damn." Shirt off and hands on his jeans, Tucker stopped, eyes sweeping over Luis. "Every time...can't believe how lucky I am to get to see you like this."

"Sweet talker." Luis made fast work of his remaining clothes before leaning in for another kiss. "And you're not so bad yourself."

Tucker truly was a feast for the senses—fuzzy chest, defined muscles, and hard cock—but even more than looking at his body, Luis was enjoying listening to him, the laughter and light banter like helium for a heart that had been way too heavy at the start of the day.

"Come here again. Right like you were." Tucker stretched out on his back on the bed again, opening his arms wide.

"Yeah? You like this?" Fully naked now, Luis straddled his waist, letting his cock drag against Tucker's abs.

"You have to ask?" Tucker bumped his hips upward and shifted so that his impressive erection nestled under Luis's ass and balls.

"Maybe I like hearing it." He laughed but he really did relish every sound Tucker made from needy gasps to dirty words. Knowing he turned Tucker on this much made his shoulders and chest lift, puffing up like some sort of erotic superhero. Experimenting to see what got more delicious sounds from Tucker, he ground against him. "Damn you feel good."

"Right back at you." Eyes locked on Luis, Tucker groaned. His hands swept over Luis's back and thighs, lingering on his ass, making Luis crave more contact.

"Want to ride you. You think you could be up for

that?" Much as Luis loved fucking Tucker, tonight he wanted this. He'd always loved switching things up, but he wasn't sure if Tucker felt the same way.

"Is that a trick question?" Tucker was already twisting for the nightstand drawer.

Accepting the supplies from Tucker, Luis chuckled at his ready interest. "I'll take that as a yes."

"Tell me what you like, how to get you ready." Tucker's earnestness as he danced his fingertips down Luis's spine was fucking adorable. If Luis wasn't already sure he was the perfect guy for him, Tucker turning out to be as enthusiastically versatile as Luis might have done it.

"Kiss me while I do it." Luis reached for the lube. The truly nice thing about Tucker was that Luis wasn't afraid to ask for exactly what he wanted. Tucker seemed to genuinely love indulging all of Luis's likes, and that was heady stuff.

Indeed, Tucker's eyes twinkled as he sat up enough to brush a kiss across Luis's mouth. "Should have known you'd stay a control freak."

"You complaining?" Luis raised an eyebrow as he slicked up his fingers. He liked getting fucked from time to time, but he wasn't as crazy about fingering. Lubing up and stretching always seemed to slow things down more than he liked, but aware of Tucker's eyes on him in between trading kisses, he played a little, working himself open. The kisses got hotter and he groaned as much from that as from the ass play.

"Definitely not complaining. Watching you do that is hot as hell." Tucker's lascivious grin made Luis wish his back muscles were a little more flexible, so he could give Tucker even more of a sexy show. But also the more

Tucker looked at him with such blatant lust, the more impatient Luis's body became.

"Mmm. You haven't seen anything yet." Withdrawing his fingers, he quickly wiped them on the T-shirt Tucker handed him. He loved both how naturally chivalrous Tucker was and how in sync they already were, even after only a few times together. In all things, it felt like he wanted and Tucker was right there, giving. And Tucker was also the perfect blend of leader and follower, groaning and stretching as Luis rolled the condom on him, gaze hungry but not pushing to take the fuck over.

Wanting to reward him, Luis quickly lubed Tucker's cock up, and holding it steady with his hand, he positioned himself over it. Since Tucker seemed to like watching so much, he held Tucker's gaze as he slowly lowered down, a smooth move that had them both gasping.

"Oh, fuck. Warn a guy, won't you?" Tucker's eyes fluttered shut as his head tipped back against the pillows.

"Good?" Knowing this was new to Tucker made Luis's pulse thrum, a heady mix of power and discovery. The lower Luis moved, the better Tucker's broad cock felt. Like his chest and hands, his cock was *thick*, a fun challenge to relax around and the perfect pressure against all Luis's favorite places.

"So good." Tucker's groan seemed to come from his toes as Luis took him all in and started to rock his hips.

"Yeah." It didn't take much for Luis to find a rhythm that felt amazing, shallow movements that were possibly more devastating than athletic bouncing. He loved keeping the pressure steady, adding little licks of friction that sent sparks of pleasure radiating out from his ass, up his spine, over his abs, taking over his whole body. "That's it."

And he loved that he didn't have to ask whether Tucker was liking this. His eyes, now open again, were glassy and dark, while his face was pink with a flush that started on his chest. And it wasn't merely his expression that said he was loving the fuck, but also the way his body naturally found Luis's rhythm, hips rocking, hands finding Luis's ass, urging him on.

"Fuck. No way…can't last." Tucker stilled, body going tense under Luis, hands dropping to clench at the sheets. Face grimacing, he released the bedding to fumble for the lube. He slicked up his palm and reached for Luis's cock. "Want to get you there first though. Tell me how."

"Like that." Damn, but he loved how Tucker already knew how to touch him. "Harder."

Tucker complied, but his body bowed as Luis moved faster. "Fuck. Fuck."

He wasn't lying about being close and watching him hold back was the best kind of power trip.

"Love making you curse. You feel so good."

"Yeah, you do." Even Tucker's neck was tense, every corded muscle visible. He'd stopped moving, but his breath came in harsh panting. Sexy as fuck.

"More." Luis moved into his grip, fucking his fist even as he rode Tucker's cock faster. Tucker tightened his grip, thumb sweeping over Luis's cockhead. "Damn. Damn."

Tucker echoed each of Luis's moans, barely restrained need etching his features. "Want…*need* to come. But want…you…"

"I will. Come, Tucker. Want to feel it. Let go." He honestly couldn't tell how close his own orgasm was because his whole body seemed attuned to Tucker, all his energy and focus on shattering Tucker's control. Having this sort of power over him was almost better than climax.

"Fuck." Something snapped in Tucker, his body moving again, hips bucking, free hand coming back to Luis's ass, fingers digging in. "Luis."

"Yes. Fuck. That's it. That's it." Luis rejoiced in Tucker's orgasm, urging him on, even as his own climax hit, light-speed train appearing out of nowhere. It was more of that awe-inspiring synergy. Tucker *needed* and he could *give*, and the giving was so damn good that it brought him off, spurting all over Tucker's abs.

All the tension left Tucker's body in a big whoosh as he exhaled hard and slumped against the bed. "Damn. Wow. That was…"

"Good?" Luis tried to hide his wince as he slid off Tucker's cock and stretched out next to him. It had been a long time since he'd been fucked, and his body was using the lull in the action to remind him of that. Still, though, he liked the well-fucked feeling very much, and he loved the satisfied expression on Tucker's face.

"You're underselling it. Never felt that intense before." Tucker's voice was dreamy, almost like he'd been the one getting fucked. Feeling strangely protective, Luis rubbed his arms.

"I know. Same here."

"Really?" Tucker's eyes had drifted shut, but he opened them to peer intently at Luis.

"Really." It was true. He wasn't merely flattering Tucker. He'd had a lot of sex in his life, but none that had moved him quite that much, been that emotional, or that closely in sync with the other person.

"Good." Seemingly satisfied at what he saw in Luis's face, Tucker snuggled back into him.

"Damn. You're making me torn between sleeping

messy and the smarter choice of getting reacquainted with your shower."

"Can you stay?" Sleep apparently forgotten, Tucker sat up. "I should feed you something. You missed dinner."

"Yeah, I can stay. Blaze has the automatic feeder, and I checked levels just this morning."

"Excellent. Shower then. I'll clean up too. And then I'm going to rustle up something for that dinner you missed."

"You think Wade left food? That's some serious optimism."

"Trying." Turning back to Luis, Tucker grabbed his hand tightly. "Trying to believe in everything."

His eyes said that he meant far more than whether or not there were leftovers for them to forage. And Luis got it, this weird mental space of trying to believe in a future for them, despite all the hurdles standing in the way still.

"Me too. Too easy to assume the worst," he admitted, looking away. He wanted to share Tucker's optimism, but it was hard.

"Hey." Tucker gently turned Luis's face back toward him, blessed him with a soft kiss. "Let's pray for the best instead."

"I can do that." And he would. If Tucker could trust so deeply, then so could he. Tucker was right about the *who* mattering far more than the *where*.

There would be time enough later for talking, and that attitude carried him through a shower and an impromptu late-night picnic of sandwiches and sweet, cuddly, sleepy play before drifting off together. All the way until the early morning buzzing of both their phones when he knew they were screwed. *No more time.*

* * *

Tucker knew as soon as both their phones went off that it was bad. Dawn was peeking in through his blinds, soft light that invited another hour of sleep, but that wasn't to be.

"Let me call in first," he said to Luis, who was already scrambling into clothes. His message was from Garrick.

"I'm on the way," he told Garrick as soon as he had coordinates for the fire. Another early-morning blaze near a hiking trail had to mean the chance of it being their arsonist was high. However, whatever the cause, Tucker needed to get crews on the ground and get Luis to the scene so he could do what he did best and predict the spread of the fire. "And I'll...uh...pick up Rivera along the way since I've got the better vehicle for those dirt roads."

"Uh-huh." Garrick chuckled. "I'm not going to tell if he's right there now. Your sleeping arrangements are your business."

"Thanks." He pulled on a work shirt and dug out his good boots. His hard hats and other gear was still in the SUV from the last callout. "I'll contact my crew chiefs while you call everyone else in."

"Get me the plans as soon as you have them."

After some logistics talk, Tucker ended the call and went to search out Luis, finding him already pouring coffee into travel mugs.

"Thanks. We make an efficient team." He accepted the cup, noticing that Luis had hit the perfect milk-sugar-caffeine ratio for him. "Told Garrick I was picking you up on the way."

"Technically true." Luis offered him a sleepy grin. "And I did warn—"

"I'm not caring who figures out that we're more than coworkers. Trying to keep it professional for both our sakes, but I'd give that advice to anyone else regardless of gender. Ready to hit the road?"

"Yup. Let's do it."

The site was something of a drive, and as Tucker navigated the back roads there, they took turns making the calls they needed. Tucker made sure he had ground crews on the way to dig fireline and coordinated with the interagency folks and hotshot crew chiefs. Meanwhile, Luis got the latest data and an update from the investigation.

"They've detained a suspect," he reported during a break between calls. "This was one of the areas we were closely watching, and law enforcement was able to quickly move in at the trailhead."

"Your theory was right." Tucker hadn't expected anything less because Luis was that brilliant. "Are you jealous that you don't get to make the arrest and do the questioning?"

"Maybe a little." Luis shrugged. "I enjoy the hands-on firework, but you never know. Maybe someday. And maybe if I stay—"

"I wasn't hinting at that. I meant what I said last night. I'm willing to be the one to move, so don't go job hunting yet."

Luis made a dismissive gesture. "Right now, we have a fire to fight. And an arsonist to catch. And then we can go back to worrying about the *where* part of our future."

"Yeah. I know." And he did get it—they needed to focus on the present and work, not keep going around with questions they weren't going to answer right then anyway. He tried to take some solace in the *our* that Luis had so easily tossed off there. Whatever the answer ended up being, they'd be together.

However, those questions were still in the back of his head as they arrived on site and he got to work discussing with the various crew chiefs and Adams about whether they'd need a formal fire camp. The red danger level warning meant that rapid spread was possible, but early response was promising. Still, Tucker had crews out digging more line in case they needed to do a burn to remove fuel from the fire, and additional air support was on standby too.

"We certainly moved fast." As the frantic pace slowed, Adams strode over to Tucker. "Good job getting your crews here."

"Thanks." Tucker accepted the praise, but his attention was over at a clearing where Luis was deep in discussion with some investigation personnel. Tucker was hopeful that Luis would get to see a culmination to the case before he had to depart in a few days.

Adams didn't seem in any hurry to move on, stretching his shoulders. "I'm getting too old for these early morning surprises."

"You? Old? Never," Tucker teased. He'd known Adams for at least fifteen years, through grandkids and health crises and department changes, and considered him something of a friend and mentor in addition to his boss.

"Ha. I don't know how many more seasons I've got in these old bones. Soon enough it'll be you in charge, I reckon."

"Me?" This wasn't the first time that Adams had made an offhand remark like that, but the seriousness to his tone made Tucker's back tense.

"No one better suited to it," Adams said firmly.

Tucker squinted, trying to picture that future. Meetings. Lots of meetings. Agency politics. Further from the field. Was that what he wanted? *All that routine makes you old before your time.* Wasn't that what Luis had said when they'd discussed how he'd had to give up his smoke jumper dream as a young man?

He'd been thinking about a potential move as something he could give Luis and perhaps as an empty nest solution, but maybe it was something he could give himself, resurrect old dreams, try something new. Not that there was anything wrong with Adams's job precisely, but Tucker had a restlessness to his soul as he pictured himself in the role. Just like he'd wonder what might have been if he let Luis go, the possibility was strong that he'd wonder what could have been professionally too, had he allowed himself to stretch his wings.

"Thanks. I appreciate that. But…hard to say what the future holds." His pulse galloped at the admission.

"Ah. You craving something more exciting?" Adams didn't sound terribly surprised, but then he always had joked about how Tucker would take any opportunity to get out of the office. "Always figured we might lose you to the interagency or smoke jumper folks. More action."

"Maybe. Not sure. This was the perfect job while the boys were young, and I'm not discounting how lucky I was to have it. But…might be time for me to chase some old dreams. Or find new ones." There. That was exactly what he needed to tell Luis and again his gaze flitted to where Luis was standing. He couldn't wait until this operation was a wrap and they could talk again.

Adams laughed knowingly, but if he'd noticed where Tucker kept looking, he didn't say anything about that. "You're too young for a midlife crisis, but I hear you. You're a damn good manager. You'd be an asset anywhere."

"Thanks." Tucker's attention was less on Adams's praise and more on Luis walking toward them.

"What's the latest?" Luis asked as he joined them. "The data I'm seeing suggests that we've got it contained absent some hot spot and snag flare-ups. Looks like we've avoided the worst-case scenario at least."

"Yup. Good work on your projections." Adams nodded. "And good work on the investigation. Because we were already monitoring this trail, we were able to get a faster response."

"Which let us catch a suspect. Authorities have a young man who fits the profile we've developed. Repeated applications for a smoke jumper position, but never made the grade. I'm really hopeful this will be an end to this rash of fires."

"All of us are." Letting out a weary noise, Adams wiped at his forehead. "Of course, it would be nice for you to leave with the job done. We got word late yesterday that Angeles got their way—Friday will be your travel day, and I wouldn't be surprised if they put you to work even before Monday."

Job done. Tucker had known from the day before that Luis was likely gone in a matter of days, but making it official still made his coffee slosh around in his stomach, acid rising.

"Yeah." Luis's expression was guarded, but Tucker didn't miss that brief moment when relief flashed in his eyes. He might be conflicted about leaving Tucker, but a big part of him did want to be back home. And Tucker wanted to give him that because he might be done with this job, but Tucker was far from done with him.

Chapter Twenty-Five

"Ooof!" Luis had to stifle a curse as fifteen pounds landed in his lap out of nowhere.

"Your cat is in your lap." Tucker gestured at Blaze.

Luis's laugh rumbled through his chest, a welcome lightness after the heaviness of the day. "Yeah. She's been doing that more lately."

She was heavier than she looked, a warm solid weight that somehow made hanging out on Tucker's couch that much cozier. After Luis arrived with her in tow for dinner, she'd been busy exploring Tucker's living room, seeking out all her favorite spots on his built-in shelves and investigating Walker's room upstairs before deciding to plop herself on Luis's lap.

He'd been idly surfing the various streaming options on Tucker's TV while Tucker checked his phone. The boys had eaten at Heidi's house, so it had been only the two of them to cook some steaks and clean up afterward. Domestic perfection. Luis wanted a thousand more nights like this one, not simply two.

"Maybe she's happy to be back here." Tucker was doing something on his phone, but he took a second to give Luis a playful smile.

"She's not the only one." Luis's chest lifted at getting

to tease Tucker like this. "Are you jealous my lap is full? Because nice as it is that Blaze is tolerating me, I'd happily make room for you."

"I'll wait until she moves. I do feel like I need to store up all the touches though. Two more nights." Some of the lightness escaped Tucker as he frowned.

"We'll make it work." Luis patted his thigh, hoping like hell he was right.

"We will." Tucker held up his phone. "See? I'm looking at flights for October right now."

"You're doing what?" Luis had assumed there would be visits, but it was all very nebulous in his brain, no logistics sorted out, and it had felt more aspirational than anything else. But here was Tucker *planning* to visit him, not simply waiting for the court case to bring Luis back. That meant something and Luis had to swallow hard.

"I can dwell on how much Friday is going to suck or I can use this nifty fare-finding app. Getting leave while we close out fire season here will be tricky, but October should be safe."

"Yeah." This was a little surreal and was perhaps the best evidence yet that they weren't sixteen. They had bank accounts and credit cards and access to airline tickets and good jobs with paid leave. They could do this, fluttery feeling in Luis's gut and all. "I've banked a ton of leave too. If we're not in an emergency situation, I can probably come back for a weekend even apart from a possible trial. Especially if I'm interviewing—"

"You're not." Tucker cut him off with a stern look.

"I'm not?" While he did appreciate all Tucker's offers, Luis had still been operating on the assumption that when it came down to it, he'd be the one packing up.

"No. You've got to let me job hunt first. If you apply

for the job here, you'll get it, and then that will be the easy solution." Tucker patted Luis's hand, which was still on his thigh.

"Exactly."

"Maybe I don't want the easy way out. Especially if that's not the most fair to you." Tucker's mouth twisted.

Luis wasn't entirely sure how to read his expression. "I'm less hung up on fair now. You've got a lot going on here—the house, the job, the kids..."

"Yeah, I do." Tucker made a startled noise as the cat left Luis's lap to walk between them and wiggle into the space behind their joined hands. "*Cat.* Anyway, this is why I need us to be patient. I've got to get the boys settled and back at school, talk logistics with Heidi, job hunt... It's not going to be fast."

"Which is why—"

"Fast isn't everything." Tucker leaned back as the cat made her way to the other arm of the couch, abandoning them to their very human problems. "Anything worth doing is worth doing carefully. With consideration."

"You sound exactly like your dad." That got a deeper frown and Luis immediately regretted bringing up Tucker's family. "Sorry."

"Not all of his advice sucked."

"True. But I want you *happy*, Tucker." He leaned in, trailing his fingers down Tucker's jaw. "Not obligated out of a sense of fairness or anything else like that. And asking you to give up your job, start hunting nearer to me, that feels like too much. I've seen the way Adams looks at you. He wants you to be director eventually."

"Yeah, he does. But what do I want? That's what I keep coming back to. If I don't look, I'll never know what

I might have found. You see this really wise guy told me it wasn't too late to chase my dreams."

Luis's eyes went so wide he could actually feel the stretch. "You're going to do it? The thirty-five-year-old rookie smoke jumper?"

"Well, I'm not sure if they'll have me, but I want back on the front lines of fires for sure. I want something different than hiring techs and forestry management. I miss being on a crew, and I hadn't really ever given myself space to acknowledge that. I want more adrenaline and outdoors in my days."

"That's…risky." Luis couldn't help it. His mind flashed back to Mike and how much worry sucked. Tucker potentially risking his life for a dangerous job was hardly a comforting prospect. But he also knew he couldn't keep Tucker from his dreams, and the part of him that wasn't scared shitless was so proud of him for having this realization.

"I'll be careful." Tucker met Luis's gaze, and in his eyes, Luis could see how much thought he had given this, how much he wanted it.

"You mean it, don't you? This wouldn't simply be you moving to make me happy?"

"No. I want to make *me* happy. And yeah, part of that is us together, a life together, but I also want to see if I can find a job I truly love."

"I want that for you too." Luis squeezed his hand again, less reassurance for Tucker and more anchor for himself, for all these rising emotions in him.

"Good. I don't have all the answers yet, but I want the freedom to hunt them down, be open to ones I haven't considered yet."

"I can do that for you. Give you space to find those

dreams again. Even if that means getting okay with you hurling yourself out of airplanes."

"One step at a time." Tucker gave him a fast kiss. "I'm going to start by talking about my plans at family dinner tomorrow. You're coming."

"I am? Feels like maybe I'd get in the way of that conversation."

Tucker's mouth pursed and his shoulders firmed up. "It's family dinner. You're family now or at least on your way to that status. I want you there."

Luis had to inhale sharply. His deepest wish right there, Tucker wanting it too. It was almost too much. "You want me to be family?"

"More than anything." This time Tucker's kiss was long and lingering, and Luis believed him, could feel the strength of his conviction in his possessive grip and sweetly claiming lips.

"Me too." Luis wasn't ever letting this go, not even when it got hard. They would be a family. He was ready to make that happen.

Tucker was determined to not be nervous at family dinner on Wednesday, but somehow he couldn't seem to stop the weird revving of his pulse. But at the same time, Luis by his side at the table simply felt right. Like he was supposed to be here. Like he truly was part of the family, exactly like Tucker had told him the night before. Even so, his heart rate kicked up again as the twins came barreling in, starving and full of apologies as they took their seats.

"Dude!" Wade gestured at Luis in between filling his plate with the salmon and potatoes Isaac had made. "You guys made up! I knew you'd get your heads out of your—"

"Language," Tucker warned even as he had to fight back a laugh. Wade might put it far more colorfully, but they had been rather stubborn, him especially, and he had needed his eyes opened to the possibility of getting everything he wanted.

"I'm just saying I'm happy for you guys." Wade beamed as he created a mountain of garlic mashed potatoes. "So happy that I'll sleep here tonight."

"You don't have to do that," Luis protested, sending Tucker a look. Tucker, however, wasn't going to turn down more alone time. Sure, they could cuddle quietly if the boys came back with them, but privacy had its benefits too.

"It's what…your last night together? I want it to be nice." Wade shrugged.

"Thanks. And yeah, I'm going to drive the first part tomorrow after work if I can, then the rest in a long day Friday." Luis was understandably eager to get back to help the ongoing fire situation his home office was dealing with. Tucker might want the extra night with him, but it wasn't like parting was going to be easy either way.

"And how's that going to work anyway?" Wade charged ahead into the question Tucker had been both anticipating and dreading. "If I go to Kansas, your frequent flier miles are going to be crazy high between that and California."

"Yup. Lots of visits. And…" He took a breath to steady that tap-dancing pulse of his. At least Wade had saved him the trouble of figuring out how to bring this up on his own. "I might be job hunting."

"You might be what?" Heidi's fork clattered to the table, and her *what* was echoed by several other voices.

"Right on." Wade was the only one at the table still

beaming. "If you move, the graduation trip to Disneyland is gonna be *lit*."

"Who said anything about Disneyland?" Somehow Tucker's brain latched on to that detail rather than try to sort out all the other reactions happening.

"Who said anything about *moving*?" Heidi's question was fast behind his, but Wade did a dismissive gesture.

"Dad did. Disney is going to be my price for being good with this news. That and maybe you can pick an apartment complex with a pool."

"Whoa. Slow down." Tucker wasn't quite to the where-to-live part yet. Visits, then job hunting, then they could cross the question of cohabitation. Typical Wade though to jump right to what he wanted out of this, and while dizzying, at least he was enthusiastic, unlike the others.

"Yes, how about slowing down?" Heidi gave him a censuring look he knew well. She was peeved he hadn't told her first, and he supposed that was valid. There was also a fair bit of "Tucker, be rational" in her expression and tone too.

Not enjoying being on the defensive, he held up a hand. "I didn't say I was moving tomorrow or anything. Maybe eventually though. It's on the horizon, something I want to seriously consider."

Under the table, Luis patted his leg, a welcome reassurance that they were in this together. And they were. He had to trust that the rest of the family would come around.

"I sure hope you know what you're doing." Heidi's drawn-out exhale said that she wasn't quite there yet, but her tone was more resigned than angry.

"I do." He knew better than to show doubts. He needed to be confident, not only for the kids and Heidi, but also for Luis, who needed to believe him that this was the path he wanted to take. "I'm not going to lie though, it would be easier if you guys were supportive."

Wade made an indignant sound. "Hey, don't I count? I'm already planning on being a regular on your couch. Bring on the pretty California people."

"You count, but how about you let Walker have a chance to digest this news?" Even more than Heidi's re- action, Tucker was studying Walker's impassive face, noting the way he'd gone silent and still. "I know I'm kinda throwing this out there."

Walker bit his lip and looked away. "I…uh… I need a minute. Alone."

And with that, he fled the table, food barely touched, and headed to the backyard. Tucker's heart sank all the way down to the floorboards. This wasn't the reaction he'd hoped for at all. His whole body ached, a visceral pain at the idea that he'd hurt Walker.

"I need to go after him." He stood, stopping Heidi with a hand. She had also left her chair and seemed ready to follow Walker.

"Yeah, I guess you do." She gave him a frustrated look. "Try not to make this worse."

"I'll try."

"Take your time." Luis spoke for the first time since the chaos had broken out. "Don't forget that you are a good dad."

"Thanks." That reminder did help as he made his way to the backyard where Walker was perched on the pic- nic table, hands on his knees, gaze off in the mountains in the distance.

"Hey." Tucker carefully sat next to him. "I know you said you wanted to be alone—"

"I do." Walker didn't even turn his direction.

"But we should talk. You know our thing. No one goes to bed angry. We work things out."

"We do." Walker's shoulders slumped, voice far from happy about that fact. "And I'm not *angry* exactly."

"What are you?" Tucker tried hard to keep his expression neutral. Whatever Walker wanted to express, he wanted to hear, even if it was hard.

"Sad."

Ooof. Yeah, that was a hard one all right. He could almost deal easier with an angry kid than a sad one. "Okay. Fair enough. Does it help if I say that I'm sorry you're sad?"

"I dunno." Walker's voice was soft with a hopeless edge. "Guess I figured that at least you'd be here. If I stayed, at least I'd have you."

Fuck. Walker might as well have plunged his fork into Tucker's chest. Damn. He needed a moment to quiet his breathing before he could reply. "You'll always have me. Always. Doesn't matter where I live."

"I know. But it's not the same. Might be worth it to stay if it meant seeing you and stuff."

"Walker. We're always going to have that bond. But you have to stay for *you.* Not me."

Walker waved away that advice with a flick of his hand. Big hand, bigger than Tucker's now, but still a lost little boy expression on his face. "And it's more fucking change. I just want everything to stay the same."

"I get that." Tucker didn't even have the heart to call him on the cursing, instead patting his back. "But that's not how life works."

"*I know.*" Walker shrugged away from Tucker's touch.

"I'm sorry. This is hard on you, and you're already having a rough time. I didn't mean to pile on that."

Maybe Luis was right. Maybe he should have waited to tell the boys. This was going to be hard regardless, but right then it was brutal, his desire to protect Walker at war with his conviction that he was doing the right thing.

"Are you moving because of me?" Walker twisted his upper body toward Tucker. "Because you think that will make me follow?"

"No." He honestly hadn't even considered that possibility in all his calculations. Sure, there were marine biology programs in California Walker had liked once upon a time, but Tucker wasn't about to use his move as bait. "I know it won't. You have to make your own choices. Just like I do."

"I get that." Walker's voice was calmer now and he lowered it further, almost to a whisper. "But how do you know this is really what you want to do?"

Ah. And there they got to the heart of Walker's quandary, one Tucker wished like anything he could solve for him. But maybe the best he could do was simply be a good example.

"Because I have some dreams worth chasing. I don't want to hurt you, and I'm going to do my damnedest to make things as easy as possible on you, but I need to do this."

He braced himself for a biting response from Walker, but instead Walker was silent a long moment, seeming to shrink into himself before finally whispering, "You're brave."

"Brave?" Tucker hadn't been expecting that, didn't know how to respond.

"Because it's a risk. What if it doesn't work out? What if you hate it there?"

"Those are chances I have to take. If I hate it, then I'll

readjust my plans. I'll talk to Luis, come up with something else that works."

"Because you love him?" Walker nodded, his eyes softer now.

"Yes. I do. And I know it seems quick, but I do." Ideally, he might have managed to say those words to Luis first, but it didn't make them any less true. He hadn't said them yet because he didn't want Luis to feel pressured to say them back, but his heart didn't care how fast this was. He knew what he felt. "But also…because I love me. I need to do this for me. Because I don't want to wonder 'what if' years from now."

"I get that." Walker swung his feet back and forth. "I…uh…went to that Florida school's website today. Just to see."

"Nothing wrong with looking." Tucker kept his tone mild, trying not to express excitement that wouldn't go over well with Walker's current mood.

"Yeah." Walker went silent again, but right as Tucker was about to try to fill the gap, Walker finally met his gaze. "I'm sorry about storming out. I do want you happy, Dad. I simply wish I knew what would make *me* happy too."

"I wish that too. More than anything." He clapped Walker on the shoulder, and this time Walker let him get away with the half hug, didn't recoil. "And I think you're going to find it. I believe in you."

"Thanks." Walker chewed his lip again before his gaze darted back toward the house. "I should probably get back inside."

Tucker released him. This was a lot for Walker to digest. And him too if he were honest. Probably they both needed a little break.

"I'm always going to be there for you. And if you need to talk it out more, I'm here for that too."

Standing, Walker stretched with a groan. "I might. Right now, I kinda want to go game with Wade, not think."

"I get that." Heck, Tucker was going to need his own zone-out time after this. Mindless TV and maybe some cuddling with Luis to help him calm down. "That sounds like a good plan."

"Love you, Dad."

"Love you too."

He sat there even after Walker had returned to the house, not quite ready to return to everyone, too much swirling through his head. However, he wasn't surprised when the door opened and Luis slipped out.

"How did it go?" he asked as he took a seat next to Tucker.

"Not sure," he admitted. "Good might be pushing it, but not bad either. We talked."

"If you need us to go even slower, give him more time—"

"I appreciate that. But I don't think that's what he wants either. He likes you, and he wants me to be happy. It'll be an adjustment for all of us, but I do think we'll get to a good place."

"Good. I don't ever want to come between you and your kid."

"You won't." Tucker looped an arm around his shoulder, pulled him close. The heat of the day was giving way to a soft evening breeze. "There's plenty of room in my heart for you both."

"You do have an awfully big heart. And you being a good dad is one of the things I love most about you."

"You love me?" He couldn't keep the pleasure from his voice. "It's not too soon?"

"Too soon? Tucker, we've been building to this for decades now." Luis laughed, but his eyes were serious.

"Ah. You mean we loved each other before so it was easier to fall this time?"

"Maybe, but I kind of think I'd fall for you regardless." Luis leaned into his embrace.

"Really?"

"I liked younger you a great deal, but your older self has a depth to it that made it impossible not to fall for you, so much stronger this time around."

"I like knowing that," he admitted, holding Luis closer. "And I love you too. When I loved you before, I'm not sure I really knew what the words meant. We were so young. But now… I get that it's not always going to be easy or fun. And I'm here for that. What I feel for you, it's not going away."

"I'm here for us too." Gaze darting back to the house first, Luis gave him a fast peck on the cheek.

"Then everything else will work out. Walker. My job situation. Other people's opinions. Wade's big plans." He had to believe that, had to believe deep down that they would deal with whatever life threw their way.

"I'm going to hold you to that." Luis gave him another kiss, this one on the lips, brief but potent. And as long as they had that, had that faith and love in each other, it would work out. He'd make sure of it.

Chapter Twenty-Six

June

Adjusting his sunglasses, Luis watched the sky carefully. He'd arrived early for precisely this reason, hoping to see…that. Right there.

Yeah, there it was. Incoming helicopter, a dot at first, then larger and louder as it approached the base. He couldn't be sure that Tucker was on this one, but somehow he *knew*. The bright red CAL FIRE logo became visible as the helicopter descended, pilot setting the bird gently down on the landing pad before the crew disembarked, all clad in blue uniforms with tired but smiling faces. Their faces and boots were dusty—they'd seen action, and Luis couldn't wait to hear about it. It was a rare treat these days, getting to see Tucker at work, and Luis hung back by the parking area, observing how the team joked among itself on the way to the hangar where they'd be clocking out after a long duty shift.

The pilot was a woman married to a captain on another crew, and she was first out of the building, greeted by her uniformed spouse who'd evidently been waiting, same as Luis. They gave him a wave on their way to their truck. It was still the getting-acquainted stage of meeting the coworkers, but so far everyone seemed nice, a close-knit family, many of whom had served years together.

As the evening sun starting to shift, Luis finally caught sight of Tucker.

"There's my favorite rookie," he called out as Tucker got closer.

"The other rookies are going to be jealous, you playing favorites like that," Tucker joked.

"They aren't taking me to dinner," he pointed out as he unlocked the car. Usually, given the not-tiny distance between their two jobs, they met up back at home, but Tucker had wanted to show Luis a nearby restaurant he'd discovered.

Tucker gave him a wide smile as he climbed in the passenger side. He'd evidently taken a moment inside the building to do a lightning-fast change, out of uniform and into a blue polo and jeans that showed off his impressive array of new muscles. "And thanks for meeting me. Good distraction for tomorrow."

"It's going to be fine." Luis headed away from the air base and toward the barbecue-themed eatery he'd already programmed into his GPS.

"I know. I'm just..." Tucker trailed off as he let his head fall back against the seat rest.

"Overly emotional about your babies graduating?"

"That. I just hope the flight isn't delayed. Wish I had more leave, but as the newest guy, I guess I'm lucky I got the time off at all."

"Yep. That's rookie life for you." Luis teased because he knew how much Tucker was loving the job. After spending the fall and winter getting his certifications current, he'd decided to try for the helitack firefighting unit with the state along with a few other opportunities both state and federal. He'd wanted to find something close enough to Luis's work to be feasible, and to his great delight, he'd been picked to start spring training with this crew. It wasn't smoke jumping because no parachutes were involved, but Tucker's inner adrenaline junkie seemed to love it all the same.

His role on the team was mainly fire recon, using all his years of forestry experience helping decide on a plan of attack and working with the captains to carry out the plan. His prior wildland firefighting experience had also come into play, and he joked that he was in better shape than he'd been at twenty.

It had been fun during his fall visits, watching him ramp up his already pretty decent fitness and discussing various job options on late-night phone calls. Luis couldn't lie—knowing the work was dangerous wasn't easy, but he was also so darn pleased that Tucker had figured out and gone after his dream.

"Are you going to drag the twins here too?" Luis asked as he parked at the restaurant. The long-awaited Disney graduation trip was happening later in the month when Tucker had next been able to arrange some consecutive days off.

"Probably. The portions are huge, so that should do Wade for about an hour."

"Sounds about right."

"I can't wait to see them tomorrow. I've missed them so much." There had been a few visits after Tucker accepted the job, including a longer one at spring break for the boys, but it had been several weeks since the last one, and Luis knew well that video chat simply wasn't the same thing.

"I know. They're proud of you though." Luis had been

at Tucker's the night he told the boys about the job offer, and they had both voted that he go ahead and accept it instead of waiting until after their graduation. Even now, his throat got a little tight remembering how enthusiastic both twins had been, how very much they wanted Tucker to be happy.

"I've got a great story for them too." Tucker proceeded to tell Luis all about his shift, when they'd dealt with both a spot fire as well as assisting in the rescue of some stranded hikers. He was so animated that Luis couldn't help but smile along. He worried about Tucker every day, but he also hadn't ever seen him happier either.

And later, belly full of pulled pork, as he parked in the apartment complex lot, he realized he could say the same for himself. The new place was farther out of the city, more of a drive to see his mother, but it let them each have roughly equal commutes, and more importantly it was *theirs*. They were giving Tucker a year in the job at least before they went house hunting, but they'd been careful in their selection of a rental, finding the best pool for Wade and the biggest kitchen for Luis.

Blaze was on the shelving unit near the patio door, same as always, but the kitten was there at the door to greet them and remind them it had been hours since she last saw them. Tucker had shown him the animal shelter ad for Sparky mere weeks after his arrival.

"They call her Sparky. It's meant to be."

"You're lucky I love you."

"You do, don't you?"

And thus Blaze became a grumpy big sister to Sparky, the world's most cheerful cat, who was as clingy as Blaze was aloof. Luis picked up the kitten and headed for the kitchen. Tucker trailed behind, changing the cat water dishes and handing him the can of wet food even before he asked.

"You confirmed the pet sitter, right?"

"Twice. It's not like Blaze doesn't know the drill, but Sparky will be fine. And so will you." Luis finally got to give him the kiss he'd been waiting for all evening.

"I know. I don't know why I'm so nervous." Cats taken care of, Tucker leaned into Luis's embrace.

"Because it's a big day and you want it to go perfectly for them. And it will."

"At least we'll get one more use of my shower tomorrow night," Tucker laughed. He'd been renting the house out through a vacation rental company, but had reserved the weekend for themselves.

"There is that. But the one here isn't too terrible." Luis steered him in that direction.

"You offering to take my mind off my nerves?" Tucker gave him a heated look, one that had Luis already reaching for his shirt buttons.

"Always." Abandoning his undressing efforts, he pulled Tucker in for another kiss, and as he caught sight of their reflection in the bathroom mirror, he knew the truth of his earlier realization. He was *happy*, truly happy, in a way he hadn't been a year ago. Tucker had been more than worth the wait, both to find him again, and then the months of long-distance until they'd arrived here at this place together. *Home.* That's what this was. It was a home and it was a family and it was everything Luis had ever wanted, Tucker included.

"Are you going to propose?" Wade's grin was almost as wide as the platter of food he was balancing.

"Propose?" Tucker sputtered as he glanced around.

Heidi's house was as packed as he'd ever seen it, people in every room and spilling out into the backyard, where he'd escaped to a lawn chair. Luckily no one else appeared to have heard Wade's latest outrageousness. "What on earth gave you that idea?"

"Isaac made his mac and cheese for the party. Huge pans of it. You're always calling it proposal worthy." Wade's head tilted as he considered Tucker more carefully. "Wait. You thought I meant—"

"Never you mind what I thought." Tucker gave him what he hoped was a stern stare and not a nervous one. It wasn't like he hadn't been thinking along those sorts of lines a lot lately, but he wasn't ready to share that with Wade. He was still wearing the cap from his graduation outfit, tassel waving in the breeze, the tie Heidi had forced on him already lost, and somehow looking even bigger and taller than when Tucker had seen him the previous visit.

"Are you going to ask him? Can it be at Disney while we're there? That's romantic, right? I could help you pick which ride—"

"Slow down. Please." Tucker rubbed his temples. Wade was a whirlwind, and if he wasn't careful, he'd have Tucker married off before Tucker even got a chance to pick out a ring himself.

"Fine. Steal my fun." Wade sighed dramatically as he flopped in the chair next to Tucker, narrowly avoiding disaster with his plate of food.

"I can promise you that you'll be the first to know," Tucker assured him.

"First to know what?" Heidi chose that moment to stride over, drink in hand. In a pretty purple sundress she looked way too young to be the mom of high school graduates.

"When Dad pops the question. Or Luis does." Wade's grin hadn't flagged one bit.

"Dad is not—" Tucker started to protest.

"Today? At the party?" Heidi frowned.

"Of course not. I wouldn't want to take attention off the real point of the gathering." The party was a rousing success, and if Tucker or the boys were missing Tucker's family, the house full of Heidi's family and friends was a good distraction. Tucker's parents had sent cards with small checks. He supposed that was something, but considering they lived close enough to attend the ceremony if they chose, it wasn't much.

"Oh, okay." Heidi shrugged as if either option were okay with her. "Boys have to be at the school soon to catch the bus to the safe-and-sober overnight. Think you could take them? I don't want them leaving their car there all night."

"Absolutely." Tucker was more than happy to play dad again, take them places, cheer them on. He was still a little hoarse from the graduation ceremony. He wasn't sure he'd ever been so proud as watching the boys walk across the stage, first Wade practically dancing his way toward the principal, then Walker more sedately striding but same megawatt grin.

They'd done it, he and Heidi, journeyed with the boys all the way to this moment when they were on the cusp of launching into their own adventures. It felt like a triumph, one he hadn't been so sure was possible when he'd been a teen dad all those years before.

"Do I have to go to the safe-and-sober thing?" Walker joined them. Unlike Wade, his tie was still in place and his hair nearly styled, the recent super-short cut suiting him. "I'm not sure I'm up for it."

"Dude. We got tickets weeks ago." Wade clapped him on the back. "There's going to be paintball and your last chance to see people."

"That would be the part I'm not crazy about," Walker grumbled, staring at the ground.

"The best way to show her that you're over it is to go," Wade argued, but Walker wasn't over it, might not be over it for a long time. Tucker knew from experience how deep the pain of young heartbreak could cut, and he'd do anything to shoulder Walker's pain a little.

"Want to stay in and watch movies with Luis and me?" he offered. He'd watched hours of mindless movies with Walker in January when the breakup happened. It had been the perfect storm of attractive foreign exchange student catching Mary Anne's eye, Walker deciding to apply broadly to colleges, and some minor arguments blowing up into a big breakup.

"You guys are going to get sick of me," Walker protested.

"Never. We've got your room all ready for you. I've got pictures." He dug out his phone, eager to show his and Luis's handiwork. "It's going to be a great summer."

"Yeah. It is." Walker gave a little smile as he studied the pictures on Tucker's phone. His mood had lifted as they'd firmed up the plans for the summer. While both twins were coming for the Disney trip, along with Heidi, Isaac, and Angelica, Walker was staying in California for the rest of summer, working at a nearby waterpark where he'd found a lifeguarding job.

Tucker had a feeling that the abundance of attractive young people at the waterpark had helped Walker start the healing process, start seeing a new future for himself. In the fall, he'd be moving south to the dorms at Long Beach, where he had a marine biology scholarship, but Tucker was looking forward to having him for the summer as well as the occasional weekend.

"My summer's going to be fabulous too. And that's my point, bro, we need to make the most of the time we've got left." Wade had a summer job at one of the Bend resorts, one last chance to hang with his friends, but Tucker figured the fact that Mitch's older sister was also working there had been a deciding factor in his decision.

"All right. I'll go." Walker rolled his neck and shoulders, sounding more enthusiastic. "But prepare to be obliterated by my superior paintball skills."

"You can call and I'll come get you," Tucker promised. "Any time. Even the middle of the night."

"Thanks, Dad."

"What about me?" Wade mock pouted. "Will you come get me?"

"Something tells me any call to come get *you* is going to involve trouble, but yes, you too." Tucker laughed. "Let me go find Luis for the rental car keys, and we'll get you guys back to the school."

"Awesome." Wade hefted himself out of his chair. Somehow he'd managed to pack away all his food while they'd been talking.

Tucker found Luis talking with Garrick and Rain. Heidi's expansive guest list had included several of his former work friends, and Tucker had a feeling it was to distract him from the absence of his folks, but it was a nice gesture nonetheless.

Luis decided to come along for the ride, and they made

their way through the house. "You were right. Isaac's mac and cheese truly is proposal worthy."

"It is." Their eyes met, and in that moment, Tucker knew that it wouldn't be long. Not at Disney and probably not with a huge audience, but soon. Either he'd ask or Luis would or maybe it would simply be a mutual slide into ring discussions and wedding planning, but whatever the case, there would be a yes. They already had the foundation for a life together—the place together, the cats, the room for the boys, and the hours and hours of conversations about the future they'd both like to see. No one had been more supportive of his career change than Luis, and there was no one he'd rather see at the end of his day or first thing in the morning. Luis was the one for him, and while it had taken them a meandering path with some rather serious boulders to get here, he wouldn't change a thing about their journey.

"Love you," he whispered, emotions suddenly catching up with him.

"Love you too." Luis gave him a quick kiss on the cheek. "I'm so proud of you. And the boys. It's a great day, right?"

"The best." Tucker swallowed hard because every day with Luis had the potential to be the best. It was the best of days because they were together, surrounded by people they cared about, excited about the next segment of their journey—the part they would travel together. The future was glittery with the love they shared, and he couldn't wait to experience it together.

* * * * *

Author Note

My research into the world of wildfire fighting and forestry took me deep into fire management and unusual firefighting professions. Rather than trying to copy an existing smoke-jumping base with its specific procedures, policies, and ways of handling rookies, I combined various parts of many into one fictional base and town. The town of Painter's Ridge and my forest service headquarters are entirely fictional and staffed with characters from my own imagination. However, the area's geography and attractions absolutely helped to add authenticity to the series.

While Tucker and Luis both work for the federal Forestry Department, the reality of modern fire management usually involves multiple agencies and interagency coordination at both the state and federal levels. Arson investigations in particular are very complicated with state and federal law enforcement involved along with forestry and fire personnel. Some of these details were simplified to allow the focus to remain on the characters and their growth and their story, but I did try to include as much realism as possible.

My research showed great variety in how fire behavior specialists and fire investigators are used during an active fire and in long-term and investigatory efforts. Work-related travel to meet ever-changing wildfire needs is common, but exact procedures and protocols can vary.

Finally, this book came through edits right as the world changed with the response to Covid-19. I very deliberately chose not to have these events affect the storyline, but I absolutely appreciate all our first responders and all that they do for our communities. My heart goes out to all affected by this ongoing situation.

Acknowledgments

Like with all my books, I am so grateful for the team supporting me, especially at Carina Press and the Knight Agency. My editor, Deb Nemeth, always guides me through the revision process with a deft hand and astute feedback that enables me to better meet my vision for the book. My revisions were also assisted by invaluable beta comments from Edie Danford, Karen Stivali, and David, who gave especially insightful comments on Luis's cultural background.

My behind-the-scenes team is also the best. My entire Carina Press team does an amazing job, and I am so very lucky to have all of them on board. A special thank-you to the tireless art department and publicity team and to the amazing narrators who bring my books to life for the audio market. Judith of A Novel Take PR goes above and beyond to help me, and I am so very grateful to her. A special thank-you to Abbie Nicole, whose assistance to my writerly life is making a giant difference for me.

My family remains my rock and is so appreciated for their cooperation and assistance. My life is immeasurably enriched by my friendships, especially those of my writer friends who keep me going with sprints, advice, guidance, and commiseration. I am so grateful for every person in my life who helps me do what I love. And no one makes that possible more than my readers. I can't thank readers enough for their readership and encouragement over the years. Your support via social media, reviews, notes, shares, likes, and other means makes it possible for me to continue to write stories that mean the world to me, and I don't take that for granted!

About the Author

Annabeth Albert grew up sneaking romance novels under the bedcovers. Now, she devours all subgenres of romance out in the open—no flashlights required! When she's not adding to her keeper shelf, she's a multi-published Pacific Northwest romance writer. Emotionally complex, sexy, and funny stories are her favorites both to read and to write. Annabeth loves finding happy endings for a variety of pairings and particularly loves uncovering unique main characters. In her personal life, she works a rewarding day job and wrangles two active children.

The Hotshots series joins her many other critically acclaimed and fan-favorite LGBTQ romance series. To find out what she's working on next and other fun extras, check out her website: www.annabethalbert.com or connect with Annabeth on Twitter, Facebook, Instagram, and Spotify! Also, be sure to sign up for her newsletter for free ficlets, bonus reads, and contests. The fan group, Annabeth's Angels, on Facebook is also a great place for bonus content and exclusive contests.

Newsletter: http://eepurl.com/Nb9yv.
Fan group: https://www.facebook.com/groups/annabeths-angels/

Also available from Annabeth Albert
and Carina Press

Burn Zone

*Danger lurks everywhere for Central Oregon's fire
crews, but the biggest risk of all might be losing their
hearts...*

Smoke jumper Lincoln Reid is speechless to see Jacob
Hartman among his squad's new recruits. Linc had promised his late best friend he'd stay away from his little
brother. And yet here Jacob is...and almost instantly,
the same temptation Linc has always felt around him is
causing way too many problems.

Jacob gets everyone's concerns, but he's waited years
for his shot at joining the elite smoke-jumping team,
hoping to honor his brother's memory. He's ready to
tackle any challenge Linc throws his way, and senses
the chemistry between them—chemistry Linc insists on
ignoring—is still alive and kicking. This time, Jacob's
determined to get what he wants.

Close quarters and high stakes make it difficult for
Linc to keep his resolve, never mind do so while also
making sure the rookie's safe. But the closer they get, the
more Linc's plan to leave at the end of the season risks
him breaking another promise: the one his heart wants
to make to Jacob.

Don't miss
Burn Zone *by Annabeth Albert,*
Available wherever
Carina Press ebooks are sold.

www.CarinaPress.com

Also available from Annabeth Albert
and Carina Press

High Heat

**Annabeth Albert's Hotshots series continues—the
emotions and intensity of *Chicago Fire* with the
raw, natural elements of *Man vs. Wild*.**

Smoke jumping is Garrick Nelson's life. Nothing, not
severe injuries nor the brutal physical therapy that fol-
lows, is going to stop him from getting back with his
crew. But when a lost dog shows up on his front porch,
he can't turn her away, and he can't take care of her on
his own. Thankfully, help comes in the form of his new
sexy, dog-loving neighbor. As they work together, trying to re-home their little princess, Garrick can't resist
his growing attraction for the other man, even though he
knows this guy isn't the staying type.

Rain Fisher doesn't take anything too seriously. He
dances through life, one adventure at a time, never settling in one place for too long. When his hot, conveniently
buff, neighbor shows up on his doorstep, dog in tow,
Rain's determined to not just save the adorable puppy, but
her reluctant owner as well. He never expects their flirta-
tion might tempt him into staying put once and for all...

Don't miss
High Heat *by Annabeth Albert,*
Available wherever
Carina Press ebooks are sold.

www.CarinaPress.com